A Killer Among Friends

Jade Riley Mysteries
Book 2

Andrea Barton

Copyright © 2025 Andrea Barton

Layout design and Copyright © 2025 by Next Chapter

Published 2025 by Next Chapter

Edited by Elizabeth N. Love

Author photo and cover photo by Susan Bradfield Photography

Cover design by Lordan June Pinote

This book is a work of fiction. Names, characters, places, and incidents are the product of the author's imagination or are used fictitiously. Any resemblance to actual events, locales, or persons, living or dead, is purely coincidental.

All rights reserved. No part of this book may be reproduced or transmitted in any form or by any means, electronic or mechanical, including photocopying, recording, or by any information storage and retrieval system, without the author's permission.

*To Dad,
for always believing in me,
and
to Danny,
for sharing his name and the music in his soul.*

Author's Note

If you or someone you love is experiencing suicidal thoughts, LifeLine International can help. Find your local number here:

https://lifeline-international.com/our-network/

To fit with the music theme in *A Killer Among Friends*, I've used song titles as chapter titles. For fun, I've created a Spotify playlist. If you'd like to listen along, this is the link:

https://open.spotify.com/playlist/5Svft2h1fs16CKGE3WLm1x?si=tNx3li7oRy2Eohg5ZQ8fiQ

Chapter 1
We Go Together
Jade, now

THE DRUM SOLO marked the highlight of Jade's monthly pub night at the Rock 'n' Barrel. Her friend Danny, dark-haired, dark-eyed and dark-humoured, played with the accuracy of a Swiss watch and the abandon of a drunk. He newly impressed Jade every time she heard him. But tonight, something sounded off. Not technically – he delivered a flawless performance – but his frenetic energy told Jade he was stewing over something. His drumsticks vanished in a blur. Feverish eyes appeared at odds with his deep concentration.

He finished his solo with a flourish, and as the band kicked back in, the small crowd broke into enthusiastic applause. The ensemble had three players – vocals and lead guitar, keyboard and drums – so they'd called themselves Mélange de Trois, *Mix of Three*. As Danny had told Jade, they loved the cheeky nod to ménage à trois.

They'd been doing gigs here for five years, so nerves didn't cause Danny's distress. He wore his emotions as blatantly as his lime green jacket, but Jade hadn't seen him this strung up since Elena's death. Elena had died three years ago, but her absence influenced them as strongly as her vivacious personality once had.

Where she used to instigate visits to festivals, galleries and new restaurants, they now did these things in her honour.

Jade gave herself a little shake to break free of the ever-present grief over her friend's suicide and refocused on the present: the tang of her gin and tonic, the sticky tabletop, the long wooden bar, the regulars busy sinking pints, and the cracked vinyl bench that scratched her legs. Across the booth sat Iris, Danny's twin sister, and her boyfriend Curtis, who also rated as Danny's best friend. To call them a tight-knit group didn't do them justice.

Curtis polished off his beer. 'Danny nailed it again.'

Iris snuggled closer to him as if afraid he'd vanish. 'He's such a ham, always plays up to the crowd.'

'In his element on stage.' Jade raised her glass. 'I wish I could perform like him. So uninhibited.' As an amateur ballroom dancer, she strived for fluidity when stage fright made her stiff. Now she thought about it, she realised what Danny's act had lacked. Normally, he moved freely, but tonight, tension kept him straight-backed as a British schoolmarm.

Curtis wrapped his arm tighter around Iris. 'Sometimes I wish he'd be more inhibited. The other day, he went ballistic at one of our tech guys who hadn't put in his expense claim. Way over the top.'

Jade could picture the scene. 'He can be a bit extra, but that's why we love him. And that's probably what makes him so musical.' From colourful clothing to poetic language, Danny revelled in excess.

Iris snorted. 'Mum always said his temper would get him into trouble. He's got to watch himself.' The twins sometimes bickered, but mostly they seemed closer than the average siblings; they still lived together in their early thirties. Creativity ran in their veins – where Danny used his gift in music, Iris poured her soul into work as a graphic artist. She always wore eye-catching clothes or statement jewellery. Tonight, a hot-pink bandana around her neck lifted her black jeans and shirt from mundane to hip.

Curtis nodded briefly, then addressed Jade. 'I rang that guy from the Bureau of Meteorology. He's happy to meet if you still need input for your article.' Curtis knew everyone. A master networker, he loved connecting people.

'Brilliant. I still need to do some fact-checking. Let me buy you a drink to say thanks. Beer?'

'Sure.'

'Want one?' Jade asked Iris.

'Nah, I'm good.' Iris held up her wine glass, still half full.

Jade approached the crowded bar, a classic style with glasses hanging overhead, a dark mirror at the back below a shelf of liquor, and a stained wooden countertop. She tried to attract one of the bartenders' attention – only two of them served the dozen or so waiting customers. Maybe because of her petite size, Jade often felt invisible in pubs. She shifted from one foot to the other, impatient to be served.

The drunk guy next to her leered. 'I knew I came here tonight for a reason.'

Jade gritted her teeth and forced politeness. 'The band's amazing.'

He slipped his hand around her waist. 'Wanna dance?'

She removed the jerk's arm. 'No, thanks. I'm here with friends.'

He stepped so close Jade could smell his beer breath.

She sidled away, and he moved with her. Perhaps she should stake another spot at the bar, but she'd reached the front and wanted to keep her place.

'You've got beautiful eyes.' The man touched her face.

Fed up, she brushed his stubby fingers away.

Just as she decided to return to her table empty-handed, Curtis arrived. 'Have you ordered yet?' He had the grace not to overtly play the hero. 'We should get Danny a beer. Their set will be over soon.'

The drunk man slunk away.

Jade thanked Curtis, who gave one of his bone-melting grins. 'I didn't want to interrupt in case you liked him, but...'

Jade gave an exaggerated shudder. 'Let's just get these drinks.'

Curtis boasted the golden trifecta: rich, super smart and obscenely good-looking. Even though he had five years on Jade and Elena, the girls had grown up seeing him regularly because his and Elena's parents were friends. Jade and Elena had been inseparable, so Jade had attended their gatherings. Once, when climbing from the tender boat onto Curtis's family's yacht, she'd dropped her wallet into the water. Without hesitation, he'd stripped off and dived in to save it. He'd come to the surface, droplets sparkling on his toned biceps, dark blond hair slicked back like a Greek god. In that moment, he'd become Jade's first crush. They'd never dated, but he still held a special place in her heart.

Back in their booth, they clinked glasses. Iris and Curtis shared a look of – what was it? Longing? Their clinginess struck Jade as odd. They were acting like a couple in the flush of first love, only they'd been together for two years.

Jade glanced away. She found it difficult seeing them together; Curtis had been Elena's boyfriend until she died. He'd waited a year before dating again – a decent amount of time, right? Jade couldn't expect him to mourn forever. Grief held no rules. Jade's misery had sent her running from Melbourne to spend more than a year in Houston. She'd only been back six months.

Curtis might have moved on, but Jade would never replace Elena. She had other friends, sure, but none qualified for best friend status. She always held herself aloof. Her mother gave her knowing looks and told her she couldn't hide in an emotional fortress all her life, but Jade knew better than to turn her back on the past.

The live music ended, and the volume of chatter grew as the musicians put down their instruments and made their way to the bar. Danny slid into the booth next to Jade, face gaunt, the T-shirt under his jacket tight across his pecks. Drumming kept his upper body fit.

She gave him a peck on the cheek. 'Awesome, as usual.'

'And you're charming, as usual,' he shot back.

She checked her watch. 'Nick's late. Is he coming?' Nick, Curtis and Danny had been an unbreakable trio since high school. Elena, Iris and Jade had completed the six, now reduced to five.

Danny stiffened and glanced at Curtis and Iris as if the three of them held a secret. They and Nick worked at BeanBlitz, Curtis's tech startup that developed accounting software. He'd named it as thoughtfully as Danny had named his band: Bean after bean counters from the fairytale *Jack and the Beanstalk*, and Blitz because that's what he intended to do to the market.

Jade sighed like a schoolkid with nobody to have lunch with. They probably didn't mean to exclude her, but their in-jokes and shorthand about company issues marked her as an outsider. Sometimes, she wondered why they continued to invite her to these nights out.

A beat too late, Danny answered, 'We don't think he'll make it.'

Iris added, 'He didn't come to work yesterday and hasn't been answering calls.'

Jade stirred her G&T with her straw. This explained their uptight behaviour. 'Has Nick gone off the grid like this before?'

'Never.' Iris adjusted her bandana, dark bob framing the concern on her face.

'So, what? Is he faking a sickie? Gone on a drug binge? Met someone?' Jade tried to lighten the mood – Nick wouldn't ditch work without an explanation, he didn't do drugs, and, unlike Curtis, who always had a woman on his arm, he skipped the Casanova gene – but they stared at her blankly.

'Not sure.' Curtis pulled Iris closer, and Jade realised she'd misread their signals earlier. Concern, not lust, had driven their clinginess.

She changed tack. 'Should we do something? Check his apartment?'

Curtis grimaced. 'I went there this afternoon, but he didn't answer the door, so...'

Jade didn't want to overreact, but she'd already lost one

friend, and apprehension glared large in the swig Iris took of her wine, Curtis's downcast gaze, and Danny's white-knuckled grip on the table. 'Should we call the police? They could break into his house and make sure he's okay.'

Jade liked Nick, although he frustrated her by agreeing with whatever Curtis said. She wished he'd speak his mind instead of acting like a spineless sycophant. His conversation sparkled brighter when Curtis wasn't around. To be fair, it must be difficult for him hanging out with high achievers like Curtis and Danny. Curtis had chalked up remarkable business success, and, while Danny hadn't reached the pinnacle of musical stardom he deserved, he shone as a drummer of note. Nick, the supporting actor, not the lead, joked about vanishing into obscurity next to the others, and his quips carried some truth. In his early thirties, with wire-rimmed glasses and a slight paunch, Nick already looked middle-aged. Still, he formed part of the gang, and Jade hoped he hadn't run into trouble.

Danny reached a comforting hand to her shoulder. 'He'll be okay. He wasn't ... depressed or anything.'

'We didn't think Elena was either.' Jade's response came out sharper than she intended.

Curtis winced like he'd been stung.

'Come on, I can't be the only one worrying about that.' Jade appealed to Iris for support. 'We have to do something.'

Iris cocked an eyebrow at Curtis, who clearly acted as the boss outside the office as well as in it, and said, 'We could call his parents. Someone must have a spare key. Then we could check on him.'

Curtis rubbed the stubble on his chin. 'Let's give it one more night. If we can't get hold of him tomorrow, we'll contact his folks.'

'And if we can't find him, we'll call the police,' Jade insisted.

Curtis bowed his head. 'Okay.'

Far from reassured, Jade drained her gin and tonic.

Chapter 2
No News is Good News

By Monday night, Jade still had no news of Nick. According to Curtis, Nick's parents had also been trying to get hold of him and, sick with worry, had used the spare key Nick had given them and checked his apartment. He wasn't there. They'd found no clues to his whereabouts and nothing to indicate he'd been there since the others had last seen him at work. His cat, Blackie, had been starving, so they'd taken her home with them. Distressed, they'd contacted the police, and now, Jade and her friends could do nothing but wait.

Jade faced another meal alone in her one-bedroom apartment in Elsternwick – a thriving suburb with an eclectic mix of shops and eateries that somehow managed to be both daggy and trendy. On the main street, she could indulge in food from any corner of the globe: Chinese, Japanese, Greek, Italian, Thai, Hungarian or Indian.

Her three-story cream brick apartment building had a retro vibe with a concrete carpark covered by a metal roof. Although she worried about security, being on the ground floor offered the advantage of a small courtyard behind the front fence. Lined with camellias and geraniums, it was Jade's favourite place to unwind with a glass of wine. Her kitchen adjoined a living area, where she'd crammed a small pine dining table with four chairs and a couch. Her bedroom had enough space for a queen-sized bed and chest of drawers. She'd draped a paso doble cape – black on the outside, red on the inside – over her bedhead for a splash of drama. The bathroom, with its brown floral tiles, needed an update, but she kept it clean.

She rifled through her fridge and pulled out anything suitable for a stir fry: chicken breast, onion, a limp carrot, broccoli and some wilted bok choy that looked ready for the green waste bin. Hardly an inspired meal. Much like Jade's career at present. A journalist without a story was as bad as a dancer with no music. Since returning from Houston, she'd been desperate for a solid hook. Sure, she wrote routine articles for her small community paper, such as her 'What's On' column, but she usually worked on something more substantial in the background requiring thorough investigation and deep thought. Right now, she only had the dull piece about weather patterns. It crossed her mind that Nick's disappearance could become a story, but even as the odds of him turning up with an innocent explanation dwindled, she clung to hope. Besides, if she used every private drama for a scoop, her friends would never trust her. She needed some separation between her work and personal lives.

That afternoon, she'd met with her boss, Zain, to discuss her professional development, but their discussion only highlighted her lack of direction. In Houston, she'd headed down the path of crime reporting. She loved the mental stimulation of this work but hated the associated danger. Writing about the arts or features suited her better, but didn't have the same zing, so she remained untethered. Zain had encouraged her to explore other options.

To her aggravation, he'd made it clear her American experience counted for little in Australia. 'You first need to develop local networks and credibility,' he'd said when she'd requested a meatier focus than the shenanigans of a minor celebrity.

Being told she needed to prove herself all over again made Jade want to scream. She'd left the meeting ready to quit, but her respect for Zain kept the impulse at bay. An icon in the industry, known as a stickler for the rules, he maintained the highest ethical standards. Jade wanted to learn from him but worried he'd rein her in for too long.

In the meantime, only deciding what to write stopped her from working on an article in her own time. As her thoughts drifted, the knife slipped, and Jade whipped her thumb out just in time. Unsettled, she refocused on dicing chicken, only to be interrupted by the phone.

She speed-washed her hands and answered. 'Danny, any news?'

'Hi, yeah, it's um…'

Jade rested a hand on the Laminex countertop, bracing for what his tone flagged as bad news. 'What's happened?'

'Nick's dead.'

'What?' Jade clutched the bench tighter, struggling for breath.

'The police found him in Lilydale. Out the back of a supermarket.' Danny sounded husky, as if he'd been crying.

Cold swept over Jade, and she lowered onto a stool, the knife dangling in her hand. Nick. Dead. No wonder he'd been a no-show at the pub. Hell, the last time she'd seen him, he'd been joking along with the rest of them. She couldn't imagine he'd never laugh again, never bore them with stories about Blackie the cat, never crash and burn after trying another tacky pickup line on a stranger – he had a theory about playing the odds, convinced if he hit on enough women, eventually, one of them would say yes.

Danny went on. 'They didn't tell his parents many details, but they're treating it as suspicious and will put out a public appeal for information.'

Suspicious? Had Nick been murdered? A tight band curled around Jade's chest. She couldn't believe he was gone, couldn't imagine who on earth would hate him enough to kill him.

'Oh God. How's Curtis doing? And Iris?' Jade had almost forgotten, but Iris had dated Nick briefly, years before she got together with Curtis. They'd all been friends so long that nearly every pairing had been tried like in some tacky reality TV show.

'It's been rough. And the police want to question us because, well, I guess, because we work with him.' Danny sniffed.

'Hell, that's ... are you okay?'

She leant into the following silence, waiting for his response. 'You there?'

Danny cleared his throat. 'Yeah, it's just ... it's such a shock. And the circumstances ... they can't even release his body for the funeral until after an autopsy. His parents are a mess.'

Jade toyed with the knife. 'You'll let me know when they've set a date?'

'Sure.'

'This is'—Jade couldn't find the right words—'it doesn't seem real.'

Danny's voice tremored. 'Any chance we can catch up in the next few days? I don't like being alone.'

'Sure. Just tell me when and where.'

'I'm supposed to watch a friend play at the Ruby Room on Wednesday night. Join me? Or is it too soon?'

Jade knew the jazz bar in the city. Its sultry vibe seemed strangely fitting for the occasion. 'Nick would understand we need to see each other.'

'I'll text you the details.'

She hung up, dry-mouthed. She'd barely put Elena's tragedy behind her, and now grief consumed her all over again. Another member of their circle had died. A strangled sob escaped her lips. Two deaths within the space of three years. That couldn't be normal.

Paranoia set in, and she needed to talk to someone, so she texted her mum. *Can you come over?* Jade found regular contact with her mother one of the biggest advantages of being back in Melbourne.

Within minutes, Gina responded. *Be there in fifteen. Everything okay?*

Jade was most definitely not okay, but she'd explain when her mum arrived. What was going on with her friends? They used to be healthy, happy and fun-loving. Although looking back, she realised they hadn't been truly carefree since before they lost Elena.

Chapter 3

Mamma Mia

A LOUD KNOCK reverberated from the front door. 'Yoo-hoo. It's me.' Jade's mum, Gina, didn't know how to make a quiet entrance.

Jade opened the door to her mother, who wore a vibrant yellow jumpsuit with bellbottoms. She'd chosen to direct *Mamma Mia* as the school play this year and was going through a seventies fashion phase, scoffing at the idea of reserving costumes for the stage.

Gina waltzed into the living room carrying a cardboard box with 'Jade's Keepsakes, Keep Out' scrawled on the side in black felt tip marker. She placed it on the coffee table. 'I'm clearing out the cupboards so we can sell the house. Now you're back, you can take this.' She enveloped Jade in a hug and a cloud of Chanel No. 5.

'You're selling our house?' Jade had grown up there; it held her past, her memories. Even at twenty-seven, at her parents' place, she still felt like a girl.

'We're downsizing so we can buy a place in Mansfield.'

'Mansfield? Why there?'

'Darling, you sound like a parrot. We want a weekend escape. Somewhere to retire to when we're ready. Mansfield's wonderful.

It has Lake Eildon for summer sports, Mt Buller for winter sports and interesting countryside year-round.'

Retire? Her parents were way too young. 'But you don't ski, and you hate boats—'

'Hate is a strong word, dear, and the point is, your father loves those things. It's not all about me, you know.' Jade kept her sharp retort to herself as her mother prattled on, her Sri Lankan Burgher accent growing stronger the more she warmed to her topic. 'Marriage and relationships are all about compromise, something you'll understand one day when you find yourself a nice boyfriend. What happened to that lovely young man you went out with? My friend's son, Jack, wasn't it? No, John.'

Okay, so seeing more of her mother was already wearing thin. 'It didn't work out.' Jade had met John for a coffee to appease her mother, but she didn't need the distraction of falling in love, late date nights, infatuation, arguments, and the inevitable breakup to follow. No, she needed to make business contacts and re-establish herself in Melbourne, to write stellar articles and make a name for herself. After the wrench of leaving her friends in Houston, she couldn't bear the risk of forming new friendships, let alone a romance. Saying goodbye hurt too much.

Gina tutted. 'You need to go out more, take up a hobby. You're far too focused on work.'

'I do have a hobby. What do you call dance? And I need to concentrate on work, or I'll never progress. Journalism's competitive, you know that.' Bloody hell! She didn't need criticism right now.

Perhaps realizing she'd overstepped, Gina softened her tone. 'You wanted to see me?'

'Let's sit.' Jade led her mother the ten steps to the living area, and they settled on the blue couch her brother had given her when he'd upgraded to a new one. It had faded across the top and bore a few patches – much like how she felt after her time in the US.

Gina studied Jade's face, perhaps noticing her puffy eyes and blotchy skin. 'What is it, darling? Have you been crying? Listen to me babbling on when you're upset. You can tell me anything. I won't judge. Are you pregnant? Gay? Pan? I've read all about that.'

'Mum, no. Nick's dead.'

The back of Gina's hand flew to her forehead. 'How awful.' She leant closer to Jade. 'What happened?'

Jade told her what little she knew.

'Murdered? My word. I'm so sorry. I know he was a dear friend of yours, though I never quite understood why ... he always struck me as insipid.'

'Mum!' Jade had similar thoughts, but she'd never say them out loud, especially at a time like this. The best – and worst – thing about her mother was her propensity to speak without censorship.

'Sorry, sorry, it's just, the shock. Nick. Horrendous. Are you okay?'

'No, I...' Tears sprang into Jade's eyes. 'I just can't go through this again.'

Gina drew Jade into a tight hug. 'I know it's hard, darling.'

After a few moments, Jade drew away and wiped her cheeks. 'Thanks, I needed that.'

'You're never too old for a hug from your mother.' Gina hardly paused for air before asking, 'So, who did it?' Leave it to her to get straight to the point.

'I don't know yet. I still can't get my head around the fact that he's dead.'

'We need to consider everyone who knows him. Your friends, for a start. I've always wondered about Curtis. Too successful too quickly if you ask me.'

Jade breathed deeply to summon patience. 'Do you really think Elena would have gone out with someone capable of murder?'

Gina's eyes grew wide. 'Maybe he killed her too.'

'Mum, stop. Elena suicided.'

Gina slumped. 'You always said you didn't believe it.'

'I know, but—'

'Or what about Danny? He's always been so emo. Or Iris ... didn't she date Nick? Or wait—'

'Mum!'

Her mother lifted an eyebrow. 'Mark my words. It's the rich ones, always the rich ones.'

'Enough.' Jade wanted to know who'd killed Nick, but she couldn't tackle the question while her grief scraped her raw. She needed time and space to think about it ... and quiet, something she'd never get with her mother around.

Gina went on to chat about the Mansfield properties she and Jade's dad, Keith, had inspected. To Jade's bafflement, they appeared serious about moving to the country.

When Jade started yawning, Gina stopped. 'Will you be okay, my sweet? I snuck away to see you, but I've got to get back. I need to go to school early tomorrow morning. The sets won't design themselves, you know.'

'I'll be fine. Thanks for coming.'

Gina hugged her again. 'Don't forget we're going to see *Chicago* on Monday night.'

Jade couldn't possibly forget; Gina had reminded her every time they'd spoken since she'd booked the tickets. 'Yep. Can't wait.'

Gina gave Jade a once-over. 'Why are you wearing black? I know you're in mourning, but find something a bit more colourful for the theatre, okay? You have such gorgeous eyes'—they changed from blue to green depending on Jade's outfit—'wear something to make them pop.'

'Sure.' Jade found it easier to agree than argue.

'Right then.' Gina bestowed a kiss on each of Jade's cheeks, drew her into another bear hug, then bustled out the door, leaving Jade reeling as all the possibilities her mother had raised jostled in her mind.

Back on the couch, Jade closed her eyes, and images of Nick

played behind her eyelids. The time he bought his first sports car – a BMW M3 – and drove Jade to Mornington so sedately she'd needed to smother her laughter. The night they went out to celebrate Curtis offering Nick a job, and all he could do was sit there grinning over his beer. Nick. Someone had *killed* him. The shock of it made Jade's heartbeat thud in her ears, and she went light-headed.

Eager to think about something – anything – else, her attention turned to the box on the coffee table. She'd packed it before she left for Houston and could barely remember what she'd put in it. Kneeling, she tore off the packing tape with a satisfying rip and pulled the flaps apart.

One by one, she lifted out a couple of university assignments, a few articles she'd written, an old resume, an out-of-date diary and her blazer pocket adorned with school colours. One of Danny's demo CDs, 'Dance Junkie', caught her eye. After hunting through her chest of drawers in the bedroom for a DVD reader that plugged into her laptop, she pressed play and sat on the floor, back against the couch, to sift through a few more keepsakes.

The music brought a flood of memories, and before long, she forgot about the box and listened to the lyrics of the titular track.

> *If a day goes by and I haven't had a dance,*
> *I feel sad and blue coz that day has no romance.*
> *Day two rolls past and my body starts to shake,*
> *After three and four I've had more than I can take.*
> *Withdrawn and sad, I need a fix in haste,*
> *I'm crazed and caged coz these days have been a waste.*
> *I'll hunt for a woman who'll follow my lead,*
> *I'll grab her hand, and she'll give me what I need.*

Hold your drugs,
Hold your drink,
All I want
Is my dance fix.
Coz I'm a dance junkie,
My moves are kind of funky.
I'm a strong, tough guy
Who can make you feel high.

Jade chuckled at Danny's words. Not the least bit strong and tough, he did have a gift of making her feel high with acts of kindness. Once, he'd bought her a green stone at a garage sale, believing it to be jade. It was too smooth and perfect to be real, but that didn't make the gesture any less charming.

She closed her eyes and let her mind drift back to Elena's twenty-fourth birthday when Jade, Elena and the gang had celebrated at a nightclub in South Yarra – six months before Elena's death.

The friends let loose, happy to escape the pressures of their jobs for a night out. Curtis, always eager to support his friends, charmed the DJ into playing the demo of 'Dance Junkie'. Danny looked ready to burst with pride, and the six of them, sweaty and pumped full of adrenaline, formed a circle, arms around each other, and sang themselves hoarse.

Elena danced with abandon, fuelled by alcohol and her obvious passion for Curtis, almost manic in how fully she embraced the moment. Danny, Curtis and Iris seemed almost as uninhibited, while Jade suffered a twinge of envy because even as she joined in, her level of escapism stayed tempered. Despite her ballroom dance training, or maybe because of it, Jade worked better with choreography than improvising. Only Nick seemed less comfortable than she, his movements stiff and jerky. He made

Jade squirm by holding her too close – socially awkward, he lacked awareness of personal space. Although he tried hard, he never quite read the room.

As the evening wore on, Nick and Iris cozied up to each other. Previously, Iris had said she had no interest in him, so Jade didn't understand why she seemed to revel in his attention – until she caught her glancing repeatedly at Curtis in a futile attempt to make him jealous. Curtis, oblivious of the whole painful act, focused fully on Elena. Still, Iris played her role so convincingly that soon, she and Nick started kissing, marking the start of their romance.

With Elena and Curtis already a pair, Jade commiserated with Danny. 'Looks like we're the leftovers.'

He raised his eyebrows. 'Leftovers can be thrown together to make a lovely meal.'

'I'm not settling for second best. I want freshly cooked pasta. No, wait, not pasta. Curry. I want spicy hot chicken korma.'

Danny laughed. 'I'd be happy with pizza.'

'Right, well, I tell you what. If we get our meal of preference, all good. If not, and we're still hungry in ten years, let's reassess.'

He brushed the hair out of his eyes and held out his hand. They shook on it, both knowing passion would never happen. They had a strong friendship, sure, but no magic danced between them.

Three years later, Danny still had a messed-up love life. He'd been not-so-secretly in love with Elena for the last year before she'd died. Previously, he'd had many girlfriends, but although a raft of women threw themselves at him, he took no interest.

For her part, Jade had dated several men, but as soon as she flagged a negative trait – too clingy, too remote or too self-involved – she broke up with them. They rarely lasted more than a month. Her mum accused Jade of being a master at avoiding intimacy, but Jade saw no value in allowing someone into her life when it would all end in disaster. She preferred the single life to being miserable in love.

And Nick? Jade couldn't recall him dating again after he'd broken up with Iris a month or two later. And now, he'd never kiss another woman. In hindsight, his short-lived relationship with Iris probably remained the romantic highlight of his life. Impossibly sad.

Jade refocused on her keepsakes. A sparkling piece of jewellery drew her eyes. Elena's charm bracelet. Blinking tears, Jade shoved everything back inside and closed the box before her memories swallowed her whole. She'd dealt with enough of the past for one night.

Chapter 4

And All That Jazz

JADE SLIPPED into The Ruby Room, a jazz club tucked into the basement of one of Melbourne's cobbled laneways, and scanned the patrons to find Danny. Seven signature ruby paintings, crafted in thick acrylic, shimmered in the dim light. About a metre high and half the width, each showed a musical instrument against a charcoal background. Dollops of metallic red representing sparkling rubies embellished the singer's dress, the keys of the saxophone and trumpet, the pegs of the bass and guitar, the piano maker's name and the trombone's bell.

'Cool, aren't they?'

Jade whirled around to find Danny had snuck up beside her. 'You startled me.'

'We're all a bit edgy.' An aura of melancholy enveloped him, and pain dulled his eyes. Jade understood. Her raw grief for Nick merged with her ever-present sorrow over Elena, which had faded over time but now formed part of her, a tattoo on her heart. And Danny? He'd always adored Elena, pining for her with all the subtlety of a skywriter. No question, he'd taken her death hard, and now, another of his best friends had left them.

They hugged, and he held onto her like a life raft.

'I saved us a spot.' He led her by the hand through a maze of tables filled with people dressed in black – in Melbourne black was gold – to a prize position beside the stage.

'Awesome seats.' Jade could almost reach out and touch the double bass resting upright in a stand.

Before she could offer to buy drinks, Danny went to the bar and returned with two gin and tonics.

She accepted hers with gratitude. 'Who's the friend you came to watch?'

'Sammy, our lead singer. He originally trained in jazz and plays here, too, vocals and sax. The guy's a musical genius.'

Jade had interviewed Sammy a few years earlier when she'd written a piece about Mélange de Trois. 'It'll be fun seeing him playing a different style. How about you? I know you're still drumming up a storm, but are you still songwriting?'

Danny gave a self-deprecating laugh. 'I haven't composed anything for ages, not since ... well, not since Elena.'

'When you're ready, you'll go back to it. You're crazy talented.'

He grimaced. 'How about you? Still ballroom dancing?'

'Yeah, but the instructor I had before I went away has moved on, so I'm trying out a new one.' Jade missed her teacher from Houston, their bond impossible to replicate.

Danny slumped lower in his chair. 'I don't want to be a downer, but after what's happened, it's hard to pretend everything's okay. I can't believe we've lost another friend.'

'You must have read my mind.' Jade had started to wonder if her mother had hit on the truth by connecting the two deaths. 'The thing I can't wrap my head around is somebody did this. We can't blame a car accident or cancer. Somebody killed him and dumped him out the back of a supermarket like a piece of trash. I want to know who.'

'The police interviewed Curtis, Iris and me today. Horrible.'

The ground shifted beneath Jade's feet. Nick had been murdered, and statistics said he knew his killer, which increased the odds Jade knew him or her too. Hearing about Danny and the others being questioned brought this into sharp relief. 'Did the police tell you how he died? The news reports haven't said.'

Danny winced. 'They wouldn't reveal cause of death, but they found him in an industrial bin.'

'Hell! Who did this?' Jade's mind raced, trying to connect hazy dots.

The band emerged from backstage to a burst of applause. Sammy and the other musicians took their spots and struck a bold opening chord. Then another. After the third, the bass picked a rhythm, soon joined by the drummer. Sammy crooned about liquid love.

Danny gestured to the few couples swaying on the small dancefloor. 'Shall we?'

'Sure.' Jade's questions for Danny were multiplying, and dancing would draw their heads together so they could talk without interrupting the musicians.

She followed Danny to the floor, and they entered a comfortable dance hold. His slender frame had several inches on hers. Despite the situation, the joy of connecting with a partner caught her off-guard. Danny made her feel safe; he'd never misinterpret a rumba as something more. They could simply enjoy the music.

For a few minutes, she put her chaotic thoughts on ice and appreciated the quiet, dreamy number. Sammy's voice had the soothing quality of tropical ocean waves, and Jade enjoyed Danny's perfect rhythm, the warmth generated by their clasped hands and his angular shoulder under her left hand. Musicality oozed from his every pore and, despite having no formal dance training, he responded naturally to the song.

'We work well together, the leftovers,' Danny whispered in her ear.

'You remember?'

'Always.'

Jade laughed. She'd never turn to Danny if she didn't find someone else; while comfortable together, they lacked chemistry. Besides, the police were interviewing him about Nick. God, he could be a murderer. No, they must have got it wrong. Sure, he had a temper, but he wasn't capable of such violence.

Now the silence had been broken, Jade refocused. 'I can't stop thinking about who killed Nick. Do you think it's someone we know?'

Danny drew her closer. 'The police act like it's one of us. It's freaking me out.'

'Could it be related to work?'

Danny led Jade into a turn. When she faced him again, he said, 'I'm not sure.'

'Is it possible? Because I can't figure out why someone would want to kill him. He was so ... vanilla.'

Danny's steps slowed. 'Everyone has secrets.'

'Even you?'

He fell out of time with the music. 'Don't you see me as dark and mysterious?'

Danny's humour made her uneasy. She waited until they regained their rhythm before pressing further. 'Feels like there's a lot you're not telling me. What the hell goes on over there at Bean-Blitz?' Suddenly, rather than envying her friends' togetherness, she felt relieved to be apart from it.

'Look, I ... it's not straightforward. I don't know what happened, but—'

'Spit it out, Danny.'

'Wait until the set's over. I can't think clearly with the music so loud.'

Jade inclined her head to their table, too caught up in her spiralling suspicions to continue dancing. 'Another drink?'

Danny agreed, and they sat quietly until the musicians finished to generous applause. Sammy put his saxophone on a stand and came to say hello.

'I'm loving the show. Your solos are out of this world.' Jade spoke the truth, all the while wishing he'd leave, burning with impatience to grill Danny.

'You're too kind.' Sammy turned his attention to Danny. 'Would you like to play a song with us?'

'Mate, you know I don't do jazz.'

Jade wished they'd keep it short, smiling to hide her exasperation as Sammy replied, 'You undersell yourself. You'd manage one song.'

'Not today.'

A look passed between them, and to his credit, Sammy took the hint. 'Righto.'

'Sammy!' a woman called from an adjoining table.

He excused himself and went to greet her.

As soon as they were alone, Jade rounded on Danny. 'What's going on?'

'I'll tell you, but first, promise not to publish this information.'

Jade opened her mouth to object; she'd never write about her friends for a career break. But her face burned. Of course, she'd considered writing Nick's story – she had an insider perspective on his murder. It sounded predatory, but if she figured out who killed him, it would be a major coup. She needed to balance blind ambition with being a trustworthy confidante.

'Promise, or I won't tell you,' Danny insisted. 'Once I finish, you'll understand.'

'Okay, okay, I promise.' Jade sat forward, hopeful that once everything came out, he'd release her from their agreement.

'Are you sure you're ready for this?'

'You're scaring me. Just get on with it.'

Danny drew a deep breath. 'First up, Curtis isn't the clean superstar he makes out.'

'What do you mean? Did he kill Nick?' It couldn't be Curtis. Danny must have it all wrong.

He held up his hands. 'Whoa! I'm not saying that. I mean, it's possible, but I don't know for sure. What I do know is he's guilty of financial crimes.'

Jade baulked. Curtis, a criminal? She'd known him all her life.

True, he'd always had a slipperiness about him, but Jade thought he limited this to minor matters: he'd park in disabled parking spaces, he'd copy one-liners from his friends and bask in the laughs as if he'd made them up himself, or he'd travel without swiping his travel card between rarely manned train stations. Maybe she should have been suspicious about BeanBlitz's exponential growth, higher than anyone expected. Rumours had circulated about the source of his Midas touch even before Elena died. But breaking the law? What the hell did he do?

Chapter 5

Be Prepared

Danny, Six months before Elena's death

MUSIC WASHED OVER ME, and the lyrics from Sheryl Crow's 'The First Cut is the Deepest' pierced like pinpricks. All night I'd acted normal, but Elena and her untamed red hair held me captive. From across the room, I checked out her smooth, flat stomach above low-rise jeans. She draped her arm over Curtis in easy familiarity, and I ground my teeth at the thought of their intimacy.

We were lounging around in the Carlton home Elena shared with Jade, little more than student accommodation. The single-fronted Victorian terrace house in near-original condition had threadbare carpets, peeling paint, and couches with springs ready to burst through the fabric. At least it included the luxury of an inside toilet, although Elena had once taken us to the garden to show us the outhouse, still intact, despite the weeds barricading the splintered wooden door. Before long, she'd upgrade to something more upmarket. She'd already graduated and held a fancy role with Dragonworthy, a top investment company.

I didn't understand her job, but Curtis appeared endlessly fascinated by it and spent hours grilling her, while I tuned out and composed music in my head – usually something maudlin about unrequited love. Every now and then, I'd add a humorous flourish to my tune just to prove I didn't take myself too seriously, but who was I kidding? Love hurt.

My twin sister, Iris, wrapped her arms around her current flame, my mate Nick. They'd just got together, and already, she was heading down the path of smothering him like her previous boyfriends. It wouldn't last; Iris typically crushed hard then lost interest. I gave them three weeks. We weren't identical – obviously – but our dark hair, almond eyes and brooding natures left no question of our close relationship. We had different styles, though; she looked chic in a shift dress with a bold floral design, while I had more of a hippy vibe with hair on the longer side, loose pants and a V-neck shirt with embroidery around the cuffs and collar. I didn't present the image people expected from a rock drummer, and while many of my fellow musicians experimented with drugs, I'd seen too many of them come unstuck that way, so I kept to alcohol. Others probably saw me as a nerd, but I didn't care. I had no desire to end up in rehab.

Nick was rabbiting on about his amazing job with Curtis, who'd founded BeanBlitz. Physically, Nick looked unremarkable: average height, average build, medium brown hair. His podgy face made him seem older than a man in his early thirties. I couldn't believe we'd aged so much; some days I felt like a grandpa, others still like a schoolkid.

Nick, usually deadpan, not super-expressive like me, gushed, 'You should've seen Curtis at our investor meeting. He made the company sound like we had the brains of NASA with a concept to match. They practically had their check books out on the spot.'

I chuckled at Curtis. 'You've always known how to suck people in. Remember when you got Mr Halliday'—our high school principal—'to take the whole of year twelve to the beach for environmental day?'

The three of us had been mates since year seven, so although I had no interest in IT, I felt on the outside, not being part of Curtis's team. Early on, he'd invited me to join, but I'd declined, too intent on my flailing music career.

Just as I thought about leaving, Jade came through the front door in a pencil skirt and shirt.

Elena asked her to join us, but Jade made a beeline for her bedroom, saying, 'I've got to get out of this gear before I suffocate.'

The two of them acted weirdly formal with each other as if they'd been fighting, which, although they tried to hide it, I sensed had happened a lot lately.

A few minutes later, Jade emerged wearing tracksuit pants and a hoodie and darted into the kitchen. I thought about following her in there for a chat, but before this translated into action, she came out again, holding a steaming plate of leftover pasta.

When I caught her eye, she smiled warmly. 'Hey, Danny. How's work?'

She'd written an article about my band, so I kind of owed her – we were struggling to get noticed, and Jade's media splash had provided a brief boost. Still, I didn't come close to making a living. I'd given myself until the end of the year to earn more, or I'd have to become a music teacher, and I didn't have the patience for a role like that. September had come, bringing a cold, wet spring, and schools had already advertised positions for the following year. I should have been home applying for jobs instead of lounging around, wallowing in unrequited love for Elena.

I mustered a grin. 'We're having fun. A couple of gigs a month.' The local pub didn't pay us for those appearances, so we weren't exactly killing it.

'Don't give up. You guys are great.' Her spontaneous encouragement gave me hope.

I gestured to the couch, inviting her to sit, but she grimaced. 'Sorry. I've gotta catch up on some research.' She worked harder than anyone else I knew. It couldn't be healthy.

As she headed away, Curtis called, 'You're not joining us?'

His smarmy charm grated because I recognised his insincerity. Curtis didn't trust journalists, so although Jade was one of us, he sometimes avoided her. I didn't have a clue what made him shy of the press – he loved all eyes on him – but Curtis could be unpredictable.

Jade left, and something subtle shifted in the atmosphere, like now that the adult had gone to bed, the kids could party. Never mind that Jade, like Elena, was five years younger than the rest of us.

Curtis got up. 'Beer, anyone?'

After handing longnecks around, he sprawled on the couch next to me. 'You still thinking about working in some hole of a school?'

I lifted my drink in a mock toast.

'What if you had another way to earn a crust?' His gaze took in the room, but I sensed his awareness of me in his peripheral vision, assessing my reaction.

'You offering me a job?'

He grinned.

I sat up straighter. 'I don't know the first thing about IT. Besides, aren't you a startup? How can you afford more staff?'

'Mate, never underestimate the underdog. I got this. Bean-Blitz is living up to its name. We're exploding. I need people. You could start part-time if that suits and build up or down, depending on what happens with the band.'

'But what would I do? Serenade your clients?' Despite my nonchalance, a hopeful drumbeat started in my head, accompanied by a long-held note. I swore I should be writing film scores – a job in the movies would be heaven – but I guessed that wasn't what Curtis had in mind.

'Ya clown, you make out like you don't have a business brain, but I haven't forgotten your math grades at school. Plus, you did half a commerce degree.' I'd dropped out to concentrate on music. 'I need a spreadsheet junkie, and you've got the smarts.'

His offer was worth considering. I enjoyed playing with numbers, but more so, I really didn't want a future filled with snotty-nosed kids practicing scales. 'It's all above board? I mean—'

Curtis looked offended. 'Who do you think I am? It's a serious business.' The speed of his response made me wonder what the heck he was up to, but I brushed it off and heard what I wanted to hear. 'Come to my place tomorrow, and I'll show you what's involved.'

He was doing me a favour, but I couldn't shake the sensation of being manipulated. At high school, we once did a group project together. I did most of the work, yet somehow, the teacher singled out Curtis for all the praise. Call me superstitious, but when 'Be Prepared' from *The Lion King* piped over the cheap speakers at Elena's, I should have paid closer attention.

Chapter 6

Zorba the Greek

As it turned out, working for Curtis reminded me of performing in a band with a prima donna singer – we all supported him to make him shine. To begin with, we met in his living room, but three months later, he splashed out and rented a flashy office in South Yarra, an inner-city suburb with panache.

The day Curtis picked up the keys, he and I stood in the doorway surveying the layout. Offices lined two walls, interrupted by a kitchenette and the boardroom with furnishings of tempered glass and black leather. The magnificent corner office already had Curtis's name on it. Work cubicles took up the rest of the space; their faux wooden floors and minimalist Scandi-inspired desks made from light wood and white metal frames looked brand new.

Curtis gestured proudly. 'Isn't it a ripper?'

I stared out the floor-to-ceiling windows at the view of the city skyline, gobsmacked. 'How can we afford it?'

'Steve owns the building. He cut me a deal.' Steve, Elena's stepdad, finance guru and real-estate mogul, also happened to be friends with Curtis's parents. When Curtis was seeking investors for BeanBlitz, Steve had jumped in feet first and become a company director, alongside Elena's mother.

'Nothing like a good bit of nepotism.'

Curtis gave me a reproachful glare. 'He's one of our directors, so he wants us to succeed.'

I tried to bring him back to earth. 'We don't have an income yet.' He seemed to forget we were a startup, not some oil-rich corporate. Our product had yet to hit the market. Okay, so I hadn't completed my commerce degree, but I'd been doing the books long enough to know our expenses were accelerating faster than the theme song from *Zorba the Greek*. 'We'll need a new investor.'

An enigmatic grin spread across Curtis's face. 'Don't you worry about that.'

I wanted to know more, but before I could ask, he crossed the floor, set his bag on the kitchen bench, and took a bottle of Moët and Chandon from the fridge. He popped the cork and poured, sending bubbles cascading over the rims of two glasses.

'A toast'—he raised his glass regally—'to BeanBlitz, the start of the Haycroft empire!'

Men on a mission, we clinked glasses. His enthusiasm, difficult to resist, made me temporarily veer away from my dreams of musical stardom. I envied his lashings of confidence. Maybe if, like him, I acted as though I owned the world, I'd achieve the success I craved.

'When do the others get here?' We wouldn't have needed so much space for just the two of us, but, with further disregard for our budget, Curtis had recruited more staff.

'After ten. I want to make sure everything's ready first.' He shuffled his feet, a sure sign of mischief.

'What's going on?'

'I don't want to blindside you, so...' He hesitated a whisker longer before breaking out his salesman smile. 'I offered Iris a job.'

'Really?' Too surprised to know whether I was pleased or furious, I sure as hell didn't feel comfortable with the situation. My sister, a creative soul, a graphic designer and brilliant photographer, also had a degree of vulnerability. For reasons I couldn't quite articulate, I wanted to shield her from Curtis.

'It happened spontaneously. We were chatting, and I saw her potential.' While Curtis liked to appear impulsive, I knew he was far too calculating to leave a hiring decision to chance. Everyone he took on had a gift that made them perfect for their role: Nick, the most meticulous person I'd ever met, worked in operations; the software engineers' IQs landed off the charts; and Curtis's vision made him a brilliant CEO. Only my talent didn't fit. A musician in accounts? Go figure. Sure, I could handle numbers, but I didn't have the same level of expertise as the others. Still, Curtis could always identify people's strengths and weaknesses and used them accordingly.

'What role will she do?'

The answer seemed obvious even before he replied, 'Sales and marketing.' Mum always said Iris had 'the gift of the gab'.

'But she's already got a job. She loves her work.' While her personal life resembled a train wreck, she'd aced her degree and landed steady work in corporates ever since, unlike her graphic design cohorts from college, most of whom had drifted into other careers or side-hustles.

Curtis crossed his arms. 'She's resigned but has to work out her notice, so she won't start for a couple of months.'

I resolved to speak to Iris.

Just then, Steve breezed through the door in dark wash jeans and a blue woollen crew neck. He took one look at Curtis and burst out laughing – the only difference in their outfits, down to their RM Williams boots, came from the sage colour of Curtis's top. I stood beside them in my leaf-print shirt over white linen pants, leather necklace with a raw quartz pendant, and hair flopping down over my eyes. I'd never fit in with this crew.

Only after Steve finally stopped bonding with Curtis did he acknowledge me. 'Good to see you, Danny. How's the band?'

'We're doing okay.' To my bafflement, my musical life was looking up. Aria Belle, one of Australia's homegrown pop stars, had come to our show, and after, she'd enquired about the rights to a song I wrote, 'Dance Junkie', one of my rare lighter pieces that didn't include a single reference to unrequited love. If I looked hard enough, I'd find a message in there somewhere, but back to the point – if Aria put it on an album, I'd have every chance of a hit on my hands. Optimism bubbled brighter than the champagne Curtis was busy pouring for Steve.

We toasted again.

Steve drew himself tall. 'Curtis, Danny, may this space give you the impetus to grow your business into a lasting concern. Remember me when you're in Australia's top one hundred companies.' He used the same charm offensive as Curtis, which won women's hearts and men's confidence. Only the hardening effects of time set them apart from each other. Age had toughened Steve to the point of ruthlessness, while Curtis retained some soft edges.

Two such similar men might be expected to develop rivalry, a Scar versus Simba dynamic, if you will, but it seemed Steve viewed Curtis as an asset rather than a threat, so he'd assumed more of a fatherly Mufasa role. And yes, I'm a little obsessed with *The Lion King* – people underestimate it because it's a kids' movie, but really, it's *Hamlet* in disguise.

Steve clapped an arm around Curtis. 'I'm proud of you, son.'

Son? A term of endearment, or was he already viewing Curtis as his son-in-law? I conjured an image of Elena in a bridal gown gazing lovingly into Curtis's eyes. Oh God! I had to stop torturing myself.

I barely kept up with Steve and Curtis's mutual backslapping, too caught up in the mournful ballad playing in my head. Before I knew it, they'd emptied the bottle, and Steve was guiding Curtis to the corner office for 'a quick word', leaving me to clean up, a half-empty drink in my hand. A hot blast of fury coloured my cheeks. Steve's careless dismissal of me made me want to shake him until he noticed me – really noticed me, like he wanted me to have a future with Elena. I held my champagne flute by the stem, tempted to smash it on the side of the sink, picturing shattered glass littering the basin, shards of crystal catching the light.

I started counting to ten, the only useful tip I'd learnt from the anger management training my mother had made me do as an adolescent.

As I reached seven, my phone rang. An unknown number. I only answered in the off chance it had something to do with my song.

'Danny?' I didn't recognise the woman's voice.

'Yes, this is he.' How did I manage to sound so pompous?

'I'm Mary, Aria Belle's manager. We just adore your song, "Dance Junkie". We'd like to record it.' I rose from agony to ecstasy fast as a bird in flight – now there was a line I could use as a lyric.

After we arranged to meet, I downed the rest of my glass in one go.

Chapter 7

The Little Drummer Boy

SAMMY HAD SCORED our regular gig at our local, the Rock 'n' Barrel, because he knew the owner, and we drew enough of a crowd to keep our spot. Here, I lost myself in the warm arms of music, soothed by abstract emotions rather than the barbs of reality.

Today, my reality wasn't hard to face: Aria Bell planned to make a hit of my song, and I'd convinced myself she'd then ask for more. When I sat down to write, new songs flowed like a river after rain. To celebrate my imminent fame, I'd invited Curtis, Elena and Iris – who'd come alone as she'd already split up with Nick – to watch us play.

I could tell the breakup had upset Iris because she refused to talk about it and pretended not to care. Usually, she was all too willing to whine about her exes. She'd only joined me at the pub because I'd promised not to invite Nick or ask about him – although I still planned to corner her about her decision to work for Curtis.

For now, as I played, my awareness centred on Elena. My performance always elevated a notch around her, my sensations heightened by her presence. I floated on a cloud of notes, ready for my solo, invigorated by the melodic bassline and buffeted by our singer's husky voice. Sammy, the legend.

I silently dedicated my starring moment to Elena, a love letter in sound. Baring my soul, I began with a flurry of beats, the patter of rain on a metal roof. Sunlight burst through the clouds, brightening the sound, increasing the pace. I reached further skyward in a blaze of passion so hot it sounded almost brash, only to sour and plummet to a slower pace. The band kicked back in, and the audience applauded.

Until the day I overheard my band members talking about 'the Elena factor', I used to think I kept my infatuation private, which didn't bode well for my future as a professional poker player.

The crowd lapped us up, and before I knew it, our first set finished. I left my drumsticks on the snare and joined my friends in their booth at the back, where empty plates and a forest of beer and cocktail glasses showed how liberal they'd been with their credit cards. I caught a waft of Elena's perfume, fresh as the sea breeze, above the background reek of hot chips and stale beer. If we were alone, I'd have asked her the brand.

'Great show!' Elena's compliment lifted my spirits higher, but even as I bathed in her praise, I clocked her radiance had dimmed. I didn't doubt her sincerity, but I'd studied Elena so closely that I noted her low mood.

Curtis cleared his throat. 'To the man of the moment. Congrats on the Aria Belle song, and well played tonight.'

Elena shifted infinitesimally away from him. Had they argued? A butterfly of hope stirred in my chest. Yet, even as I wished for their relationship to choke, I berated myself for disloyalty to Curtis, and I wished no heartbreak on Elena.

'Hear, hear!' Iris slapped me on the back, catching me off guard and bumping me into the table.

I righted myself. 'Steady on.'

Iris chuckled. 'Who's for another drink?'

After she took everyone's order, I seized the opportunity to speak to her alone. 'I'll come with you. See if I can get us a discount.'

We ordered the drinks: cosmopolitans for Elena and Iris, tequila shots for Curtis and me.

I adopted a casual air. 'So, you're coming to work for Curtis?'

'I wondered how long you would take to bring that up. What's your problem with it?' She played with the diamantes on her denim shirt. On anyone else, the outfit would have looked tacky, but she'd picked a classy design and could have been a model for *Vogue*.

'Who said I have a problem? I just want to make sure you've thought it through.'

'Can't help yourself, can you? Always have to act the big brother. You do know I was born first?'

Man, did Iris love to gloat about our birth order. Per family folklore, Dad said Iris popped out like she couldn't wait to escape the womb, while I, evidently more reluctant to face the world, required medical intervention. With the benefit of hindsight, I'd say I was wiser. Not that our childhood held any more trauma than anyone else's, but I seemed to bruise easily – not physically, but words punched their weight on me, music dragged me through a minefield of emotion, and I couldn't watch a sad movie without tears leaking down my cheeks. I've been told that society needs people like me to attune to the environment and keep others safe, but to date, I seemed to be the one in need of protection.

I tried to articulate my worries. 'BeanBlitz is a startup. It could all come crashing down.' The pop music playing over the speakers grated, eating into my skull.

'Don't be such a hypocrite. You work for Curtis.'

'My stakes are lower. I was basically unemployed before this. You have an amazing, reliable job. Why risk it?'

'Because startups are exciting. Fun. I can always go back to some boring old corporate role.' Her confidence took her wherever she wanted to go. She'd sucked all the self-assurance out of the gene pool, leaving me lacking. Curtis and she matched in that regard, and ... it hit me with gale force: was she in love with him? I'd seen the way she gazed at him. The idea of him having a hold over my sister made me reach for the barstool behind me.

'You okay?' she asked. 'You've gone pale.'

'I'm fine. You're not interested in him, are you?'

Iris burst into a full-throated belly laugh, although her tone sounded off-key. 'Curtis? You've got to be kidding.'

I glanced at the man in question, who, back stiff, seemed to have moved further apart from Elena than before.

Iris followed my line of sight. 'Something's up with them. They've been sniping at each other all night.'

I must have given her an accusatory stare because she pulled an innocent face. 'Hey, nothing to do with me.'

'All I can say is, thank God Elena isn't coming to work for him as well.' Our gang had become a bit too involved, working together and playing together; something felt vaguely incestuous about it.

As the bartender finished putting our drinks on a tray, Iris motioned with her head. 'I've got to go to the loo. See you back at the table.'

Grateful to have a moment alone to collect my thoughts, I meandered back, balancing the tray with care – it would be just like me to spill the whole thing – so I didn't catch a snatch of Curtis and Elena's conversation on purpose.

'How could you do that to me?' Her whisper vented a world of hurt.

'You're overreacting.' Curtis placed a hand on her shoulder, but she shrugged it away.

I should have minded my own business and cut off the conversation, but I stood mutely, listening, my mind leapfrogging itself to guess what Curtis had done: cheated on her, belittled her, hurt her? God help me if he'd laid a finger on her, I couldn't be held responsible for my actions. Another problem with being sensitive – my temper sometimes ran away with me. I once got suspended from school for fighting. In my defence, the guy I hit had been bullying Iris, so—

'You used me.' Elena glowered with a fury I'd never witnessed in her. Whatever Curtis had done must have been bad.

He tried to pacify her. 'Now isn't the time to discuss this. What's done is done.'

'Easy for you to say. I did nothing, but I'm implicated—'

'Enough. I get it, you're mad, and I'm sorry, but...' He looked over his shoulder, right at me.

I delivered the tray as if I'd just arrived from the bar. 'For you, madame, sir.'

Smooth as double whipped cream, Curtis picked up his tequila and skulled it with a quick, 'Cheers.'

Elena blinked the moisture from her emerald eyes and sipped her choice of poison. 'Here's to your rip-roaring success, Danny. You deserve this.' Under the dim lights, the colour of her cosmopolitan deepened; she could have been drinking blood.

How I longed to ease her pain, but I couldn't even ask what had happened in front of Curtis. To dig deeper, I'd have to admit I'd been eavesdropping. She seemed angry about being implicated in something, so it didn't sound like an affair, but what else could he have done? She didn't work for him, unlike most of us.

As I took to the stage for my second set, I tried to stop my mind from wandering down shadowy alleyways. No question, my next solo would be a whole heap darker than the last.

Chapter 8

Baby Did a Bad Bad Thing

THREE WEEKS in a row on our nights out, Elena drank herself sick. I even saw her popping a pill, probably ecstasy. She seemed to need an escape, and I longed to offer her one. Each time our group went out, I hovered, ready to sidle up to check on her, but whenever I came close, Curtis arrived before I could speak, standing protectively like a security guard. I half-expected him to follow Elena to the bathroom. It bordered on creepy.

Desperate to speak to her alone, I agreed to go for a run around the Tan with her on a day I knew Curtis wasn't available. Every Melbourne runner has done the Tan at some stage – a four-kilometre track around the Melbourne Botanic Gardens – but not a sporty person, I'd never even walked it. How would I manage such a feat?

I arrived at our assigned meeting place at the ungodly hour of six the next morning, bouncing on my toes, trying not to appear like a hack. The summer morning held a taste of the forecast scorcher, the earth having retained its heat from the day before. In my shorts and singlet, my limbs bright white, I clearly couldn't claim to be an outdoor boy. Despite my thin legs, I had a solid chest and arms. All those hours at a drum kit counted for something.

Elena jogged up to me, stunning as ever. 'You ready?'

'Raring.' Ha! What a liar.

As she drew closer, I spotted the bags under her eyes and the faint sallow tinge to her skin. My concern grew. I'd been right to fret; she showed signs of extreme stress. She kept moving, so I started running. Oh boy!

She set a steady pace, and I worked hard to keep up. All my oxygen went to my limbs, leaving none for talking. I resigned myself to waiting and focused on not embarrassing myself. Gravel crunched beneath my feet in a satisfying beat, and I found myself tapping a paradiddle in my head.

We wound past lush gumtrees and oaks, which invited further exploration of the gardens. Fitness freaks in Lycra filled the surprisingly busy, wide track – the beautiful people ensuring they remained beautiful. I had no idea so many madmen came out at this hour.

Buoyed by a sense of well-being, I enjoyed the rhythmic pounding, as if by running fast enough and far enough, I could exorcise my demons. In my dreamworld, Elena would be untroubled. Curtis would have nothing to hide. In fact, Curtis would be dating someone else entirely – definitely not Iris – and Elena and I would run off to Barbados. This was like therapy. Why hadn't I joined this running crowd sooner?

My euphoria lasted about five minutes before my breath grew jagged in my chest. Far from therapy, this now resembled torture. Beside me, Elena maintained speed, barely raising a sweat. God, she was gorgeous. I could bear getting up this early just to see her.

I kept going for ten or twelve excruciating minutes until we reached the Anderson Street Hill, where my lack of fitness caught up with me. I slowed to a walk, trying not to gasp air too greedily so I could maintain some dignity.

Elena matched my reduced pace, laughing, a precious tinkle with a rough edge. 'I guess you haven't been for a run in a while.'

'Not in a long time. It's scary how out of shape I am.'

'Why'd you agree to come?' The morning sun caught on the

golden flecks in her green eyes. I couldn't tell whether her sad gaze came from pity for my fruitless crush or the secrets I longed to pry out of her. Probably both.

I faced forward, eyes down as if I'd find the right words etched in the ground. 'Truth is, I'm worried about you. I...' Hell, I was making a mess of this. I needed to play it straight. I faced her. 'Are you okay?'

She found my gaze. 'Why do you ask?'

We stood, the stream of joggers parting around us, and I sensed that whatever I said next would make or break, a password to give access to her innermost thoughts or lock me out for good. 'Can we keep this conversation between us? I don't want to overstep and hurt you or Curtis.'

Her forehead wrinkled, and I wanted to reach across and smooth out the creases, but she nodded, so I went on. 'Please don't think I'm judging you, I'm not, but I've noticed you're drinking more and'—her frown deepened, so I veered in a different direction—'every time I try to talk to you, it's like Curtis wants to stop me from catching you alone. I just, well, I hope I'm wrong, but you seem troubled. Curtis is my mate, and I don't want to be disloyal ... but if he's ... I don't know, if he's hurting you in some way, please tell me, and we'll find a way to make it right.' I gulped, unsure whether my elevated pulse came from the run or my garbled attempt to win Elena's trust.

She didn't respond right away, but I could tell her mind was whirling from the way her eyes darted around my face, then dropped to my sneakers.

I hadn't realised I was holding my breath until she resumed hiking up the hill. Damn, I'd made her defensive and lost her. My opportunity to help had vanished fast as a rock plunging to the bottom of the ocean. Shoulders sagging, I trudged alongside her, trying to figure out how to redeem myself.

She turned. 'This is between us, right?'

'Yes, yes, of course.'

'Even if it's ... no, don't worry.'

I reached for her arm. 'Elena, please. I'll keep quiet. Whatever you say.'

She strode on, eyes forward, but at least she slowed down. 'Even about something illegal?'

I figured she was talking about the drugs, and I'd never dob her in. 'No worries.'

But she did look worried. This time, when she fell silent, I gave her time. Clearly, she needed to think this through, and I didn't want to rush her.

At last, she met my gaze. 'Let's get away from these people.'

She took a path into the gardens and said nothing more until she found a bench overlooking a lake. Under different circumstances, the soft morning light, the gentle breeze sending ripples across the water, and the ducks gliding across the surface could have been romantic, but the dark undercurrents of our conversation, the sweat drying on my body, and Elena's grave demeanour made it sombre.

She glanced over her shoulder before speaking. Nobody stood within earshot. 'Do you know where I work?'

'An investment company.'

'Right, which means I have access to privileged information.'

I nodded, fingers interwoven, concerned about where she was leading.

'I'm super-careful to keep this knowledge to myself. The need for confidentiality is ingrained in us at work. Breaking it can lead to charges of insider trading.'

'I'm sensing a "but".'

Elena chewed her bottom lip before answering. 'I'm such a sucker. I thought I could trust him, but I never should've said anything.'

'Curtis?' Suddenly, his better-than-a-fairytale finances made sense.

Staring out over the lake, she nodded. 'I only told him to show off. In a million years, I never would've guessed he'd use that information.'

My fingers clenched. 'Why don't you leave him?'

'I tried to break up with him, but he begged me not to, and ... I still love him. When I found out, I threatened to turn him in, but he said I'd come out of it worse than he would, and he's right. I knew the rules, and I broke them. So reckless.'

'That's not fair. More likely, he just didn't want to be implicated.' As I said it, my brain locked into gear. 'Wait, what company did you tell him about?' But I already knew the answer.

She named Blok Tech, whose stock had skyrocketed after a recent management hire, and my head sank into my hands. I groaned. Because Curtis didn't place those trades. I did. He hired me instead of a better-qualified candidate because he knew I'd be too gullible to see through his misdeeds.

She clutched my wrist. 'You didn't?'

The slight pressure of her fingers stoked my attraction for her even as I recalled the seemingly innocuous day. 'Curtis asked me to do it. I never thought...' If I hadn't been so preoccupied trying to make a success of Mélange de Trois and my song-writing career – constantly composing love anthems in my head instead of concentrating on the numbers swimming before my eyes – I might have been more concerned that startlingly favourable trades financed our extravagant spending. Curtis had told me he had a good advisor, and I'd never questioned him further.

'What other companies have you told him about? We've done well in other shares too.'

Elena cocked her head. 'Which ones?'

I scoured my memory. 'Welltopia'—Elena nodded, expression pained—'and ... what was their name? A grocery store.'

'Not Foodplay?'

'That's the one.'

She looked shattered. 'ASIC will have a field day.' Elena didn't need to explain the seriousness of messing with the Australian Securities and Investments Commission.

As the enormity of what had happened sank in, Elena blinked, and a shimmering tear trailed down her cheek. I reached across and brushed it away with my thumb, trembling at the intimacy.

It was off-limits to go after a mate's girlfriend.

Except when your mate had implicated you and his girlfriend in financial crimes.

Chapter 9

Dirty Deeds Done Dirt Cheap
Jade, now

IN THE RUBY ROOM, Jade stared at Danny, surrounded by a hum of conversation and the tinkle of glasses. Although he sat right across from her, he seemed far, far away. On what planet would he call Curtis a criminal?

'What exactly did Curtis do?'

Danny's eyes darted around the club before he answered. 'He used confidential information Elena had told him to make money on the stock market.'

'You're kidding! Insider trading. And he involved Elena?'

'Uh-huh. And that's not all. He asked me to place those trades, so I'm involved, while he's completely removed from it.'

Jade's sense of reality swayed off-kilter. While she found it unfathomable that Curtis had dragged Danny and Elena into his scheme, it explained why Elena had been drinking more and acting out. Jade tried to wash down a surge of anger with a swig of her drink, but it didn't work.

'This must have happened at least three years ago. Why are you still working for him? You could've turned him in to ASIC or the feds.' Jade knew from an article she'd written that financial crimes were notoriously difficult to prosecute; it could take years to accumulate enough evidence. All the same, there must be a way to prove Curtis engineered it.'

'I wanted to, but Curtis is smart. Nothing links him to it. Elena and I would've ended up in jail.' Danny pushed his hair out of his eyes. 'I hoped we'd got away with those trades, but Nick's murder has thrown a spotlight on BeanBlitz, and now I'm afraid it'll all come out.'

Suddenly, it made sense why the police were interviewing BeanBlitz employees about Nick's death. 'If Nick had found out about these trades … could Curtis have killed him to keep it quiet?' The words came out before Jade had fully thought it through. She was becoming more like her mother every day. At least she showed enough caution to make sure nobody around them sat close enough to hear over the background music.

'I'm not sure. Curtis can be a dick, obviously, but there's a huge leap from victimless crimes like insider trading to murder.'

Jade's simmering anger boiled harder. 'Do you really buy into the rhetoric of a victimless crime?'

'What do you mean?'

'For a start, what about you and Elena?' Jade picked the slice of lime off the top of her drink and sucked it dry.

'True, but you know what I mean. Nobody was killed.'

'Danny, open your eyes. Elena died. What if this drama tipped her over the edge?' Danny flinched, and the couple next to them turned to stare, so Jade lowered her voice. 'Even if that wasn't the case, what about other traders, the company stock and the impact on other businesses. It undermines the integrity of the stock market. I know it's not murder, but it's not nothing.'

Danny looked abashed. 'I never really worried about the flow-on effects. You won't tell anyone, will you?'

Jade wished she hadn't made that crazy promise. Curtis deserved to be exposed for his treachery. 'Cross my heart. But please, keep an eye on Curtis. The penalties for insider trading – I'm sure you've researched it – for big amounts, he could get a jail sentence.'

'I know.'

'People do crazy stuff to avoid doing time. I've written about cases where, after a small initial crime, the perpetrator did something worse to cover it up, then covered up the cover-up and...' She gestured at the sky.

He shifted in his seat. 'I can see how that happens.'

Suffocated by the crowded room, the moody ambience and Curtis's duplicity, Jade tugged down the neck of her long-sleeved top. 'If not Curtis, who do you reckon killed Nick? Did he have enemies, people with grudges against him?'

'I dunno, but he must have pissed someone off.'

Jade ran through typical murder motives: money, passion or retribution. 'I don't remember him having any long-term girlfriends, do you?'

'No.'

'Didn't he go out with Iris for a while?'

Danny bristled. 'You're not suggesting...? They dated for like five minutes. It didn't last.'

'Sorry, that came out wrong. Iris would never...' All the same, Jade flagged the possibility for further consideration. 'Any other ideas?'

Danny took a moment to respond, giving Jade the sense he was holding back. He had proved capable of subterfuge; after all, he'd hidden these poisonous secrets for three years. And Elena had taken Curtis's crimes to her grave. How had Jade missed all this? She felt the disorientation of waking up after sleeping through half a movie.

At last, Danny said, 'You know Nick, he was a bit of a loner.'

'What's it they say about still waters? He must've done something or witnessed something to make him a target.'

A muscle in Danny's jaw tightened.

'What are you not telling me?'

'Nothing.' Danny responded too quickly, convincing Jade he was nursing other secrets. Did he know who killed Nick?

She felt compelled to warn him. 'If Curtis is behind it, you could be in danger.'

'And if he finds out you suspect him, you could be too.'

Christ! Danny was right. But Curtis was her friend; he'd never harm her, would he? Then again, if he'd hurt Nick...

Thankfully, the band started their second set, and the saxophone's breathy tones wrapped around her, seductive, with a sense of longing. Jade used the break in conversation to digest what Danny had told her.

A terrible thought hit with gale force: if Nick knew about the insider trading and threatened to go public, Danny and Curtis had the same motive to kill him. She studied Danny's familiar face, his smooth skin, and slightly crooked nose from the time he'd ended up in a pub brawl. Could he have killed Nick? Placing the offending trades made him more heavily implicated than Curtis. On the other hand, if Danny had murdered Nick to cover up financial crimes, he wouldn't have told Jade about them. Unless he figured she'd find out herself, and he'd got in first so he could make her swear not to break the story. No, she was overthinking it. Danny would never be so conniving.

As she wrestled with her confusion, she speculated how Elena must have felt, betrayed by her boyfriend, Curtis. If only she'd brought Jade into her confidence. Together, they'd have found a way forward.

The shock of Nick's death had brought back the debilitating pain Jade had suffered after Elena died at just twenty-four – the nausea that took her appetite, the countless questions that stole her sleep, and the bottomless tears that made her doubt she'd ever get through a day without crying. None of Elena's friends or family had survived her death unscathed.

The coroner had blamed it on the sleeping tablets in her system, but Jade couldn't understand why Elena had taken all those pills. She'd graduated with top marks in a commerce degree and had been snapped up to work at Dragonworthy, the state's top investment company. Poised for success, she'd had every reason to live. Some people excelled at masking their true mental state, but Elena, so fresh and vibrant, had seemed far from depressed. Jade had urged the police to carry out a more thorough investigation, but they'd overruled her, and Elena's parents, who held more weight with the authorities, hadn't supported her request.

In the following months, Jade's counsellor had suggested she might be in denial. Jade knew if she admitted Elena had killed herself, she'd need to accept a level of blame. She could have done so many things differently, been a better friend in so many ways. For a start, she should have taken more notice of what was going on around her instead of being so career-focused. Sure, she'd spotted Elena's behaviour changes – moody and secretive, she'd been drinking far more than usual – but Jade had put it down to her intense relationship with Curtis.

Since then, rather than easing back on work hours, Jade had doubled down and thrown all her energy into her job, with high but knowable demands, unlike the stakes of friendship, where you could let someone down without even realizing it.

The band played a lengthy set, each song conjuring sounds of lost love, burning lust or hot summer nights. A high note on the saxophone almost reduced her to tears, but at last, Sammy announced the final number, an up-tempo piece that earned a standing ovation.

Jade finished the last of her drink, by then, mainly melted ice. She anticipated Sammy approaching again, but as if sensing their need for privacy, he nodded a greeting and drifted on.

'I wish we could have a do-over and make everything right for Elena,' she whispered, half to herself, half to Danny.

He made a sound close to a moan. 'Me too. What would you do differently?'

Jade drew on her straw, only to realise she was sucking air. She tried to answer truthfully. 'I'd be more present. Elena was in trouble, but I missed the signs or misread them.'

Danny slumped lower, sorrow written on his face and in his

posture. Doubtless, like her, he felt guilty of oversight and inattention, the failings of a friend too caught up in his own life to recognise Elena's unravelling mental health. She leant closer and placed a gentle hand on his arm.

He thumped his empty glass back on the table. 'Thing is, I knew exactly what was bothering her, but I didn't make it right. I made it worse.' He studied his hands. 'Ever since Elena died, I've been wondering whether she killed herself because of what Curtis did.'

'I'm thinking the same, but if she did, wouldn't she have left a letter so Curtis didn't get away with it?'

'That would've exposed me, and she'd never...'

Possibly Elena had returned Danny's affection. One night, Jade had arrived home and caught the two of them emerging from Elena's bedroom looking flushed. She'd suspected a post-coital glow, but in retrospect, perhaps they'd been discussing Curtis's betrayal. 'Did you two ever get together? I—'

'No, never! Despite everything, Curtis was still my mate.'

'Right.' Could Danny's infatuation with Elena have veered into something unhealthy? Jade started imagining a *Romeo and Juliet* scenario but snapped herself out of it. The music, the alcohol and Nick's murder had tipped her ideas into the realms of fantasy. She needed to step back.

Rather than slowing down, her brain sped up. Jade had never accepted Elena's suicide. What if she didn't kill herself? What if she'd threatened to go to the authorities? What measures would Curtis or Danny have taken to silence her? If Curtis had killed Nick to save himself from jail, he could have killed Elena for the same reason. Identical logic could be used for Danny. A chill swept up Jade's legs as if someone had opened the door and let in the winter night air. She couldn't tell if she was on to something or overreaching, her imagination soaring in a desperate attempt at redemption – because if Elena had been murdered, Jade's failures as a friend hadn't played a part in her death.

'What if Elena found something to use against Curtis that

didn't implicate you or her? If she'd threatened Curtis, would he have hurt her?'

Danny stared into his empty glass. 'You think Curtis made her take those pills?'

'Maybe.'

Danny's mouth opened, then shut a few times, the words not quite making their way out. He stiffened. 'I don't know what to think anymore.'

The crowd had thinned, and the bar staff began collecting empty glasses.

Jade heaved a sigh. 'We should wrap this up.'

'Yeah. And sorry, I know what I've told you is a lot. Thanks for listening.'

She placed a comforting hand on his arm. 'Don't be sorry. Anytime. Really. It's always good to see you.'

They left soon after, with Jade reluctantly putting Curtis and Danny on her list of suspects. Did she now have two murders to solve, not one?

Chapter 10

Private Investigations

While working from home the next day, Jade's emotions went into freefall. She organised her notes to write a review of local properties for sale, but memory snippets of happier times floated through her head, like the day Nick had planted clues for Elena and Jade's murder mystery dinner, or when Nick, Curtis and Danny had dressed as the three musketeers for a costume party. She mulled over her conversation with Danny about their group's web of romances, business relationships … and insider trading.

Unable to hold it all in her head, she grabbed her laptop and sank into the couch. Hands poised over the keys, she acknowledged she wanted to write about Nick's death despite her promise to Danny. Even as she baulked at the idea of benefiting from the case, she recognised the markings of a winning story. The murder had already attracted media attention, but her connections to the central players gave her unique insight. More than that – or perhaps to justify her moral queasiness over exploiting her friend's tragedy – if she found a connection to Elena's death, she owed it to her friend to dig deeper.

Jade tried to imagine what Elena would advise about these

ethics, but she could only hear what her boss, Zain, would say about the importance of objectivity. He'd question her ability to remain unbiased when two people she cared about lay dead, and another had committed financial crimes. If she wanted to work on this article, she might need to expose any misdeeds her friends had swept into dark corners.

Also ambivalent about diving into another crime story, she reflected on the last time she'd become involved in such a case. She'd been held at gunpoint. Twice. She should leave this to the police. Still, all her best stories started with her willingness to court danger, and this could be her breakthrough in Melbourne, as long as her personal interest didn't override her professionalism.

So far, Curtis led the pack as her chief suspect, and Jade couldn't claim impartiality about him. She remembered admiring him at a New Year's Eve party at Elena's home when she was about eighteen. Amid the streamers and balloons, Curtis had mingled, as comfortable with the parents as the younger crowd. He'd seemed unattainable, so much older and more sophisticated. Something about the haunted look in his eyes drew Jade in and made her want to nurture him. His mother had died when he was a teenager, so maybe that had led to his little-boy-lost vibe. No matter what he did, she couldn't stay angry with Curtis.

Jade had confided in Elena about her crush, which had made her squirm in retrospect when Elena and Curtis had started dating several years later. Their romance had hurt less than Elena's lies of omission. When the truth had come out, Jade realised they'd been on-again-off-again for months. So much for a friendship with no secrets. As a girl, Jade had developed an idealistic notion of trust, and she was lucky to have reached her twenties before her beliefs had been challenged, but when her desire for absolute honesty had been violated, she'd floundered.

All Jade's disagreements with Elena had stemmed from that first betrayal. Her friend's relationship with Curtis had driven a wedge between them, not only from the subterfuge, but he'd consumed so much of Elena's time that she'd neglected everything else. The couple often invited friends over and kept Jade awake until late. When Jade complained, Elena shrugged and said Jade could have joined them. It wasn't like Jade to yell – she avoided conflict as she'd dodge a rabid dog – but these discussions frequently ended with Jade raising her voice and Elena slamming her bedroom door.

Only now, after Danny's revelation, did Jade understand what Elena had been going through: her boyfriend had made her an accomplice to a crime.

Jade sat on the floor next to her keepsakes box and, choking a sob, pulled out Elena's silver bracelet with charms of the Disneyland castle, the Eiffel Tower and Big Ben. Beside them, a heart, a peace symbol and a bird. The empty links left spaces Elena might have filled, if only...

But then, Elena never would have completed the bracelet, because a few weeks before she'd died, she'd given it to Jade.

Jade and Elena lounged on Elena's bed in their shared Carlton rental on one of the rare occasions Elena wasn't with Curtis. Sunlight streamed onto the large wall print of daffodils – Elena's favourite flower – and sparkled on Elena's bracelet.

'You're still my best friend.' Elena's use of the word 'still' gave Jade pause.

'You're my bestie too.' Their desperate need to articulate their friendship made Jade shift on the spot. 'Are you okay?'

'I'm fine.' Elena smiled too brightly.

'It's just...' How could Jade explain without sounding childish? They never found time to read the same books anymore, when for years they'd devoured every new mystery novel and compared notes. They no longer tried new recipes together, swapped clothes, and knew the minutiae of each other's lives. But

Elena's irritability and the amount she drank concerned Jade the most. If Curtis made her as happy as she professed, why did she seem so miserable?

Elena took off her bracelet and held it up. 'I want you to have this.'

'But you adore that bracelet.'

Elena tapped the travel charms. 'I've been to these places. You haven't.'

Jade chafed. Elena knew she was sensitive about never having left Australia, so why rub it in?

'I want you to have this so you can travel vicariously until you get there for real. And these others'—she touched them in turn—'love, peace and freedom. You can visit these too. I love this bracelet. And I love you. I want you to have it.' Elena gestured for Jade to hold out her arm and clasped it on.

It hung heavily around Jade's wrist. 'Thank you. I ... I don't know what to say.' The generous gesture made her stomach turn. She couldn't name the emotion making her nauseous, but it felt ominously close to the ugly spikes of jealousy she'd experienced the day her parents gave her brother a bike for his birthday when she'd desperately wanted one herself. Not only did Elena own such a symbolic piece of jewellery, but she'd been overseas to experience everything it represented, and now, she was giving it away with grace and equanimity. Jade hadn't been sure whether she envied the object or the person, or if the stakes reached even higher.

After the funeral, the heft of the bracelet had been too much for Jade to bear, and she'd tucked it into her keepsakes box. Now she reclasped it around her wrist, ashamed of her younger self. She'd felt patronised, but Elena had simply meant it as a sweet gesture ... unless she'd given it as a parting gift.

Jade hadn't paid enough attention to Elena then, but she had every intention of making up for it now. She'd start by speaking to Curtis and Iris with carefully crafted questions to see what they revealed. Then, she'd approach Steve Gillespie, Elena's stepdad. As Curtis's mentor and BeanBlitz board member, Steve probably had insight about Curtis's integrity and where his limits lay.

He and Elena's mother, Moira, were like Jade's second family. Sadly, like so many parents who'd suffered the loss of a child, they'd divorced after Elena's death. At first, Jade had been unsure whether they'd want to see her after they'd lost their daughter – a constant reminder of all the stages of life Elena would miss – but Moira had clung to her with a desperation Jade couldn't ignore. Even while Jade had been overseas, Moira had called monthly. And Steve, who Jade had guessed would drift away, still harnessed her support as his go-to person for collecting his mail and watering the plants when he went out of town. When Jade had mentioned this to her grief counsellor, the older woman had suggested he was using her as a proxy daughter, but Jade had a more cynical analysis. Much as she liked Steve, he always played an angle. She'd written articles to help him sell his properties, so possibly he maintained their relationship to keep a journalist in the fold. Most likely, the truth lay somewhere in between.

She called Curtis to set up a time to meet, but he didn't answer. Iris, same thing. She shot off quick text messages instead.

When she tried Steve, a message told her his phone was switched off or not in use. Odd. Surely, he wouldn't have gone away without telling her, or the letterbox would overflow.

She messaged Danny. *Any idea where Steve is? His phone's switched off.*

As she waited for a reply, she played with Elena's bracelet. The idea of Elena in Paris warmed her heart.

Her phone pinged with Danny's reply. *Haven't seen Steve since last week.*

Worried? she texted back.

Curtis is annoyed with him. He should be here while the company is mourning for Nick.

A knot of anxiety formed in Jade's stomach, the sense of another tragedy looming. Before she could think better of it, she jumped up and grabbed her handbag, planning to drop by Steve's home. Hopefully, she'd find some simple explanation, but she wanted to play it safe.

Chapter 11

House of Cards

A BRISK WIND cut through Jade's jacket as she parked her grey Honda outside Steve's home. Closed blinds gave the old house the appearance of a sleepy geriatric. She hoped that despite not answering her calls, he'd be there, and they'd soon be laughing about her worries over a glass of wine.

Steve's wealth, charm and charisma weren't reflected in the weatherboard façade, which hadn't been painted in years. Jade couldn't understand why he hadn't updated it; he had no shortage of cash. The other properties in the quiet, affluent Brighton neighbourhood jostled for attention – designer homes that looked like boxes stacked on boxes or renovated period houses. The cars in the street competed for status as the top European brand and model. A burglar casing the area would never bother with Steve's place. Jade assumed that was the point.

As she opened the front gate, she spotted a pile of newspapers on the front lawn that had been delivered and not picked up. She hitched her handbag strap higher on her shoulder.

A woman bustled out of the house next door, shopping bag in tow. 'Hi, Jade. You collecting the mail? Steve hasn't been around for days.' Everybody needed a nosey neighbour like Dorothy, who noticed anything out of place.

'When did you last see him?'

Dorothy wrinkled her nose. 'Last week sometime, Thursday, no, Friday. I was heading out for lunch and waved as he drove away.'

'Thanks for telling me. I just popped over to say hi, but I'll take in the mail while I'm here. He must've forgotten to call me.' Jade knew the spot for the spare key and the code for the alarm.

She counted the newspapers. Six. He'd been gone for six days, which tallied with Dorothy's account. She caught her breath. When had Nick died? The others had said he'd been missing since Friday. Today was Thursday. Six days. Steve had been gone since the day Nick had likely been murdered. Coincidence? Jade thought not. He knew both the victim and BeanBlitz. Then again, he could have just forgotten to arrange for the mail and newspaper to be collected.

Dorothy hovered by her gate. 'I do hope he's okay.'

'I'm sure he's fine,' Jade said with more conviction than she felt.

'Righto. I'm off down the street.' Dorothy gave a cheery wave. 'See you soon.'

Jade rang the doorbell just in case, hugging her arms to her chest for warmth. She listened for footsteps but only caught a magpie warbling and the faint rumble of highway traffic. If he'd had a health crisis, he could be lying inside waiting for help. He'd lived alone since leaving Elena's mum. In his late fifties or early sixties, he was probably too young to suffer from a fall or a stroke, but who knew?

She knocked and called, 'Steve.'

No response.

Jade walked back to the letterbox in the picket fence and pulled open the back flap to find several envelopes addressed to Mr Steve Gillespie and a collection of gaudy brochures boasting specials at chain supermarkets, office suppliers or department stores. Mail in hand, she gathered the newspapers and returned to the front verandah. Piling her stash next to the door, she stooped to reach under a pot plant in the corner. The wilted peace lily evidently hadn't been watered since Steve had left. Bingo – she picked up a bright blue key.

Not until she'd slotted the key in the lock did she hesitate. She hated the idea of marching into someone's house uninvited. She could call the police – stumbling across a corpse would give her nightmares for weeks – but they'd probably laugh at her paranoia.

She opened the door with unsteady hands and stepped inside. The musty smell suggested it hadn't been aired in days. At least no overtones of rotting flesh assaulted her. The closed blinds made the entrance hall gloomy, although a shaft of light filtered through from the back of the house. As her eyes adjusted, Jade flicked the light switch to reveal familiar parquetry floors, restored architraves and contemporary hallstand. Immaculate. Much more Steve's style than the run-down exterior. Jade picked up the letters and newspapers from the doorstep and placed them on the hallstand, then checked the door wasn't security-locked and swung it shut. She kept her jacket on against the chill.

The beep of an alarm made Jade jump. She opened the security panel and dialled the number: Elena's birthday.

Pure, godly silence.

Sweating now despite the cold, she resolved to do a quick sweep of the house to make sure Steve wasn't lying in a pool of blood. She stared along the hallway – two doors on the left and two on the right. It opened out to the family room.

'Steve?' Even as she called, she knew she'd receive no answer.

She pushed open the first door on her right – his bedroom. The crumpled navy silk sheets on the king bed hinted he'd left in a hurry. Holding her breath, she checked the ensuite, then the walk-in robe. Relieved to find no sign of a corpse, she spotted gaps in the wardrobe. Steve must have packed a bag. Maybe he'd simply gone away for business. Or pleasure.

Hurrying back to the hallway, she opened the first door on the left to see Elena's bedroom had been converted to a guestroom with a sage green doona. Dust on the maple bedside tables with matching dresser showed Steve rarely had guests.

The next door on the left led to a study. Books, folders and photo albums lined the floor-to-ceiling shelves, while neat piles of paperwork sat on the desk. The room conjured a vivid memory of a night when Moira and Steve had left for dinner, promising to be home by ten, leaving teenaged Jade and Elena delirious with freedom. Three hours of parent-free bliss. Elena had told Jade that Steve – she'd been told to call him Dad but used his name as a small act of rebellion – had been acting suspiciously, taking calls in his study with the door shut and switching computer screens when she walked in. Spies on a mission, they'd searched his study. Not really expecting to find anything, they'd come across a divorce letter from Moira's lawyer. Shocked, they'd put it back and made a pact to ignore it. Nothing more had come of it until after Elena's death.

Shaking off the memory, Jade opened the second door on the right to an empty bathroom.

She reached the open-plan family room and kitchen with its high ceilings, flawless cabinetry and leather furniture. The vast timber floors could have served as a dance studio. Thank God, no gruesome discovery marred its style.

Moving to the wall of windows opening onto the landscaped garden, she checked for signs of life. Water trickled over rocks and into a pool designed like a natural waterhole. A country oasis in the middle of suburbia. Beside it, life-sized statues of a horse and foal painted lurid pink and orange grazed on artificial grass. Jade hadn't noticed them before; they must be a recent purchase.

She scanned the kitchen. Metres of black granite benchtops held a coffee machine, a SodaStream and a wooden knife block – she checked and found all knives present. No rotting fruit on the counter. No clues about Steve's whereabouts. She opened the fridge to see no out-of-date milk, so he hadn't left in too much of a rush.

Her eyes strayed to a couple of framed photos on the wall. A keen photographer, Steve often strutted around with expensive camera gear. As a self-conscious teenager, Jade had hated having her photo taken, especially next to rail-thin Elena, but Steve had been persistent.

Evidently, he hadn't taken the one on the left because he stared straight into the camera, arm wrapped around a much younger Moira. He wore an elegant tux, while Elena's mother looked radiant in an off-the-shoulder gown, hair in a chignon. Steve was one of those men women never forgot. Jade's mother swooned over him and claimed he must be Cary Grant's double, but he'd made Jade cringe the way he flaunted money, showering Moira and Elena with gifts, taking them on expensive holidays, and moving them into this house, which had been freshly renovated back then. Elena had said she tolerated him because he made her mum happy – and she didn't seem to mind his opulent lifestyle – but she missed living with her birth dad, Peter.

The other photo showed Moira on a beach, head thrown back in laughter, with Elena beside her, a mirror image, only in a skimpy green bikini and a dolphin pendant necklace. Mother and daughter had the same thick hair, stance and reckless joy. The rock pool behind them identified the location as Sorrento back beach. Jade had spent many vacations in Moira and Steve's unassuming beach house. Even now, she could feel the warm sand underfoot and hear waves crashing on the shore, seagulls squawking overhead. Jade's family couldn't afford a holiday house, not on teachers' wages; their holidays had been spent camping or renting cheap cabins. She'd felt like an interloper with Elena's family at first, but they'd treated her as one of them, so she'd soon relaxed.

Obviously, Steve still cared about his ex-family to keep these pictures in such prominent positions, but tragedy had torn them apart. After they'd split up, Moira had moved back into the house she'd kept in her divorce from Peter.

Jade filled a jug with water and drenched the peace lily out the front. Hopefully, Steve was fine, but a part of her brain, the irritating part that kept her awake at night whispering doomsday scenarios, kept questioning whether he'd suffered the same fate as Nick. God, she hoped he hadn't met a grizzly fate.

As Jade returned the jug, it hit her. Sorrento. Steve might have gone there. She opened the drawer where he kept the keys, and sure enough, she couldn't find the set with the anchor on it. Her next step became clear: although too late today, she could do a daytrip to Sorrento tomorrow.

As she reset the alarm, pulled the door closed behind her and replaced the key under the lonely peace lily, the thrill of the chase kicked in.

Chapter 12
Life is a Highway

JADE SIPPED her water bottle as she sped along the freeway at the wheel of her Honda hatchback. Steve's phone had remained offline, so she'd left for Sorrento. Despite her seaside destination, her mood better suited a visit to the dentist. Nick was dead, Curtis was a white-collar criminal, and she couldn't help anticipating more unpleasant surprises.

She put her phone on hands-free and dialled Zain to make excuses about why she wouldn't be in the office. While she'd have preferred not to mention Nick's story until she saw how it panned out, spending the day on the Peninsula made it hard to avoid.

Zain answered with a perky, 'Jade, what's up?'

She wiped a sweaty palm on her faded jeans and put it back on the wheel. 'I'm driving to Sorrento to follow a lead.' A white Jag sports car sped past her, and she checked her speedometer – right on the limit, but the other car made her feel like she was crawling. 'Have you heard about the Nick Matrakis murder?'

'Hard to miss.'

'I know one of the board members for BeanBlitz, the company where Nick worked. I'm meeting him at his Sorrento home.' Jade hoped like hell Steve would be there – she'd be mortified to return to work empty-handed. She presented her trip as a firm arrangement rather than a hunch, as she didn't want to explain her concern for Steve or to admit she'd searched his house. Her gesture to put Steve's mail inside could be misconstrued as a break-in – Zain was exacting when it came to these details – and she didn't need the drama.

'How well do you know this person?'

'We're sort of family friends.' She downplayed it; Zain would disapprove if he understood her close relationship with Steve.

'Hmmm.' Jade pictured his neat, dark eyebrows almost meeting in the middle, the way they did when he disapproved of an idea. 'Have your meeting, then let's discuss it before you go any further. Monday?'

'Sure. Monday it is.' Jade desperately needed a concrete lead by then.

Iris had responded to Jade's text saying she was too upset to talk, but Curtis had yet to reply. She tried calling again, but he still didn't answer.

As she turned onto Point Nepean Road, rain splattered the windscreen. Drizzle blurred her view across the bay to the city, and the sea melted into the horizon. The wipers' *swoosh* created a hypnotic effect. Yellow in her peripheral vision drew her eyes to the bouquet of daffodils on the passenger seat. She planned to visit Elena's grave in the Sorrento cemetery after seeing Steve.

For the rest of the trip, memories danced in Jade's head. After becoming friends in grade two, she and Elena had remained close through high school and university. They'd learnt to cook, drink and clean a house together; swapped stories about work and their hopes for relationships; and held passionate conversations about everything from politics to their favourite movies.

Jade returned to the present as she parked in front of Steve's beach house. The two-story sandstone home bore no resemblance to the simple cottage Jade remembered as a child. Steve had told her he'd rebuilt it, but she hadn't seen it since. She darted through the downpour to shelter on the front porch. After ringing the doorbell, she brushed raindrops from her jacket.

A curtain fluttered in the front window before the door opened, and Steve, with his shock of dark hair, grey stubble and wrinkled brow, peered around it like a fugitive.

'Jade? Why are you here? I mean ... come in.' He held the door open.

As she crossed the threshold, he glanced up and down the street before shutting the door behind them. No question, he was in hiding. Jade's shoulders tightened; Steve wouldn't be scared for no reason.

'May I?' He took her jacket and hung it by the door. His height made the surplus inches around his waist hardly noticeable. 'What a wonderful surprise. I still can't believe how grown up you look.'

A pang of survivor's guilt hit Jade for continuing her climb into adulthood without his stepdaughter. She gave him a hug. 'It's good to see you.'

'Follow me. Coffee?'

The timber floors, ceiling-high windows, and warm tones of the living room reminded her of his Brighton home. She guessed he'd used the same interior designer. 'This rebuild is magnificent.'

'Thank you. It took three years from concept to completion, but I'm happy with the result.' His voice sounded like honey laced with brandy.

He bustled around the kitchen preparing a cappuccino for him and a hot chocolate for her. The flashy coffee machine on the kitchen bench likely required a licence to drive. All the while, his eyes roved between the windows and the back door.

With the drinks ready, he ushered Jade to the cluster of armchairs overlooking the backyard. She sat, looking at the wide, simple garden – nothing like his Brighton oasis. A drooping she-oak dominated the space, one of the few plants remaining from Jade's childhood. She and Elena had climbed it, had picnics beneath it, and planned to build a tree house in it, though they never progressed further than lodging an old cardboard box in a nook between two boughs. Jade had once fallen off a high branch and cut her knee. She caressed the scar through her jeans.

Steve tapped his forefinger on his mug. 'So, what brings you here?'

'I've been trying to reach you—'

'I lost my phone. Slipped out of my hand while I was walking along the Sorrento pier. Can you believe it?'

No, she couldn't. The way he avoided her gaze suggested a lie, but she couldn't figure out why he'd bother. 'When I couldn't get through, I went to your house. The mail was overflowing, so I put it inside.'

'Thanks.' He slapped his forehead. 'I forgot to ask you to take care of it.'

'When I couldn't get onto you, I guessed you'd be here, so I came to check.'

'I'm fine, really, you shouldn't have.'

'I wouldn't normally, but ... I assume you know about Nick?'

He grimaced. 'Just awful.'

'I'm so glad you're okay. Also'—although reluctant to mention her crass idea of writing about Nick, if she wanted to use anything Steve said, she had an obligation to do so—'I'm chasing a few leads to see whether I can shed light on the case in a way to encourage someone to come forward. I mean, I know it's already in the news, but...' Aware she was babbling, she stopped.

Steve stalked to the window and stared at the weeping clouds before turning back to her. 'Please don't quote me without my permission.'

'I'll check with you before I put anything in print.' She took a notepad and pen out of her handbag. 'The police have questioned Curtis and others at BeanBlitz. Why do you think they're so interested in the company?'

Steve frowned, looking years older than usual. 'Well, I...'

When it became clear he wasn't going to answer, she went on, hoping to find out whether he knew about Curtis's trades. 'There's always been speculation about how the company grew so quickly. Are you aware of any deals that weren't quite right? Anything untoward?' She pressed her pen into the page, suddenly breathless. In her rush to find Steve, she'd assumed he'd done no wrong, but now, she couldn't help wondering why he'd abandoned the company in their time of need. What if he'd colluded with Curtis's scheme?

A wave of emotion washed across Steve's face as he returned to his chair. 'Look, don't dive any deeper into this.' He seized one of her hands.

She resisted pulling away. 'Has someone threatened you? Is that why you're here?'

Steve drew back, clenching his fists. 'Please, leave. You don't understand what you're getting involved in.'

Softly, Jade asked, 'Who are you afraid of?'

He didn't answer.

Rain drummed on the lawn, puddling in dips and streaming down pathways through a wire fence to the back lane. Jade kept her gaze on the downpour, sensing he'd find it easier to speak without her eyes glued to him.

He remained quiet.

She tucked her notepad away and tried another tack. 'I'll keep everything you say off the record. Knowing you're okay is more important than any story.'

'It's not that. I know you're a journalist and need material, but I don't want to put you in danger. Moira would never forgive me.' Interesting, he still cared about Moira's opinion despite their divorce, just as the photos in his Brighton home had suggested.

'Don't worry about me. I'm perfectly safe.'

Thunder rumbled as Steve lowered his voice. 'I have evidence that Curtis did some shady trades. If the police question me, I'll have to tell them, but Curtis has advised me – strongly advised me – not to speak up.'

A tremor of unease raced through her. 'But Nick's murder ... you don't think Curtis did that?'

Steve smiled weakly, and Jade's hands felt as though they'd

been plunged in the icy puddles forming outside. She'd hypothesised with Danny about Curtis, but it had seemed theoretical. Now, with Steve so afraid, the possibility seemed more concrete. How could Curtis – the same Curtis she'd admired from afar since a teenager, who Elena had dated for over a year, who made them all laugh so hard they cried, and who'd had the vision to create BeanBlitz and employ half his friends – be capable of murder? Then again, traits like his entrepreneurial drive and charismatic leadership also qualified him for a life of crime.

Jade had long since given up her crush on Curtis. She saw past his polished façade and recognised his faults and strengths: his propensity to home in on the most influential person at a party; his need to suck all the air out of the room without leaving any for others; and his ability to bend people to his will. He drank hard, drove fast and spent crazy amounts of money, yet he genuinely tried to help people through connections, jobs and gifts. Jade had barely accepted that Curtis had conducted illegal trades; she still couldn't reconcile him being a murder suspect. Zain's voice played in her ear, reminding her to remain objective. Steve wouldn't act like a cornered animal for no reason.

She leant forward. 'If he's dangerous, you won't be safe here. I found you. Curtis won't have any trouble tracking you down.'

'I've been here six days, and so far, you're the only one who's arrived.' Steve rubbed his upper arms. 'You need to leave. I don't want you mixed up in this.'

Jade wished he'd stop treating her like a child. He clearly knew more than he was saying. 'Let me help you. If Curtis killed Nick, we need to know.'

'I won't go on the record. Curtis would … please, go home. This is my problem. I'll find my way out of it.'

'One more thing.' Jade wavered, unsure whether to raise her suspicions about Elena. She didn't want to upset him unnecessarily, but with his intimate connections to BeanBlitz, he might have some insight. 'I could be way off base here, but…' She chewed the inside of her cheek, still uncertain whether to go on.

'But what?'

'I don't want to hurt you by bringing this up, but if Curtis killed Nick to cover up the trades he made with information from Elena, do you think he could've killed Elena too?' In the end, her words came out in a rush.

For nearly a full minute, neither of them spoke. Jade waited with bated breath while a multitude of emotions crossed Steve's face. She could almost see the cogs turning in his brain.

He finally broke the silence. 'I don't think so.' He spoke slowly, clearly choosing his words with great care. 'Whatever Curtis is capable of, he wouldn't have hurt Elena.'

Jade accepted her theory would gain no traction, so she asked nothing further.

He stood, motioning to the door. 'I couldn't protect Elena from herself, but I can protect you.'

Jade picked up her bag, considering her options. Steve had evidence that implicated Curtis in financial crimes. She itched to get her hands on it. 'Can you at least give me some information to follow up?'

He avoided her gaze. 'I'm sorry.'

She sighed, ready – and honestly, a bit relieved – to make a temporary retreat. 'How can I get hold of you?'

'Use my new number. I ditched my old phone so Curtis can't track me.' Steve dictated it, and Jade saved it on her phone.

With nothing left to say, Steve walked her to the door.

After she stepped outside, she turned back. 'Call me if you change your mind or think of anything I can follow up. *Anything.*'

He nodded, and she headed back into the wet weather, rattled but more determined than ever to uncover the truth.

Chapter 13

Only The Good Die Young

THE RAIN HAD SLOWED to a light drizzle, diffusing the late morning light and giving the seaside town the faded tones of a black-and-white photograph. A subtle glare remained, so Jade polished her sunglasses, checking for smudges before putting them on. She drove to the Sorrento cemetery at the end of the street and pulled up beside the wrought iron gates. A chain had been wrapped around the handles to keep cars out, but a separate pedestrian gate gave easy access.

As teenagers, Jade and Elena had snuck in here at night, expeditions instigated by Elena. Jade had gone along, a willing, if anxious, participant. They'd told ghost stories against a tapestry of tombstones, creaking gum trees and cloudy moonlight, as the breeze stirred their imaginations. Back then, sheltered by youth and inexperience, they'd deemed monsters make-believe. Now, Jade knew better. And today, Elena had drawn her back here again.

Jade wove between the rows of graves, clutching the bouquet of daffodils. A flock of seagulls sheltering under a tree took flight in a rush of flapping wings and loud squawks. She ducked, then cringed, grateful nobody had witnessed her overreaction. Nick's murder had made her jumpy.

She still resisted viewing Curtis as a suspect. The night before, she'd researched the potential penalties for insider trading. They ranged from severe fines to ten years' jail time – a solid motive. But he was her friend. They hung out together. The idea that someone so familiar could be capable of such evil made her question her ability to read people. She'd trusted him.

Jade reached Elena's grave and knelt to place the flowers, wiping her face, which was wet from more than the rain. Memories flooded of daffodils on a coffin, the casket lurching on its ropes as the pallbearers lowered it into the dark grave. Elena's friends had stepped forward one at a time to throw a yellow bloom into her resting place. When Jade's turn had come, she'd swayed on the edge, half-wanting to fall into the hole where her best friend lay, half wanting to scream, 'How dare you leave me? You had everything! Why did you throw it all away?' Fury and alternating sadness had battered her with an intensity that left her breathless.

As if to punish herself, she'd replayed cross words from their recent arguments that stained the history of their friendship. If she'd had even an inkling Elena teetered on the brink of making this decision, she'd have shown more patience. How could she have been so blind?

Three years later, grief and guilt clung to the recesses of Jade's mind like mildew. The unfairness – that Jade should live, while Elena remained cold in the ground – struck her with gale force. At the same time, she longed to live well. Not merely to exist, but to live a life that counted. A life of value to help people like Elena.

Her mind wandered to the first time she'd had dinner at Elena's house when they'd become friends. She'd been amazed by her books, the best collection of mysteries she'd seen outside a library – nearly the whole Nancy Drew and The Hardy Boys collections. Jade had borrowed a different one every time she went over. Even as an adult, Elena had filled her bookshelves with thrillers and whodunits. How horribly ironic her life had ended alone in a room filled with those stories. Why Elena had killed herself remained the greatest unanswered question in Jade's life, one she returned to time and time again.

The idea that her friend had been murdered had upended these established patterns of thought. It didn't really help – didn't bring Elena back – but at least it offered relief from crippling self-blame.

She read the gold lettering on the dark granite headstone in front of her.

In loving memory of Elena Tiffany Kelly.
Beloved daughter of Moira and Peter Kelly.
May you find everlasting peace.

Moira contrasted greatly with Jade's mother, Gina. Where Gina wore all bold colours and flowing kaftans, Moira selected button-up blouses and pearls. Where Gina encouraged free-thinking and left-leaning politics, Moira held conservative views. But the two mothers had been friends as long as Jade and Elena. Moira used to be a nurse, although she hadn't worked in that capacity since she'd married Steve. He'd involved her in his companies, presumably for tax purposes, even though Jade had never seen her as having a business mind. Still, as a BeanBlitz board member, she might know about Curtis's financial crimes. Perhaps Jade should arrange to see her.

Jade adored Peter, Elena's birth father. His unruly hair, bushy eyebrows, glasses, daggy cardigans and mismatched socks gave him the air of a mad inventor, the Willy Wonka of machinery. When not at the research centre where he worked, or locked in his studio, he told stories in a soft rumbling voice. Elena and Jade had been drawn to him like filings to a magnet, eager listeners to his anecdotes about Australian explorers, gold mining and engineering feats. At the funeral, he'd been smartly dressed but sickly pale. Even his hair, more white than red by then, had been neatly combed. Moira and he had declared a truce and stood together, united in grief. As a child, Elena had spent every other weekend with him, so Jade had known him well. Sadly, she rarely saw him these days. She resolved to make time to see him too.

Shivering now, her jacket inadequate against the cold, Jade slipped into her car.

As she drove back up Ozone Avenue, she noticed a gunmetal grey SUV parked outside Steve's house. A man dressed in black climbed out. Jade looked more closely and nearly veered off the road. Curtis. She'd recognise his erect posture any day of the week. His grim expression made it clear he meant trouble.

He tucked something into the back of his jeans. Shit! A gun? Jade shrank lower in her seat so he wouldn't notice her.

Steve needed help. She had to get to him before Curtis did.

Chapter 14

Life on the Edge

Jade faced forward so Curtis wouldn't notice her, desperately hoping he'd be too preoccupied to recognise her car. Instinct told her to speed past the SUV, but logic kept her low-key. She maintained her steady pace while her mind took off fast as a bullet train.

She recalled a laneway out the back of the house. Steve could escape that way. She took the corner, then, one hand on the wheel, fumbled through her handbag on the passenger seat for her phone and called Steve.

As soon as he answered, she said, 'It's Jade. Curtis is out the front. He has a gun.'

'A gun? Fuck!'

'I'm driving to the laneway. Meet me there.'

Steve cursed again.

'Bring your phone and run.' Jade hung up.

After rounding a second corner, she reached the back lane to find Steve scrambling through the wire fence. He jumped into the passenger seat and shifted her handbag into the footwell.

Jade gestured ahead. 'Does this road go through? I can't remember.'

'No.'

Jade reversed back out the laneway, then cruised past the turn to Ozone Avenue.

Curtis stood in Steve's driveway, arms crossed – he must have rung the doorbell and got no response. He tracked the Honda and caught Jade's eye before she could look away.

'Jade, stop!' He sprinted towards her.

Jade accelerated too fast, tyres screeching.

'Careful!' Steve cried.

She inched off the pedal to take the next corner. 'Front beach or the back way?' The busy front road offered safety in numbers, but they'd get stuck in traffic on the main street.

Steve confirmed her choice. 'The back way.'

Sweat trickled from Jade's armpits as she swerved through the roundabout onto Melbourne Road. She glanced in the rear-view mirror. 'No sign of him yet.'

Steve swivelled to check the road. 'Hurry.'

Jade pressed the accelerator harder, and they tore through the Sorrento backstreets lined with tea trees to the six-lane Mornington Peninsula Freeway that carved a scar through rural properties en route to the city. Long straight fences separated plump cattle from speeding vehicles. A hawk circled overhead. If they didn't get caught in traffic, Jade guessed they'd reach home in about an hour.

Speed and emotion formed a heady cocktail, so Jade kept a firm grip on the steering wheel. 'Where should we go? You won't be safe at your place.' She considered asking Steve to her apartment, but it felt inappropriate, and she didn't want to invite danger into her home.

'I don't know.'

'A police station?'

'If I agree to testify, Curtis will find me.' Steve's voice cracked, brittle as honeycomb.

'Tell them what you know. Explain you're in danger. Ask for witness protection.'

Steve's leg jigged, but he didn't answer.

Jade backed off the pedal while they drove under an overpass armed with speed cameras. She longed to pull over and collect her thoughts but couldn't risk it. Her eyes darted to the rear-view mirror, and her pulse raced at the sight of a grey SUV.

Steve fidgeted. 'We don't have time to mess around. If he catches us … you're right. Police protection is the only way.'

'Okay, I'll go to the Bayside police station. Why is Curtis so worried about your testimony?'

Steve checked his watch before launching in. 'It happened three or four years ago. Curtis made a series of wildly successful trades.'

Jade knew all this from Danny, but she couldn't betray his confidence, so she played along. 'Could they be legit?'

'One or two outstanding calls can be talent or good luck, but ten or twelve? Nobody's that smart or lucky.' His voice sped up as he warmed to his tale.

'So what? Inside information?'

'That's my guess.'

'Who from?'

Steve squirmed. 'Something Elena said made me wonder.'

Jade reached the end of the freeway and stopped at the first set of traffic lights. The sudden stillness after speed made her dizzy. 'Elena? What's she got to do with this? She never worked for Curtis.' She glanced at Steve to gauge his reaction. He seemed agitated, chest rising and falling too quickly.

'You're missing the point. No matter where the information came from, those trades give Curtis a motive.' Steve gulped air. 'Because Nick threatened to tell the authorities.'

'Bloody hell!'

'The arsehole killed Nick, I tell you. He…' Steve winced as if his memories caused physical pain.

'Slow down and take a breath,' Jade said, as much for her own benefit as for Steve's. Her heart jackhammered.

Steve clasped his hands to his knees as Jade gave him time to regain his composure. The passing scenery had changed from farmland to industrial estates; they'd already reached the suburbs.

When he seemed calmer, Jade asked, 'What happened? Did you witness the murder?'

'No, but I saw the body. In the office. I came into the boardroom and found Curtis standing over Nick, holding a phone charging cable. Curtis had ... oh God, Curtis had strangled Nick.'

Jade drove on in silence, hopes of Curtis's innocence disappearing like early morning fog under a rising sun. 'Maybe he found Nick already dead. Was anyone else around?'

'No. It was late. We'd stayed back for a meeting.' Steve faced Jade, and she felt his eyes boring into her. 'You're a good person, Jade. I know he's your friend, and you don't want to believe this, but there's more. When I told him to call an ambulance, he refused. Shoved me away from the body. Threatened me and made me promise to leave and tell no one. I should've stood up to him, should've insisted, but under pressure ... I was in shock ... wasn't thinking straight. I can only assume he dumped the body after I left. I ran before I could get called in for questioning. Curtis must've tracked me down because he didn't trust me to stay quiet.'

A grey SUV pulled up five cars behind them, but Jade couldn't tell if it was Curtis. 'Look back, is that him?'

'Fuck, yes. Hurry! We're nearly there.'

The lights changed, and Jade took off. For a time, only the engine growl could be heard, the automatic gear changes too smooth to detect, as if the car, too, were holding its breath.

Jade swung right through a minuscule gap in the traffic and floored it. Car horns honked.

Steve braced against the momentum pulling him into his door. 'What are you doing?'

'We can't let him know we're going to the police.' She took the next left, then the first right.

Steve clung to the door handle to stay upright. 'Where'd you learn to drive like this?'

Jade gave a wry grimace. Not a confident driver, adrenaline seemed to work in her favour. 'I've studied with the best: James Bond, Jack Reacher, Ethan Hawke. Is he still behind us?'

He checked through the back window. 'No.'

She drove on, hyper-vigilant, scanning the roads. Several times her stomach clenched – did everyone in Sandringham drive a near-black SUV? – but none matched Curtis's model.

At last, she slammed on the brakes in front of the Bayside police station.

Chapter 15

Mr Policeman

JADE AND STEVE rushed inside the police station, ready to blurt out their story, but not a soul could be seen. The austere foyer, all glass and tiles, had no soft surfaces. The doors, elevator and reception window were closed, reception unmanned.

'Read this.' Jade pointed to a notice in the middle of the reception window.

> *We can see you but are busy attending to other business. Please only press the button in an emergency.*

'Are you fucking kidding me?' Steve's nostrils flared. 'Our tax dollars hard at work. Yes, it's a freaking emergency.' He rammed his finger on the button, eyes skipping from reception to the windows and back again.

Jade checked outside. No sign of the SUV. Surely, Curtis wouldn't follow them into the police station, not with a gun in tow.

Several minutes later, a young police officer – a constable according to his silver name badge – ambled out to the desk, looking so bored Jade half-expected him to yawn. 'Can I help you?'

Steve stepped forward, a sheen of sweat glazing his forehead. 'I want to make a statement about the Nick Matrakis murder. It's urgent. I'm being followed.'

The constable's chest puffed fuller, as if suddenly proud of his navy uniform. He jotted Steve's details on a notepad. 'Wait here, I'll call my superior.'

Alone again, Jade's damp palms and sense of helplessness reminded her of the day she'd found Elena dead on her bedroom floor – nobody there when she needed support. She resolutely shoved those bleak memories back into a dark corner of her brain.

At last, a sturdy police officer marched into the foyer. 'Steve Gillespie?' She had a no-nonsense steadiness about her.

Steve nodded and strode forward, fear written into his tousled good looks.

The police officer regarded him closely. 'You want to make a statement relating to Nick Matrakis?'

'I do. I need protection. Can you help me?'

'Depends on your information.'

Jade stepped forward. 'He's in danger. There must be something you can do.'

The police officer raised an eyebrow. 'And you are?' Jade couldn't read whether she was amused or annoyed.

'Jade Riley. Family friend.'

'Thank you, Jade. Please leave your details with the constable at the front desk. We'll contact you if we need anything further.'

Steve gave Jade a firm hug. 'Thanks a million. You just saved my life.' He seemed older, in need of care, where she usually saw him in control, living large. Their sudden role reversal caught her off guard.

As she let go of him, a lump formed in her throat. 'How will I know what happens? Will you be allowed to call?'

'I will if I can. If I don't, assume I'm in protection.'

Jade watched Steve and the police officer leave the foyer with a weird pang of separation anxiety. She hoped she'd done the right thing. If they didn't give him protection, and Curtis found out they'd been to the police, he'd be in even more danger.

As she drove home, the likelihood of Curtis's guilt made Jade reassess her memories in case they'd been distorted through the prism of time. She rehashed their recent conversations, searching for evidence of ill intent, but found it near impossible to recast him in the role of villain. Wait ... that night at the pub when Jade had found out Nick was missing – if Curtis already knew Nick was dead, why did he pretend otherwise? He'd lied not only to Jade, but to Danny and Iris.

Further, Steve had found him holding the murder weapon. If Curtis had come in after Nick had been killed, surely he'd have reported the murder to the police. Unless he wanted to protect someone else. Her thoughts turned to Danny, the other person on her suspect list. His story about the insider trading tallied with Steve's but also gave him motive.

Another possibility crossed her mind: Steve could be lying. And he'd only do that if he'd killed Nick. Her stomach curdled. Steve had been her second dad, although she'd always held reservations about him out of loyalty to Elena's birth dad, Peter. Her sense of bewilderment grew. She'd known these people her whole life, but after uncovering a few of their secrets, they all felt like strangers. Her world had morphed into a twilight zone where nobody could be trusted.

Chapter 16

Sunday Morning Coming Down

On Sunday morning, Jade practiced a tricky dance move in her living room. Pushing the chairs hard against the table created just enough space between them and the bench to complete a cha cha spot turn. All the while, she craved updates about the murder, waiting for the television news, the sound muted.

She hoped Steve had been accepted into interim witness protection. His new phone had been disconnected, he hadn't called her, and when she'd driven past his house – which she'd done five times – she saw no sign of habitation. From what she could ascertain on the internet, to keep his location secure, he'd need to avoid all communication because phones and even IP addresses could be traced.

Practicing her Latin moves allowed Jade to avoid grappling with her strange sense of dislocation after another key person had been uprooted from her life. Steve, out of contact with everyone, must feel more isolated than a prisoner.

The high point of her weekend had been a foxtrot class on Saturday afternoon. She'd been so intent on mastering a new routine that for forty-five minutes, she nearly forgot about Nick's murder. Aside from that, she'd managed some work, watched reruns of *Friends*, and deflected a barrage of texts from Gina, who was trying to persuade her to set up a dating app profile.

Jade had watched every news bulletin, taut with tension, half-expecting to hear Curtis had been arrested, even though she knew the police needed time to compile and validate Steve's evidence before they'd act. They must have taken him seriously because a frantic Danny had called to say the police had searched the office and asked about insider trading. He'd assumed the tip had come from Steve, even though Jade didn't mention she'd taken him to the police.

The splash of headlines from when Nick's murder first hit nearly a week earlier had subsided, and today they only played a short rerun from an interview at a press conference with Nick's parents.

Jade stopped mid-step, pulled on her Ugg boots and sat on her blue couch, glued to the television as Nick's mother, tear-stained and pallid, spoke into the microphone on the table in front of her.

'Anyone who knew Nick would remember him as kind, thoughtful and loving. It's beyond my comprehension—' A sob choked her words, and she broke eye contact with the camera and picked up a glass of water with a shaking hand.

Her husband wrapped his arm around her and took over. 'We can't understand why anyone would want to hurt Nick. He worked hard, stayed out of trouble and had a steady group of friends. Please, if anyone has knowledge of what happened, or how he ended up in a'—he glanced at Nick's mum, face twitching in a battle to control his emotions—'how he came to be found in Lilydale, we implore you to come forward.'

The television screen switched back to the newsroom, where the glamorous newsreader said, 'That was Tom and Betty Matrakis, parents of Nick Matrakis, the man found murdered in Lilydale last Friday. If anyone has information relating to his death, please call Crime Stoppers at the number on the bottom of your screen.'

The news moved on to a five-car pileup on the Western Freeway, and Jade flicked it off, unable to deal with further tragedy. Seriously, watching the news could make anyone depressed.

Her phone rang – Curtis – the fifth time he'd called since Friday. Jade didn't answer, conflicted over her allegiances to Danny, Steve and Curtis. Curtis left another message, but she didn't bother listening to it; it would be the same as the others, demanding to know why the hell she'd driven away from him at Sorrento. On edge, she kept expecting him to land on her doorstep, but so far, he'd stayed away. She needed to call back, both as a friend and for her article, but she procrastinated, chilled by the idea of facing a potential murderer.

She checked her text messages – Iris had confirmed morning tea at Turtle Rock Café on Tuesday morning – and turned to her unread emails. She scrolled through several newsletters, deleted them, and tagged a few advertisements as junk. The next one came from The World of Writing, titled 'Writing Tips'. She didn't remember a company with that name, but she often received unsolicited information from various writing schools, so she opened it, expecting more junk.

It contained four words: *Stop investigating Nick's death.*

At first, she didn't know how to react. It must be a joke. Hardly anyone knew she was considering the story, just Danny, Steve and her boss. Zain wouldn't send a weird email – he'd simply instruct her to drop it. Steve had already told her to back off, so why would he bother? And Danny had given her information but made her promise to stay off the record. If none of them had sent it, perhaps one of their connections had done so. Was someone watching her?

Unease hit like fingers down a chalkboard. How many people did this involve? She must be getting close, or there'd be no reason to scare her.

She reread the email. It seemed unfinished, like there should have been an 'or else'. The writer had stopped short of issuing a warning. Perhaps they'd known it would prevent her from reporting it – and they were right, because even as she considered telling the police, she dismissed it. This person's mind games seemed far more sinister than a blatant: *Stop investigating Nick's death, or you'll be next.*

Chapter 17

Complicated

ON MONDAY MORNING, Jade sat in front of Zain's desk in the only enclosed office on the open-plan floor teeming with people. She needed to pitch her story, but her mind kept skipping back to the warning email.

'Have you made progress with the Nick Matrakis murder?' As always, Zain jumped straight to business, no small talk or fidgeting, sharp eyes trained on her. Sandy-haired and round-faced, he sat with perfect posture.

Nerves atingle, she launched into the rehearsed spiel of her meagre offerings. 'As I mentioned, I know one of the BeanBlitz board members, Steve Gillespie. Actually, I know two of them. I'm meeting the other one shortly, Moira Gillespie.'

'They're married?'

'Divorced.'

'Awkward.'

'Right.' Jade looked down at the tidy desktop between them, clear except for a computer, a notepad and an in-tray. No photos, no mementoes. Zain valued action, not sentiment. 'I get the sense Moira's more of a figurehead. Anyway, I saw Steve on Friday. He didn't witness the murder, but claims he caught Curtis Haycroft, the BeanBlitz CEO, hovering over Nick holding the phone charging cable used to strangle him.'

Zain raised a single eyebrow into a perfect arc. 'I assume there's a "but" or you'd have filed this story on Friday.'

'He won't go on the record.'

'Can you change his mind?'

Jade had debated whether to tell Zain about Steve going to the police. She didn't want to be pressured by a headline-hungry editor into revealing anything without Steve's permission, but while everyone else in her life seemed determined to undermine her confidence in people, she trusted Zain. He'd never do anything unethical or put someone at risk. Her greater worry was he'd pull her off the story out of concern for her safety. 'I don't have access to him now. He's asked for witness protection.'

Zain studied her more closely, chin resting on his hand. 'What about the other director, Moira? Any chance she'll make a statement?'

'I'll tell you after today. I also met with one of Nick's best friends, Danny Wyatt. He knew nothing about the murder but accused Curtis of insider trading. Again, off the record.' She switched her spinning ring, a present from Elena, from her middle finger to her thumb and twirled the spinners.

Zain turned his gaze from Jade to the window. Grateful for a break from his scrutiny, Jade studied the busy street below them. Traffic lined all the way to the end of the block.

Her reprieve didn't last long, and within seconds, his eyes caught hers again. 'It appears your friends will confide in you, but unless you get them to commit, you have no story. What's more, as you know, subjectivity distorts our perception of events. Are you sure you can pull this off?'

Jade had the same concerns, but she couldn't let this go. She needed to know who'd killed Nick, even if it was Curtis. If not him, she wanted to clear his name. Further, suspicions about Elena's death had taken hold like a pit bull and wouldn't let go. If Elena had been murdered, she owed it to her friend to prove it.

She hadn't planned to tell Zain her Elena theory, but the words tumbled out of her mouth before she could stop them. 'I need to do this story. It could be linked to another death three years ago. My best friend suicided, but now I'm questioning whether someone murdered her. She was dating Curtis at the time and told him inside information in confidence. He used it to place successful trades without her knowledge.'

'Doesn't that add credence to the possibility of suicide? Her sense of betrayal must have been overwhelming.'

'That's one way of seeing it, but what if she threatened to turn him in? He'd have done jail time. One of my theories about Nick's murder is that Curtis killed Nick to stay out of jail, and he had the same reason to kill Elena.'

'We deal in facts, not conjecture. How did she die?'

'An overdose. Ambien.'

'Any evidence of a struggle? Could someone have forced her?'

'Anything's possible.'

Jade didn't want to talk about finding Elena after her death. Even now, the gut-wrench nearly knocked her off her feet. She'd seen no signs of violence, but some elements made no sense: Jade never understood where the drugs came from; the number of tablets Elena took weren't enough to kill her; and they'd never found a suicide note – although she'd subsequently learnt notes weren't as common in real life as in movies. Further, nobody could explain why the spare key had been sitting on Elena's bedside table. The obvious answer – Elena had left her key at home, so she'd used the spare – made no sense to Jade. The pair had shared a running joke about Jade resorting to the spare key six times in the two years they'd lived together, while Elena had never needed it. The rest of the gang had denied using the key that day, and when Jade had floated the idea that someone else had let themselves in, they'd looked at her with pity and offered her a glass of wine.

'There were a few unexplained circumstances.'

Zain steepled his fingers and tapped the forefingers. 'Is the idea of Elena being murdered more palatable than suicide?'

He'd targeted Jade's sore spot with the accuracy of a sharpshooter. 'I'm taking that into account—'

Jade's phone rang. She rushed to silence it, then stopped. 'It's Curtis.' She'd been avoiding his calls, but right now, she desperately needed credibility with Zain, and contact with one of the key players offered a priceless opportunity.

Zain nodded. 'Answer it.'

Jade stood and walked to the window, phone to her ear. 'Curtis. At last, talk about telephone tag. You okay?'

'What do you think?' His sarcasm dripped over the line. 'Steve's threatening to implicate me in Nick's murder, you're helping him avoid my questions, and the police don't seem to have anything better to do than hassle me. I don't know what the hell Steve's told them, but they searched the office on Friday and questioned me again.'

Jade immediately regretted siding with Steve until she remembered Curtis had used Elena for financial gain and implicated Danny in the process. Worse, Steve had caught him with the murder weapon. And she'd seen him with a gun at Sorrento. Not so innocent. She should view everything he told her with scepticism. But she also needed him onside. 'I'm so sorry for what you're going through.'

'Would you like to catch up? Or are you avoiding me like everyone else?'

'No, no, not at all.' Of course, she'd been avoiding him, but scared or not, she needed to step up. Zain was listening, and she wanted to impress. 'Let's meet.'

He snorted. 'Always after a good story, I suppose.'

Jade coloured. 'Well, I—'

'Maybe you can help.'

'Sure. When and where?' Jade looked to Zain for a reaction, who gave a thumbs-up, but she wished she'd been more specific; she didn't want to meet in private with a possible murderer.

He must have encountered this response from others because he said, 'Let's go for a walk along the beach. Elwood Pier? Tomorrow around four?'

'That works.'

'Hey, do you know where Steve is?' Curtis sounded casual, but Jade caught the tension in his voice.

She couldn't tell him the truth. Witness protection should keep Steve safe, but the fewer people who knew about it, the less chance of him being exposed. 'No idea, why?'

'You drove off with him, so I—'

'Let's chat tomorrow.'

'Right.' He sounded flat, perhaps disappointed she hadn't been more forthcoming. 'See you then.'

She hung up and told Zain the outcome, hoping he'd be pleased.

He sat back, arms crossed, scrutinizing her closely. 'Hold your meetings with Moira and Curtis, then let's speak again. I'm concerned you're too close to this. And be aware, if Curtis used confidential information from his girlfriend, he'll use you, too, so be careful.'

'I will.'

'And Jade, consider writing a different kind of article. You have unique access to people who've experienced the murder of a loved one. Consider a feature piece on the impact of crime. Talk to Curtis about how it feels to be accused of his best friend's murder.'

Jade thanked him and left. She loved Zain's lateral thinking, but his suggestion of writing a soft article rather than something with greater impact annoyed her. Deep down, she knew she was struggling to remain objective, but that didn't mean she shouldn't try or wasn't capable. Either way, she needed to know who killed Nick, especially if it led to the truth about Elena.

Although everything pointed to Curtis, ever since her night at the Ruby Room with Danny, something had itched at the back of her mind. He'd given her the distinct impression of hiding something about his relationship with Elena. And she wanted to know what it was.

Chapter 18

Mister Cellophane
Danny, one month before Elena's death

I GUESSED it would be a crap day from the way it began: my agent called to say Aria Belle had decided not to release my song. This meant I wouldn't get the exposure I'd hoped for, not to mention the royalties, just when I longed to escape my job with Curtis. I should have known my potential breakthrough sounded too good to be true, and I cursed myself for telling everyone and celebrating before I'd signed a contract.

I reached for my phone and tapped a text to Elena. *They're pulling my song from the album.*

We'd grown closer since she'd told me about the insider trading, and spoke or messaged daily. Often, she didn't reply immediately, caught up in meetings, but today, she did. Perhaps she understood how hard this would hit me.

So sorry. Catch up after work? Come to my place at 6, I can c u before I go out.

The rest of the stifling summer day dragged slower than the last dance at a disco. As soon as I finished work, I raced home to shower and change – not that I was planning anything intimate, but I wanted Elena to see me at my best, especially now my music career lay crumpled at my feet.

I didn't expect Elena to make the same effort, but when she

opened the door, I smelt hints of shampoo and toothpaste. I almost moaned with longing, then scolded myself – she'd probably freshened up to see Curtis later.

She drew me over the threshold and into a hug. 'I'm so sorry about your song. Don't give up. You'll make it in the end. If not with this piece, then with the next, or the one after that.' My despair eased. One of the many things I loved about Elena was her unshakeable belief in my talent.

Inside the rundown terrace house, she poured two glasses of sauvignon blanc, handed one across the kitchen bench to me, then tapped hers against mine. 'To failure. May it make us stronger.'

I took a long sip, the cool liquid a balm. 'You're too much.' She *was* too much – too joyful, too beautiful, too much fun, but most of all, too hard to resist. My thoughts evolved into song lyrics, but I didn't want to disappear down that rabbit hole. I wanted to remain one hundred percent present in the moment, so I made a mental note of the concept and focused on Elena. 'Where's Jade?'

'She has dance after work on Thursdays.'

'Right.' I sipped more wine as an unspoken whisper of possibility echoed between us. But I couldn't seriously entertain the possibility of Elena and me; she was already in a relationship. With my best friend. Ex-best friend. My friendship with Curtis might be in question, but as the saying goes, two wrongs don't make a right.

'Where are you going tonight?' I asked when the silence grew too thick.

'Curtis wants to check out a new bar.'

'Right.' Instead of sounding like a proverbial broken record, I needed to get out of my head and improve my conversational skills. 'I finished a new song last week.' Oh hell, why did I bring that up? The lyrics explored friendship and betrayal, inspired by none other than our mutual frenemy, Curtis.

'What's it about?'

I hummed a few bars.

She hummed it back to me. 'Catchy.' She pointed to the shabby couch, took her glass and a packet of Twisties, and we sat together. 'Sing a bit more.'

'It's not ready. I need to work on it longer.'

She searched my eyes as if reading my intent. Seemingly satisfied, she opened the Twisties and offered them to me.

I laughed. 'I haven't eaten one of these in years. Takes me back to being a kid.'

'They're my favourite.'

Most other women I hung out with worried about their weight too much to eat junk food, so I found her disregard for calories refreshing. God, she was gorgeous, not only in appearance, but her infectious enthusiasm made her great company. Her summery perfume carried wafts of magnolia blossom. The warmth, the wine, and my proximity to Elena made my cheeks burn.

Elena must have noticed my flush because she said, 'Sorry about the heat. We don't have air-conditioning.' She turned to kneel on the couch and reached for the sash window behind us. 'This might help.'

The window jammed, and much as Elena wrestled with it, she couldn't lift it. I knelt next to her to help, and my arm brushed against hers. We froze, arms bound together with a force so palpable I could almost see the threads of silk. I told myself not to cross the line, but I'd never wanted anything so much.

Although we rested skin to skin, Curtis stood between us as surely as if he'd snuck into the room to push us apart. Elena took a sharp intake of air, and I tore my arm away from hers and leant forward to lift the window.

To my embarrassment, I couldn't budge the frame either.

Elena laughed – a tinkle like a wind chime – and put a hand on mine. 'Let's close it, then try again.'

Together, we pushed the window down, and this time when we drew it up, it slid freely. We'd had a run of hot days, leading to one of those humid, still nights when the weather hoarded its energy for a thunderstorm. The fresh air didn't help the temperature inside at all.

I resettled on the couch, instructing myself to behave. 'It'll cool down once the rain comes.' So I hoped.

'Has Curtis asked you to do any more trades?' she asked.

Unsure whether to be relieved or disappointed at the change of topic, I sipped my wine. 'Yes. A mining company. Is that from you?'

Elena nodded. 'I try to avoid telling him anything about work, but he keeps pressing me.' She interlaced her fingers and pressed her palms outward. 'He's so easy to talk to. I don't know how to stop it.'

A wave of fury at Curtis, the manipulator, rose in me, but I wrestled it back under control. I didn't want Elena to see my ugly temper in full force. 'We could confront him together. Tell him we've rumbled him and ask him to cut it out.'

She sprang back. 'Hell no! Then he'd know we've been talking behind his back.'

'What's wrong with that? We're friends. We're allowed to talk.'

'Yes, but ... he might misinterpret and think we're'—she nudged me—'you know. He asked me about you the other day.'

My senses jumped to high alert. I found it gratifying to be considered a threat by a person as cocky as Curtis. What had Elena said or done to make him question her about me? 'That's crazy. He knows I'd never touch you.' Yet, my fingers itched to do just that. I clutched the velour armrest to stop from reaching out.

She sat back, feigning offence. 'What, never?'

'You're my mate's girlfriend.'

'What if I wasn't?'

A loaded question. 'You know I adore you, but I'm a victim of circumstance.'

I swore if she moved a whisker closer, all bets were off. Warped logic made me figure that if she made the first move, I wouldn't be culpable. Maybe she thought the same because she, too, held still, so neither of us took the initiative.

Our standoff lasted for what felt like an hour but was probably only seconds.

I gulped. 'I should go.'

Elena swallowed. 'Yeah, I need to get ready for Curtis.'

We stood in unison and moved towards the door, trancelike. The humidity, tension and laden conversation slowed my steps as though wading through mud.

She gave a sympathetic smile. 'I'm sorry about your song.'

I'd almost forgotten about 'Dance Junkie'. My addiction wasn't dance. 'I'm sorry too.'

We reached for the door handle at the same instant, as though trained by the same choreographer. My anticipation spiked, just like when I walked on stage – the sense that one wrong move could bring down the whole band, but if I played things right, I could achieve greatness.

This time, when our hands met, neither of us held back. I couldn't tell you who made the first move because we drew together as one. Our fingers clasped, lips met and bodies pulled close with raw, unbridled hunger.

She drew apart only long enough to grab my hand and lead me to her bedroom.

I didn't speak. Didn't pause. Didn't acknowledge this was all kinds of wrong.

Elena didn't either.

Frantically, we clawed each other's clothes off and fell onto her bed, rushing to make this happen before one of us had second thoughts.

I wanted it to last. This might be our only opportunity, so I imprinted every sensation, nuance and gasp into my memory to replay later: the smoothness of her skin, the sweetness of her breath, the ferocity of her grasp, the tangle of her hair in my fingers, and the way my body hummed. Naked, save a silver necklace with a dolphin pendant, Elena moved with joyful abandon.

We went on, kissing, panting and licking; clutching, grabbing and pounding; all the way to a glorious finale.

Even as I tried to draw it out, it finished too soon. It wasn't enough; I craved more. I never wanted to leave this room. If only I could lie beside her forever, heady with her scent, my legs and arms entwined with hers.

Elena, beautiful, troubled Elena, had been mine for one glorious moment.

I soaked in the bliss of it and took in the kaleidoscope of competing colours in the room: blue and violet bedclothes, knick-knacks in everything from hot pink to orange, and green curtains. The wall art stood out, a photograph of a field of daffodils that drew one flower into sharp focus and blurred the rest into a golden sea. A bottle of Dolce & Gabbana's Dolce Garden sat on her dressing table – her secret weapon that turned my knees to water. I made a mental note of it in case I ever needed to buy her a gift. This room, this moment and this woman gave me a taste of heaven.

She snapped out of it before I did. 'You have to leave.'

Her abruptness didn't faze me. Nothing could spoil it. We dressed in silence and shared a last lingering kiss before heading to the door just as a key sounded in the lock.

Jade came in, gussied up in work clothes, a laptop bag hanging from her shoulder. She grinned when she saw me. 'Hi, Elena, Danny.'

'You're home early.' Elena spoke a bit too loudly.

'My class got cancelled.' Jade looked at me with thinly disguised curiosity. 'Staying for dinner?'

I remained so blissed out I struggled to conjure an acceptable answer. 'No, I just came round for a quick chat. Elena's going out.'

'Shame. See you soon.' Jade headed to the kitchen, making no effort to disguise her smile.

I'd guessed it would be a crap day from the way it began, but it turned out to be the best day of my life.

Chapter 19

Tainted Love

THE WHOLE DAY after my thrilling visit with Elena, I found myself humming a new tune. Words and motifs swirled around my brain, inadequate to articulate my rapture. Elena, gorgeous, unattainable Elena, had slept with me. Unable to contain my ballooning emotions and reluctant to spend time with Curtis, I achieved zero productivity at work and left early.

Back home, with Iris still at the office, I had the apartment to myself, so I didn't have to worry about making noise. I observed my room clinically, comparing it to Elena's. Like hers, it had strident and varied tones, a jumble of colours from posters of bands, my electric blue drum kit and my unmade bed. The angular lines lacked the softness of hers, the scent more of a dirty sock vibe than high-end perfume. But it was mine, and I loved it.

I sat at my precious Ludwig drums, which consumed all the floorspace in my bedroom – gifted to me by my father, who always backed my talent – and tried to find the right rhythm for the song I'd scribbled in my notebook, 'You're Too Much'.

I tried a quick tempo, but it had the wrong vibe and lost the longing in the lyrics, so I slowed it down. That didn't work either; it sounded more like a ballad. At last, I found a midpoint that captured playful desire rather than pining. And something else crept in, something I hadn't even acknowledged to myself, a wonderful, soaring, blossoming sensation. Hope. The burgeoning wishful thinking that maybe, just maybe, one day, perhaps not immediately, but some glorious day in the future, Elena and I might be a couple.

I'd never call myself a singer, but I could keep enough of a tune to sketch out the song.

> *I tell ya, baby, you're too much,*
> *I say you're way too much.*
> *You tempt me far too much,*
> *I wanna feel your touch.*

Okay, call it tacky, but what rock song doesn't have a few soppy lyrics? The accompanying harmonies played in my head. I reached for my phone to call Sammy to see if we could turn my idea into something real, but it rang as I picked it up from my bedside table. Elena. My soul circled even higher. She must have known I was thinking of her; clearly, we had ESP.

Staring at the posters of my band heroes from the eighties and nineties that lined my bedroom walls, I answered, 'Hi, beautiful.'

'Hi. Do you have a minute?' She sounded sad. I'd hoped for a mirror to my euphoria, so I immediately detected trouble.

'Everything okay?'

'Yeah, I just...'

My elation took a nosedive. Her hesitation, her tone ... I could see what was coming, and I wanted to block the words before they escaped her mouth. Once out, she couldn't take them back. They would shred my emotions. I wanted her to break up with Curtis, the lying, cheating scum who'd tricked us into being complicit in his money-making scheme. We deserved a fairytale ending, an elopement to a Pacific Island where I could play gigs at a fancy resort and Elena could teach people how to avoid financial scandals.

But before I could stem her flow of words, she continued.

'Yesterday was amazing. I'll always cherish the memory of it, but—'

'Stop! I don't want to hear it. How can you stay with him after what he's done?' I stood, tipping my stool over behind me.

'The guilt's killing me. I'm sick to my stomach. I can't do this.' The tremor in her voice tore at my heartstrings, but I had to say my piece.

'Guilt? What about what Curtis did? Even if you don't care about him implicating you, he hurt me too. He's trapped me.' I pushed past my drum kit and paced the crowded room as best I could.

'Please, don't make this harder than it needs to be. I'm falling apart.' The pain in her voice drew tears to my eyes. 'Even if I break up with him, we can't be together. It's against every code.'

I closed my door, pressed my back against it and sank to the floor. 'What about the code for not using your girlfriend to get inside information on the stock market? What about the code for not using your best mate to place those trades? Elena, wake up, he's evil.'

Her breath sounded shaky over the phone line. 'He's not. I had it out with him last night, and he explained everything. He's just a big kid who got carried away and did some stupid things. It was a game. Nobody got hurt.'

A game? Nobody? What about me? 'What sort of magic dust did he sprinkle on you? This wasn't an accident. He knew exactly what he was doing.'

'He didn't think it through. Never in a million years would he hurt me. Or you. He wanted to start his company, and bending this rule made it possible. If we say nothing, the chance of anybody in authority finding out is remote. He promised never to do it again.'

'And you believe him?'

'I do.'

I groaned. 'He's really got you conned, hasn't he?'

'Bottom line, I still love him.'

'But not me?' I regretted the words as soon as I said them; I shouldn't have to plead for her affection. Nor did I need my hopes dashed further.

'I really do care about you, Danny. In another lifetime, we could be together, but I'm already committed.'

So, there it was: Elena chose Curtis, the criminal, over me. I'd given it my best shot, and she had turned me down. 'You didn't tell him about us, did you?'

'No, and please, I beg you, can this stay between us? It'd kill him.'

Good. I would happily kill him. Murder him in his sleep. 'I won't keep quiet to protect him, but I will out of respect for you.'

The call ended. We had nothing left to say. Elena was too much, and I was not enough. I tore up the page with the song I'd been working on and lay on my bed in bleak silence.

Chapter 20

Empty Chairs at Empty Tables
Jade, now

Jade darted into Talking Heads café and found it filled to the brim with chattering patrons, the sharp tang of coffee and bustling wait staff. Her pulse spiked when she spotted Elena's mother in an Oxford shirt and pearls. Ever since Elena had died, grief had been etched into Moira's face, the shadows under her eyes and the taut tendons in her neck. Jade's mum had said her friend had struggled emotionally, especially after her split from Steve, and today, she seemed more uptight than usual.

Jade approached warily, not wanting to disrupt whatever fragile balance Moira had found. At the same time, she wanted to know who Moira thought had killed Nick and to test her theory about Elena's death. Nothing they did could bring Elena back, yet if Jade had guessed right about Elena being murdered, Moira should be the first to know. The truth might give her a degree of closure.

Speaking of truth, Jade had to be careful how much to tell Moira. She certainly wouldn't break her promise to Danny and reveal Elena's involvement in illegal trading, but should she divulge Steve's location? The fewer people who knew about witness protection, the better. Still, he cared about her, and Jade suspected she reciprocated the feeling. From what he'd told Jade, they sat on the BeanBlitz board together and kept in regular contact. Possibly, she already knew about Curtis's trades.

After the icy wind outside, the heated air made Jade slip off her puffer jacket as she wove through the mismatched furniture. Next to Moira's immaculate presentation, Jade's jeans and chambray shirt looked decidedly scruffy, and her hair, mussed by the wind, only emphasised Moira's hair-sprayed do.

Jade kissed Moira on both cheeks. 'Thanks for meeting me.' She hung her jacket on the back of her chair and sat. Elena left a void between them as tangible as a warm body. She should have been with them, full of energy and vitality.

'It's always lovely to see you.' Moira's plum-in-the-mouth accent made Jade smile. Elena, as a precocious teen, had mimicked her mother behind her back, while to her face, she'd used an exaggerated ocker accent. Moira always responded, *I didn't send you to a private girls' school so you could sound like someone from the Western suburbs*, which was a little rich, as Moira had grown up in Broadmeadows. 'But it's been an awful time. I'm still in shock. Are you okay?'

Jade wavered over whether to take Moira's lead and dive into sensitive topics or to attempt more small talk. She followed her gut and launched in. 'I'm a bit all over the place, to be honest. Since I returned to Melbourne, I've been searching for a story to cover, and now I'm wondering if I should ... well, Nick's murder means more to me than anything else. I know the people, so I can dig deeper than other reporters and, hopefully, find out more.' Jade opened her mouth to ask if she could record their conversation, but Moira's frown showed strong disapproval, so rather than risk being shut down, she ploughed ahead without it. 'I assume you know the police have spoken to Curtis and some of the others. What do you think of him?'

Moira sniffed. 'Curtis wasn't good enough for Elena, but she couldn't be told. Steve loved him and helped him set up Bean-Blitz, so at least he tried to make something of himself. But look at him now, a murder suspect, no less.'

The police still hadn't named official suspects, and being questioned didn't make Curtis one, but evidently, Moira viewed him that way.

The server came to take their order – coffee for Moira, peppermint tea for Jade, and an apple muffin to share – so Jade waited a few minutes before asking, 'Could Curtis have killed Nick?'

'Well, he's been questioned by the police and, as far as I can tell, they don't have any other credible options.'

'But what do *you* think? Is Curtis capable of murder?' Unless Steve was mistaken or lying, it had to be him.

Moira blinked, eyes dull with confusion. 'You never know who people really are, do you?'

'Are you still on the BeanBlitz board?' Jade had learnt to check every detail.

'I'm a director. We set it up when I was married to Steve to distribute our income for tax purposes and never got around to changing it. I see him every other month at director meetings.' Moira's eyes lit up, and her animation made Jade guess she wasn't over Steve. Not by a long shot.

'People always said BeanBlitz grew big too quickly. Were you aware of Curtis doing anything dodgy?'

Moira toyed with her pearls, either unaware or unperturbed how overdressed she looked next to the other customers in jeans or exercise wear. 'Back then, we applauded him. Thought he'd made shrewd market assessments. But Steve started to wonder. That happened around the time Elena died, so if I'm honest, I was preoccupied and didn't examine the trading thing too closely.'

'With the benefit of hindsight, is it possible?'

She shrugged. 'I should call Steve and see what he thinks.'

'Ah...' Jade needed to make a snap decision. If Moira tried to contact Steve and couldn't get through, she'd stress about it. To avoid giving her this additional anxiety, Jade said, 'You won't get onto him.'

The server brought their drinks. 'Sorry it's taken so long. We're swamped. One of our casuals is off sick.'

As soon as she'd left, Moira asked, 'What's up with Steve?'

After securing a promise of confidentiality, Jade launched into an overview of her trip to Sorrento, her meeting with Steve, seeing Curtis and the getaway to the Bayside police station. She kept it brief and left out Elena's involvement.

By the time she'd finished, Moira had flushed bright red and the vein on her temple pulsed. 'So, Curtis did kill Nick.'

'It seems that way, unless Steve jumped to conclusions, or—'

'Wait, are you trying to pin something on Steve?' Moira turned on Jade as though she'd physically threatened her.

'No, no, of course not'—although Moira's response had raised Jade's suspicions—'I'm just trying to sift through the facts. Who do you think did it?'

'If Steve blames Curtis, he must be right. He wouldn't make such an allegation lightly.' Moira's hand fluttered to her neck. 'Nick must have uncovered evidence about Curtis's trades. What else did Steve say? Who else was in the boardroom?'

'The boardroom?'

'You said Steve found Curtis in the boardroom.'

Jade thought back. She'd mentioned the office but didn't recall saying anything more specific. She mentally kicked herself for not recording the conversation. A pitiful mistake. Because if she hadn't pinned down the location, how did Moira know where it happened? For now, she didn't want their conversation to lose momentum, so she tucked away the concern to dissect later. 'Oh, right, yes. Steve said everyone else had gone home. He and Curtis had stayed back for a meeting or something.'

'Steve is always so generous with his time. Curtis would be nothing without his mentoring.'

They ate and drank quietly for a few moments with only the sounds of chatter and the squeal of a chair on the wooden floor intruding. Jade tried to figure out the gentlest way of introducing her theory about Elena. It might work better if she could lead

Moira to the idea without stating it overtly. 'These past few years have been rough. And now, another loss.'

'You're far too young to have lost two friends to tragedy.'

'Right, it's almost as if...'

Moira looked at her sharply. 'As if what?'

'Well, like we're jinxed or something.'

'You know better than that, Jade. There's no such thing as a jinx.' Moira had never been keen on fanciful ideas, always calling superstitions ridiculous. She'd scolded Jade and Elena as youngsters if they held their breath driving past a cemetery or freaked out after seeing a black cat.

'So what, it's just an unlucky coincidence?' Jade sipped her tea, hoping the peppermint would soothe her fluttery stomach. 'Or are you suggesting a connection?'

'Well, I...' Moira stalled. 'But that would mean ... wait ... if they're connected, then ... oh my God, do you think someone murdered Elena?'

Jade kept her voice even. 'I don't know.'

'Let's say Curtis killed Nick. If he's capable of murder ... what if he's done it before?'

Jade clasped her fingers to keep them steady. 'Slow down.'

'But why would Curtis kill Elena?'

Jade broke off a piece of muffin and toyed with it. 'What if she found out about the trades? How far would he have gone to avoid jail time?'

'I wouldn't put anything past him.' Moira blinked quickly, clearly bewildered by the course of the conversation.

Jade reproached herself for manipulating her. 'People will probably think we're in denial, but—'

'We had an autopsy.' Moira gulped. 'They said she died from an overdose.'

'The pills killed her, but what if someone forced her to take them and made it look like suicide?' Jade had promised herself she'd get through this meeting without breaking down, but as she recalled the scene – Elena on the ground, the pill packets on her bedside table, nothing out of place, no sign of a struggle – her eyes brimmed with tears. They'd never figured out where the pills came from. And Jade's research showed that for Ambien to be lethal, it required more tablets than Elena had taken. 'Could you show me the coroner's report?'

'I ... yes. I'll dig it up and email it to you. We should check into this more closely. My Elena. I never accepted that she did it.'

Jade enjoyed a small surge of triumph that Moira had followed her logic, yet she winced, aware the years hadn't diminished her crushing guilt about Elena's suicide. Danny had said the same, and it seemed Moira had a similar response. 'We need to be careful we're not seeing what we want to see, but are you okay if I dig into this?'

A fire blazed in Moira's eyes. 'I want to know what happened. She's my daughter.'

Jade wasn't sure what she'd have done if Moira had begged her to leave it alone, but having her endorsement made the job easier.

But Moira hadn't finished. 'If Curtis hurt her, I'll—'

A sinking sensation hit Jade. If Moira turned vigilante, then involving her had been a grave mistake.

Jade jumped into damage control. 'We can't assume anything. Even if Curtis killed Nick, that doesn't mean he murdered Elena; it only means the possibility's worth exploring.'

Moira gripped her coffee mug so tightly Jade expected it to break. 'Please, keep me up to date.'

Jade nodded with a taut smile of solidarity.

'What are you going to do next?' Moira asked.

'I want to find out who killed Nick. If it's unrelated to Elena, we're probably wrong. We could be wrong, anyway. It's only a hunch.' Jade spoke faster, unsure how the emotional toll of murder versus suicide would land. Would it help to have someone else to blame, or would she and Moira be consumed by fury? 'I'd like to speak to her dad – Peter – to see whether he remembers anything relevant. Do you keep in touch?'

Moira's paper-thin eyelids flickered. 'We see each other from time to time, although I always come away depressed. Why do you think I left him?'

Jade assumed she meant the question rhetorically but answered regardless. 'I don't know. What happened?'

As a child, Jade had seen divorce as a frightfully sophisticated thing to do. It terrified her. Usually, her parents kept their fights behind closed doors, but on the odd occasions when her mum couldn't contain herself and their squabbles had bubbled over in front of the kids, Jade had catastrophised and imagined the fallout of a separation. Which parent would she live with? Where would she spend her holidays? Moira and Peter, meanwhile, had trapped Elena in a relentless tug-of-war, and Jade, although curious, had been too young to grasp the nuances of their estrangement.

Moira grimaced. 'You really don't know?'

Jade combed her brain for snippets of conversation from her sleepovers with Elena. She had only been eleven when Peter left, and her memories had faded over the years, but Elena had repeated her parents' platitudes and scoffed at them: *We both still love you, we just can't live with each other anymore.* She'd made out she didn't care, but Jade could tell she'd been devastated. For two whole weeks, she'd refused to train for netball. Back then, they'd lived for netball. But while Elena had mentioned arguments and tempers flaring, no real explanation had been given. 'We were kids. Nobody told us anything.'

'He cheated on me.'

'Oh, I'm so sorry to hear that.' Badly timed peals of laughter came from a table across the room.

'It was horribly tawdry. The local gym instructor, would you believe? He didn't even go to the gym. They met on a train. It only lasted a few weeks, but the damage remained. I found out later he'd been made redundant from his job the week before. If I'd known, I might have been more forgiving.' Her lips tightened into a severe line. 'Then again, maybe not.'

Elena's dad had stopped working as an engineer and announced he planned to write crime fiction. All these years later,

Jade had never seen Peter's name on the spine of a novel. Perhaps he lacked the discipline and hadn't stuck with it. She doubted a lack of talent; he could turn any incident into a grand story, like the time he drove his car down a dirt road in Alice Springs, got bogged and had to call the police to get towed out.

Moira touched her pearls again as if noticing them for the first time. 'These came from Peter. His grandmother's. He let me keep them in the divorce on the understanding they'd go to Elena. No matter how he treated me, he always loved his daughter.' She wiped her mouth with a napkin. 'Do you mind if I join you when you see him? I want to hear whether he has any insight about Elena.'

Jade would have preferred to go alone – it would be easier to reconnect with Peter one-on-one – but she couldn't find a polite way to decline. They parted ways with Moira promising to arrange lunch with him in the next few days, and Jade wishing like crazy she'd recorded their conversation so she could check whether she'd mentioned the damn boardroom.

Chapter 21

They Both Reached for The Gun

JADE, prosecco in hand, revelled in the theatre bustle as she chatted with her parents during intermission for *Chicago*. She'd worn a sage green dress to please her mother and blended in with the other theatregoers, whose attire varied from casual to evening gowns and slick suits. Red carpet, high ornate ceilings and chandeliers gave her the sense of stepping back in time.

The delicious irony of them having booked months in advance for a show about murder didn't escape her. Art imitating life. Or was it the other way around? 'Cell Block Tango' replayed in her head. She'd envied the performers during the number; tango was one of her favourite dances.

Gina, still channelling *Mamma Mia*, wiped her forehead, sending the wide sleeve of her polyester tie-dye dress flapping. 'I'm not taken with the actor playing Roxie, she's a bit too polished. Roxie should be more brash and raw. But Velma, mwah'—she touched her fingers to her lips and blew an air kiss—'magnifique.'

Part of the fun of attending shows with her parents included analysing the performance. Gina, as an industry insider, shared forthright opinions about every element of the production from set design to lighting. A small-time actor in her youth, she'd given up her fledgling TV career to become a drama teacher after falling pregnant with Jade. Whenever Gina mentioned her great sacrifice – and the references were frequent – Jade suffered guilt pangs. A few years back, Jade and her brother had re-watched Gina's collection of TV appearances over a bottle of wine. For the first time, they'd recognised their mother's unfortunate lack of talent. She laboured over every movement, word and reaction, making her performances hopelessly contrived. The siblings' gales of laughter came from relief they hadn't been responsible for hamstringing the next Cate Blanchett. Despite their amusement, Jade's heart ached for her mother – to be so passionate about acting but unable to realise her dreams must have been a terrible frustration. Yet, in teaching, she'd found her true gift. Her students adored her.

'They're both excellent, but the true magic of the show is the music.' Intoxicated by showtunes, Jade's father, Keith, usually less effusive than his wife, almost matched her enthusiasm.

'I'll drink to that'—Gina toasted then kissed Keith full on the lips—'it's a real toe-tapper.'

Jade recognised her luck in having parents who'd remained married, and more so, who still got along, but sometimes their public displays of affection could be downright embarrassing.

'Don't roll your eyes at us'—Gina must have caught her at it—'one day you'll be just the same. I know things didn't work out with Jack ... no, John, but if you're interested, I can set you up with one of the teachers at school. He broke up with his girlfriend a while back, so he'd be ready for—'

Jade held up a hand. 'I'm not interested. My friend just died. I'm not in the headspace for romance.'

Chastised, Gina, guzzled her prosecco. 'All I'm saying is you need to get out more. It's not good for someone your age to spend so much time alone. What did you do last Friday night? Saturday?'

Jade knew admitting she'd stayed in and watched reruns of *Friends* wouldn't cut it. 'I went to the Ruby Room with Danny on Wednesday.'

Rather than focusing on her mother, Jade stewed over the connections between the show and Nick's death: the way a clever spin – like how the lawyer in *Chicago* created reasonable doubt by suggesting the shooter and victim both reached for the gun – could help someone get away with murder. She wanted to use this insight to decipher fact from manipulation in what Curtis, Steve and Danny had told her.

Gina touched Jade's arm. 'You're quiet. What's going on inside that busy brain of yours?'

'I saw Moira today.'

'How was she?'

'You know how she can be ... a bit reserved. She...' Jade hesitated, unsure whether to hold this conversation in public, but nobody in the crowded lobby paid them any attention, all too busy in their own groups, sipping drinks or devouring Magnum ice-creams. 'Nick's death has stirred up a lot of angst from the past. I just ... we wondered if, as you suggested, Mum, there might be a link between Nick's death and Elena's.'

Keith and Gina exchanged a glance, and immediately, Jade wished she'd kept her mouth shut.

'Don't look at me like that. You said it first.' Jade stared accusingly at her mother. 'Remember? The night you came over after we found out about Nick.'

Gina spluttered denials, but Keith cut in before she could reach full flight. 'What sort of link?'

Jade stepped closer to her parents and lowered her voice. 'Steve thinks Curtis killed Nick to cover up financial crimes he committed while Elena was alive. What if she'd threatened to turn Curtis in? He'd have had a strong motive to keep her quiet.'

Keith narrowed his eyes. 'Are you writing a story about this?'

'Yes.'

'Is that wise?'

'Dad, I'm a journalist. That's what I do.'

'Which reminds me, I bought you a present.' Keith reached

into the inside pocket of his jacket and pulled out a blue object about the size of a car key.

'You bought me a car? Dad, you shouldn't have.'

'You wish. No, it's a personal safety alarm.' He held it proudly and pointed to the button in the middle. 'Press this for an ear-piercing squeal. It'll draw attention and, hopefully, scare your attacker away. Obviously, I can't demonstrate it here, but I tried it at home and—'

'He nearly deafened me.' Gina put her hands over her ears.

'Oh.' Instinctively, Jade wanted to reject it, as if conceding the need for it would brand her weak, but then she remembered the warning email and figured it might come in handy. Besides, her dad looked so earnest she couldn't bear to respond with anything less than gratitude. 'Thanks, that's really thoughtful.'

He handed it over, and she tucked it into the side pocket of her handbag.

'If you want my opinion about Nick's murder'—Gina didn't wait to see if anyone did—'I'm not sure it's connected to Elena's death because my money's on Moira.'

'Moira? I thought you two were friends.' Despite her scepticism, Jade couldn't help giving some credence to Gina's wild theories – after all, she'd planted the idea about Elena's death. Jade never knew whether her mother was spouting wisdom or nonsense. And Moira did ask about the boardroom when Jade could have sworn she hadn't said it first.

'She is my friend, although to tell you the truth, I've always seen her as a bit of a money grabber. As soon as she'd finished with Peter, she moved onto Steve – and look at what a step up that gave her. Holidays. All those properties.' Gina cast a meaningful glance. How did she manage to make every gesture seem like a stage direction?

Jade recalled Moira's telltale fervour when she spoke about Steve. 'I don't think she just used him – she seems to really care about him. And even if she did, it doesn't make her a murderer.'

'Steve – now there's a shifty man if ever there was one. If not Moira, it could be him.' Gina had warmed to her subject now.

'You think Elena's stepdad killed Nick?'

Gina tilted her head. 'He's involved. He's a director of BeanBlitz.'

Jade nudged her affectionately. 'Now you're just listing everyone you know who knows Nick.'

'At the end of the day, it's always the one who seems the least suspicious who did it,' Gina said.

'I thought you said it was always the rich ones who did it,' Jade teased.

'Well, I—'

Keith snorted. 'This is real life, not one of your theatre productions.' He turned to Jade. 'Be careful. The people you're dealing with could be dangerous. The last thing we want is for you to end up in trouble like in America. We were so worried.' Jade's investigation of a crime family had placed her life in danger, and when her parents had found out, they'd tried to persuade her to catch the next plane home.

The bells chimed for the start of the second act, saving Jade from having to defend her career choice. Keith returned their glasses to the bar counter, and they followed the boisterous crowd back to their seats.

Jade sensed that a piece of the puzzle had almost fallen into place. Gina's ramblings – *Holidays. All those properties* – had set dust motes dancing in her memory. Jade just needed to figure out why.

Chapter 22

Memory

ONE OF JADE'S favourite things about her apartment was the two-minute walk to the train station and twenty-minute ride into Melbourne's CBD. Rather than battling traffic and finding a carpark, Jade swiped her ticket and jumped on the next service, leaving plenty of time to arrive for lunch with Peter and Moira.

As the train pulled out of the station, Jade's mind turned to an incident a year or so before Moira and Peter's divorce. The girls, who couldn't have been more than ten, were having a sleepover.

Elena's home overflowed with Peter's 'junk', as Moira called it. He collected radio-controlled cars and boats, old model trains, even some full-scale car engines. Jade didn't really care how motors worked, but surrounded by the smell of sump oil and the whirrs of cylinders and pistons, she sensed a world of possibilities.

The night of the sleepover, as Moira served a sumptuous roast dinner in her sparkling if well-worn kitchen, she announced Peter wouldn't join them because he was 'being difficult'. When Jade's mum said her dad was being difficult, it often meant he wouldn't let her spend money on expensive new clothes, but Jade assumed Moira wasn't talking about dresses or high heels because that wouldn't cause Peter to stay in his studio. Maybe he didn't like roast lamb. Jade did – she coated the crispy potatoes in gravy and sniffed the woody rosemary scent.

Moira kept quiet, so Jade and Elena chattered about tryouts for the school netball team.

After dinner, they wanted to watch a movie, but the VCR machine was broken. Peter had promised to fix it, but Moira explained he *still* hadn't got around to it.

'We've got plenty of other things to do.' Jade didn't want Moira to stay mad at him; arguments made her want to run and hide.

The girls went to Elena's room and hung out until time for bed. Despite the paint peeling in the corners of the ceiling and the threadbare carpet, Jade loved Elena's room with its rows of books. After stints as library monitors at school, Elena and Jade had stuck a small envelope in the back of each of Elena's tomes with a slip of paper listing the title and author. They'd even developed a lending log to hold the slip of paper until the borrower returned it – overkill because only Jade and her brother ever took out books, but when Elena developed an interest in something, she took it to the next level.

They pulled the trundle mattress from under Elena's bed and threw Jade's sleeping bag on top. After bedtime, they knew to whisper, so Moira wouldn't tell them to stop talking. A sliver of light spilled through the crack at the bottom of the bedroom door, casting an eerie glow on Elena's face. For hours, they whispered ghost stories about the spectre of Old Lady Maud in the run-down two-storey Edwardian house down the road.

Footsteps paced up and down the hallway outside Elena's room.

'Who was that?' Jade asked in a shaky whisper.

Elena shrugged. 'Mum?'

'She said she was going to bed.'

They fell quiet and listened. Jade caught the low mumble of voices in the front of the house. She crept into Elena's bed. The girls lay frozen, listening to distant chatter like the drone of a TV. Maybe Peter had fixed the VCR.

A siren sounded in the distance, and Jade gulped. It grew louder. And louder. Until it stopped right outside Elena's house.

Elena reached for Jade's hand.

'Should we check?' Jade asked.

Elena nodded.

They opened the door, crept through the kitchen, and peered down the hallway to see Moira open the front door and say, 'Thank God you're here. He's this way.'

Two men wheeled a stretcher into the house and followed Moira into Peter's studio. Jade and Elena watched, unseen. Jade felt as if her feet had been glued to the ground.

Two minutes later, the ambulance men pushed the stretcher out. Peter lay still, face grey as ashes.

Elena screamed and ran towards him. 'Daddy.'

Moira intercepted her with a hug. 'He's okay, they're taking care of him.'

Elena pushed past her mother and bent over her father. He lifted his hand in a weak wave as they wheeled him out the door.

Elena turned on Moira. 'What's the matter with him? What happened?'

'His heart, darling.' Moira held Elena by the shoulders and stared into her eyes. 'I'm going with him to the hospital. Gina's coming to take you two back to Jade's. Grab a bag and pack some clothes. I'll call and let you know how we go.'

'I want to come with you.' Elena's voice rose.

'I'm sorry, but no. Please don't make this harder than it needs to be.' Moira raced to the kitchen and grabbed her handbag.

She returned and tore out the door, shouting, 'I'll call you.'

Jade and Elena huddled by the entrance until Jade's mum arrived. Gina's serious manner and ordinary clothes immediately ranked the situation as dire.

The longest night of Jade's and Elena's young lives followed. Waiting. Talking. Not talking. Eventually falling asleep on top of the bedclothes.

Peter survived his health scare, but ever since that day, Jade pictured ghosts as grey-faced, not white like in her storybooks. When Peter came home, he seemed diminished. He told fewer anecdotes, his engine collection stopped growing, and he argued nonstop with Moira. Jade rarely saw him outside of his studio. After the divorce, he moved into a two-bedroom apartment nearby.

The train pulled in at Flinders Street station, jolting Jade out of her reverie.

Chapter 23

Warning Sign

JADE ARRIVED in the city and hurried along the windswept footpath. Six months after her return to her hometown, she still didn't feel Melbourne's warm embrace, as though it nursed a grudge against her for abandoning it. In some ways, Jade didn't fit here: she didn't drink coffee, didn't follow Australian Rules Football, and hated the cold winters. Here, life came burdened with the weight of her parents' expectations. In Houston, she'd been free to reinvent herself, to be whomever she desired. Still, the familiarity of Melbourne's shops and streets made life so much easier. She loved the thriving restaurant scene, lived beside a gorgeous bay, and had the proximity of family – even her overbearing mother. Once, she'd have added her friends to her list of home comforts, but recent events had left a question mark over who she could trust.

She reached a lane with well-worn bluestone paving, where Mock Turtle Café patrons huddled under market umbrellas warmed by outdoor heaters, and spotted Peter's messy hair and unkempt clothes.

A rush of affection overtook her as she approached his table. 'It's so good to see you.'

Wonderment transformed his face. 'My God, you're beautiful!'

Jade held back a joke about his eyesight failing; the way he squinted through his glasses suggested it might be too close to the truth. She bent to give him a quick hug and sat beside him.

'Elena would've been the same age as you. Twenty-seven.' He stared at her more intently, as if to conjure an image of his grown-up daughter.

'I think about her every day.' Jade left a respectful pause before continuing. 'What happened to the novel you started?'

'Writing doesn't pay the bills, so I went back to a desk job. I'll try again after I retire.'

'You and Elena had such vivid imaginations. She often told me ghost stories about that dilapidated house in the neighbourhood.'

He chuckled. 'I loved that old place, so full of character, but it's gone now. Did you know Steve bought it and the house next door? Knocked them down and built a block of flats. Bland and uninspiring if you ask me.'

'Yeah, I can't stand them either.'

Peter ran his hand through his nearly all white hair. 'How about you? Still a journalist?'

'Uh-huh. I'm with a local newspaper, but I want to step up.' She pulled a face. 'It's not happening as quickly as I'd like.'

Peter offered a knowing smile. 'Be patient. I was always in such a rush to get places when I was younger, but you get there and then what? Take your time and enjoy life.'

'Right.' Jade appreciated his insight but wasn't convinced. Look at Elena and Nick; their opportunities had come to a grinding halt. Who knew how long she had?

'Where are you living these days?'

She waved in the general direction. 'Elsternwick. Funnily enough, I'm in the same block you moved to after you and Moira broke up.'

'Which apartment?'

'Four on the ground floor. One with a courtyard.'

'Nice.' He noticed the charm bracelet on Jade's wrist and gasped. 'Is that...?'

Jade held out her hand. 'Yes, Elena's. She gave it to me.'

'May I?' He reached towards it.

She unclipped it and passed it to him.

Peter touched each charm in turn, eyes brimming with tears. 'She was so proud of this, and I ... I couldn't stand Steve taking her to Disneyland and Paris instead of me.'

He clipped it back on Jade's wrist, then stiffened at the sight of Moira approaching, perfectly groomed with her pearls, makeup and coiffed hair. Jade wondered if she could be guilty of more than overdressing.

'Peter, there you are, and Jade, thanks for coming.' Moira spoke a bit too loudly as she kissed Jade on each cheek and took her seat without offering Peter so much as a brief hug.

'Moira.' Peter remained cordial, despite her glacial greeting.

After they'd placed their lunch orders with the overly cheerful server, Peter said to Moira, 'You were rather mysterious on the phone. Why exactly did you want us to meet?'

Moira placed her hands on the table and launched in. 'I assume you've seen the news about Nick?'

Peter nodded. 'Terrible business.'

'The police have been questioning Curtis.'

Peter gave Moira a quizzical glance. 'I hope he's not caught up in this. He never struck me as the violent type. Always so charming. Elena adored him.'

Moira straightened. 'Turns out he's been involved in insider trading.'

'Oh.' Peter looked to Jade for direction, clearly unsure where the conversation was heading.

Before Jade could jump in, Moira continued. 'The point is, if Elena knew Curtis conducted insider trading, what if she threatened to tell the authorities? It's possible he had something to do with Elena's death. Can you remember anything Elena did or said that might implicate him?'

Jade wanted to cover Moira's mouth to shut her up, preferring to introduce the topic more obliquely. But too late. Moira had finished her brusque explanation, and Peter's jaw hung open.

Fortunately, the server arrived and served their meals – 'Here you go, nice and hot. This'll warm you up.' – which gave Peter a moment to collect himself.

Peter stared at his soup, speechless. The spoon trembled in his hand. Jade noted his jerky movements with concern – did his tremors signify anxiety, or the onset of a more serious medical condition?

Moira carefully chewed a piece of lettuce, fastidious as ever, then asked, 'So, what do you think?'

His eyes clouded. 'Why are you doing this? Dredging up all this pain. Can't we let our darling girl rest in peace?'

Jade wished they could avoid this conversation. Peter, such a kind, gentle man, didn't deserve this angst. None of them did, but something about Peter's age-weary face made him seem more susceptible to stress.

'Don't you want to know the truth?' A flicker in the fine lines around Moira's eyes made Jade study her more closely. No question, she was hiding something, possibly related to her mention of the boardroom, but Jade doubted it had anything to do with Elena.

'What if our daughter simply had mental health issues, and we didn't do enough to help her? Can you face that?' He showed no anger, just profound sadness.

Moira flinched. 'I've been living with that possibility for years, but what if it didn't happen? What if someone forced her to take those drugs? We owe it to Elena to uncover the truth. All I'm asking is for you to try to remember.'

He turned to Jade. 'What's your opinion?'

Jade knew to tread lightly. 'Elena's suicide never sat right with me. And another death in our small group of friends so soon after seems suspicious. With Curtis under the microscope for murder, we at least need to consider if this is history repeating.'

Peter kept his gaze away from Moira and lifted his spoon. 'Give me some time.' A drop of soup splashed back into the bowl. 'One thing I'll tell you for free is I'm not surprised someone took Nick out.'

'Why?' Moira asked before Jade could speak. If only Jade had been able to meet Peter without Moira's disconcerting presence. He'd surely be more forthcoming.

He glanced at the table next to them, where a couple of young men in business shirts huddled over a phone, laughing. Clearly, they weren't paying Peter any attention, so he turned back. 'Elena once said something about him behaving inappropriately.'

Again, Moira got in first. 'Did he assault her? If he did, I'd have murdered him myself. Why didn't you tell me?'

'No, no'—he gestured for her to settle down—'she was worried about a friend.'

Jade trawled through her mental catalogue of Elena's acquaintances with a connection to Nick. 'Did she say who?'

'No. She'd been told in confidence and didn't want to betray her friend's trust. I told her to encourage the young woman to report it, but as far as I know, nothing came of it.' Peter sat back. 'But he never hurt Elena, so please, let's drop the subject.'

Moira shot Jade a look of frustration but did as he asked.

Jade had always found Nick a bit handsy, but what did Elena mean by behaving inappropriately? If Peter had suggested reporting it, it must have been serious. Had Elena's friend been raped?

Underlying the shock of this ugly truth came the realization that Elena had kept more secrets. Ethically, she'd done the right thing by keeping quiet, but Nick had stayed in their friendship circle – what if he'd tried to hurt Jade? Elena could have found a way to warn her.

The clatter of cutlery, scent of coffee, and buzz of conversation crowded Jade's senses, making her fumble for small talk. 'So, how've you been?' she asked Peter.

'I get by. No dramas.'

Moira dabbed her lips with a napkin. 'Still hoarding your junk?'

His jawline tensed. 'It's not junk.'

An incident jostled for position in Jade's mind: after Peter and Moira separated, Moira had arranged a skip and dumped his engines before he'd had a chance to move them.

Jade floundered in search of a new subject. 'How's your health? No more heart trouble?' Ouch. Not the best topic. She cut open her poached egg, and the yolk bled onto the fritters.

He put down his spoon. 'My heart's fine—'

'Look!' Moira pointed at a man walking by with purple dreadlocks. 'Do you think I should get my stylist to try it out on me?'

Grateful to be on safer ground, Jade joined the banter. 'That's more my mother's style.'

'How is Gina?' Moira primped her hair. 'We're overdue a catch-up.'

Jade endured another thirty minutes of awkward small talk before they finished their meal. At last, she could say goodbye without appearing rude. Happy to escape the tension between the exes, she decided to wander past some of her favourite haunts in the arts district before returning home for her meeting with Curtis.

Chapter 24

In the City

MELBOURNE STREETS TRANSFORMED into wind tunnels during winter, assaulting Jade with a blustery breeze and a myriad of memories. Tourists, office workers and labourers were still returning from lunch, so she battled a sea of pedestrians. Around every corner, she came across restaurants or bars where she'd hung out with Elena, talking nonstop and solving the problems of the world. Elena always ate with the freedom of someone who could gorge on whatever she wanted and remain thin, while Jade took neat bites, her mother's voice ringing in her ears. 'A moment on the lips, forever on the hips.' Gina obsessed about weight – Jade's as well as her own.

Jade wandered into the laneway where she and Elena had taken turns to etch their initials into a piece of graffiti while the other kept watch. The lane still smelt of urine and garbage, but the graffiti had been long overwritten, currently upscale street art in bold fuchsia, greens and blues. Unsettled by an uncanny sense of being followed, Jade ran back to the main street, then slowed and continued to the famous clocks at the entrance of Flinders Street Station and on to Princes Bridge.

Her mind leapt back to Peter's comments about Nick. For time to think, she stepped out of the foot traffic and gazed along the Yarra River. Southbank ran along the left side, a string of restaurants, offices and hotels leading to the Casino, which hid just out of sight. To her right, the station crouched beneath the jagged city skyline. A forest of office buildings housed the headquarters of finance, insurance and telecommunications companies. The glint of sunlight reflecting off mirrored skyscrapers made her vision swirl, so she lowered her eyes as she tried to remember who Nick had hooked up with. The only person she could recall was Iris. Jade would find a subtle way to ask her about Nick when they met for coffee the next day.

Iris was now dating Curtis. He'd be livid if he'd found out Nick had raped her – could that stretch to a motive for murder? Four days had passed since she'd dropped Steve at the police station, and Curtis still hadn't been arrested. Either the authorities didn't believe Steve, or they needed further evidence before they could make their move. Unless they were making no progress because they were investigating Curtis for the wrong reason. An image of him strangling Nick made Jade shiver.

A cheer from a boatload of tourists jolted her back to her surroundings, and again, the creepy sensation of being watched struck her. Jade checked her watch. She had an hour before she had to leave to see Curtis, so she carried on to the arts precinct: Hamer Hall, round and squat like an oversized cake tin, and the State Theatre with its spire, a yellow web reaching for the heavens. The plaintive notes of a violin beckoned, and she followed the steps down to the Yarra River. Icy air blew off the water, and she zipped her puffer jacket all the way to her neck as she turned into the gloomy pathway under the bridge. She wandered past the busker, a slight woman making a powerful sound.

Footsteps echoed behind her, and a sixth sense made her arms prickle. She'd been spooked ever since the warning email but never as strongly as right now. A glance over her shoulder revealed the people behind her in silhouette. She couldn't make out their faces but strode faster, reaching into the side pocket of her bag for her personal alarm.

Finger on the button, she emerged into sunlight. Dazzled, she headed for the boatsheds. Swarms of people strolled along the Yarra banks while Lycra-clad cyclists wove along the bike path. Hopefully, nobody would approach her with so many witnesses, yet she rushed on, reluctant to take the chance.

Behind her, the violinist played on, more muted the further Jade escaped. Was that a shout? Someone calling her name? Perhaps a friend had spotted her in the crowd. Should she stop?

Hell no! Not with Nick's murderer on the loose, and not while she'd been instructed to stop her investigation. She broke into a trot. Her handbag bounced against her side, and she clutched it to hold it steady. If only she'd worn different shoes. Her boots had a small heel, not designed for running, so she clip-clopped along as loudly as a tap dancer.

She turned right to cut back up to St Kilda Road and faced the choice of stairs or a ramp. The stairs were steeper, but the ramp cut back on an angle that would keep her visible to her pursuer for longer. She trotted up the stairs, panting. Unable to maintain the pace, she slowed to a powerwalk as she turned right onto the main street, crossing the road as soon as a tram had rumbled past.

With frequent glances over her shoulder, she scurried across the bridge, hand sweaty on her personal alarm. A pigeon swooped down for a discarded potato chip, and Jade flinched. She ran to the station gates and swiped her ticket.

At the platform, her breathing returned to normal, but her pulse didn't get the message, still fired on adrenaline. She was acting paranoid, but she'd been held up at gunpoint before and didn't want it to happen again. Skittish, she startled at a loud-speaker announcement and a person jostling through the crowd. The train arrived and, with a last scan of the commuter crowd, she ducked inside a carriage.

Chapter 25

Rumour Has It

When Jade arrived home, her jitters made it too hard to concentrate. She spent half an hour in a futile effort to knock off a piece about the local football team, then went to the Elwood Pier to meet Curtis.

She arrived early, hoping the frigid air would clear her mind; she needed to be sharp to see past Curtis's charm. Walking north along the foreshore, she caught glimpses of the West Gate Bridge through low-slung clouds. The icy weather had warned most other pedestrians away, so when she stepped onto the Elwood Pier, only a few morose seagulls kept her company. They flapped away with a mournful cry as she approached. If she'd known the beach would be deserted, she'd have arranged to meet elsewhere, but it was too late to change venues now.

At the end of the pier, she stared over choppy waves. A couple of container ships had dropped anchor in the bay, transporting goods from all over the world.

If she hadn't been so wrapped up in her thoughts, she'd have noticed Curtis sooner. Instead, she heard a voice and spun around, reaching for the alarm in her handbag for the second time that day.

Curtis laughed. 'Chill. I'm not here to hurt you.'

She forced a grin, throat constricting at the realization she stood alone with a murder suspect. 'You caught me daydreaming. I was miles away.'

He gave her a once-over. 'You're looking good.'

The familiarity of his face and his relaxed posture reassured Jade even as she questioned whether she'd ever really known him at all. The Curtis she knew would never betray Elena and implicate Danny. He'd certainly never commit murder.

'I, uh, you too.' If anything, Curtis had grown more striking than ever with his dark blond hair, bright eyes, and just the right amount of stubble on his strong jaw. Jade knew it sounded shallow, but she found it hard to reconcile that someone so beautiful could be responsible for ending a life.

She recalled the footsteps under the bridge. 'Any chance you saw me in the city earlier today?'

Curtis gave a bemused frown. 'No. Last I saw you, you were driving away from Sorrento like a crazed lunatic.'

Now she thought about it, he had no reason to follow her when they'd already arranged this meeting. But if he hadn't tailed her, who had, and what did they want? She laughed uneasily. 'I'm in training for Formula One.'

'I don't suppose you've seen Steve? He's vanished since you took off with him.'

'Are you worried?' She reached for the concrete balustrade behind her, trying to appear calm.

'We should all be worried until we know who killed Nick.' He crossed his arms. 'Come on, you must have some idea. Where is he?'

'I don't know.' She'd already risked telling Moira about Steve being in witness protection, no way could she double down and tell Curtis.

He cracked his knuckles. 'Why were you with Steve in Sorrento?'

She'd prepared for this question. 'When I heard about Nick, I called Steve to check on him just like I called you and Iris. He didn't answer, so I freaked out, thinking someone had hurt him. I guessed he'd be at Sorrento and got lucky.'

'What did he say about Nick?'

Jade shifted on her feet. Curtis was interviewing her. She needed to take control. 'He didn't want to talk about Nick. Insisted the police would sort it out. But he mentioned something about insider trading. What can you tell me about that?' Revealing her knowledge of Curtis's financial crimes no longer posed such a risk now the police were investigating it. Still, she searched the shoreline, relieved to see a couple walking arm-in-arm and a cyclist riding by.

Curtis deflated. 'Look, I admit that wasn't my proudest moment, but Steve's using it to deflect from the greater issue. As I told the police, Nick knew about the trades, but he'd agreed not to make trouble because he didn't want to jeopardise the company. He loved working for BeanBlitz.'

Unconvinced, Jade moved on. 'Who do you think killed Nick?'

'If I knew, I'd have turned the arsehole over to the police, but the way Steve's acting, running away like he's been caught with his pants down, I reckon he's got something to hide.'

'Such as?'

'That's the sixty-million-dollar question. Maybe Nick had the answer. Maybe that's why he was killed.'

More and more, it seemed Nick had become a target because he knew too much. Unless someone wanted revenge for his predatory sexual behaviour.

Jade mustered her courage to try that line of investigation. 'I heard Nick assaulted a woman. Do you know if that's true?'

Fury blazed in his eyes. 'Who told you about that?'

'Elena.' The lie came out before Jade could rein it in; she didn't want to involve Peter.

Curtis's stricken expression made her add, 'Not now, obviously, back then. She didn't tell me who he hurt, just to watch out for Nick, more of a warning really.' Jade told it the way she wished it had been. 'Who told you?'

Curtis grimaced. 'I can't say.'

'It was Iris, wasn't it? You must've been livid when you found out, especially after taking Nick under your wing at the company.'

'You've got it all wrong. I'd have loved to turn that bastard into mincemeat, but Iris made me swear not to tell anyone. Then someone beat me to it.' His voice broke. 'You won't let this out, will you? Iris will think I've betrayed her. Nobody else knows. Well, except Elena.'

Jade didn't want to keep this quiet. Nick's behaviour made him a target. Iris and Curtis must have hated him. And while Curtis said nobody else knew, a secret like that was hard to contain. What if Danny had found out Nick had hurt his sister? Or what if her parents knew? Moira's explosive response when she'd thought Nick had hurt Elena offered a clue to how they might have reacted. What's more, if he'd assaulted others, a whole raft of women and their loved ones could have been lining up to take pot shots at the man. The suspect pool had suddenly expanded. Knowledge of a rape didn't make a person a murderer, but Nick's actions gave them motive.

'I respect Iris's right to privacy, but shouldn't we tell the police? This could turn the case around. I'm sure Iris would understand.'

Curtis inhaled slowly. 'We can't do that to her. If we did, she'd become the centre of the investigation, which is why she didn't accuse him publicly in the first place.'

'But the police are questioning you. Surely, she'd tell them if it helps to clear you.' As she said it, she realised the converse could be true: if Curtis had killed Nick because of the rape, the last thing he'd want is to reveal the information.

'They have the wrong end of the stick, but I didn't do it, so they can't pin it on me.' His easy shrug came from a man used to getting away with mischief, if not murder. 'She'll come forward if I get charged.'

Certain he wouldn't change his mind for now, Jade moved on. 'Can I ask you something about Elena?'

'What about her?'

Unable to hold Curtis's gaze, Jade stared out to sea, where one of the ships had almost disappeared over the horizon. 'Do you miss her?'

Curtis rested his hands on the balustrade and followed her eyeline. 'Every day. You?'

Jade nodded, the cold cutting through to her bones. If she exposed her true emotions to this friend-turned-stranger, he might inadvertently reveal something about Elena's death. But it felt all kinds of wrong to use grief as a weapon.

Before overthinking paralysed her, she pushed her worries aside and spoke from the heart. 'Always. And I feel guilty. I was her best friend. I should've helped her.'

His sorrowful eyes remained on the whitecaps chasing one another to shore. 'We've all been searching for an explanation, but maybe there isn't one.'

Jade decided to risk it. 'Or maybe there is.'

'What do you mean?'

Jade stared at a chip packet bobbing on the waves where water lapped the end of the jetty. Beneath it, a school of fish darted around seaweed. 'I'm not convinced about suicide. Never have been.'

Curtis seemed to weigh her words. 'What else could it be?' He stiffened and turned to face her. 'You think she was murdered?'

A rogue wave splashed against the pier. Jade jumped back to avoid it, but too late. She brushed seawater droplets off her jeans. 'If she was, wouldn't you want to know?'

'You're living in some kind of sick fantasy world. You feel bad you hurt Elena. We all played our part. Hell, I know I did, but we didn't kill her, she killed herself.'

'What part did you play, Curtis? What did you do?' Accusations about insider trading jockeyed for position on Jade's tongue, but she reined them in. She couldn't risk alienating him further.

'That's between me and Elena.' He jutted out his chin. 'Why now? Why are you chasing ghosts? Isn't Nick's murder enough? We need to find out who killed him, not turn Elena's death into another mystery.'

'I'm asking because Nick's been killed. How many groups of friends have two unnatural deaths within the space of three years? There must be links.'

'One suicide, one murder. There's no connection. You journalists always go after a scoop, but there's nothing to see here.' He sounded too emphatic for Jade's liking, though to be fair, he was already dealing with police interviews; he didn't need his friend to interrogate him as well.

All the same, she prepared to steer the conversation back to insider trading, but he pulled out his phone. 'Sorry, I gotta run. Nice seeing you.'

She couldn't prolong the conversation as he rushed away, the hood of his pullover blown back in a gust of wind.

'Thanks for the chat,' she said to his retreating back. She had the distinct impression he'd been anything but pleased to see her. He'd only come to find out what had happened to Steve.

For Jade, their meeting had confirmed several things: Nick had raped Iris, and Curtis knew about it. The more she mulled it over, the less likely it seemed that Curtis could have found out Nick had raped his girlfriend and allowed him to continue working at BeanBlitz without repercussions. The same could be said for Danny. Jade resolved to win Iris's confidence at morning tea the next day to find out who else knew.

Chapter 26

Don't Stand So Close to Me

AN HOUR before Jade's meeting with Iris at the Turtle Rock Café, Iris texted, *Do you mind coming to my place?*

Sure. Everything ok?

Just more private.

Buzzing with the anticipation of an impending breakthrough, Jade caught a train to Prahran. As she walked the few blocks to the apartment Iris shared with Danny, a five-story building with tight security, she glanced at her phone and saw an unread email. She opened the app, sensing trouble.

Sure enough, The World of Writing had sent a message titled 'Writing Tips 2'. This time, they'd written more than four words.

I asked you to stop investigating Nick's murder.

I'm watching you.

If you keep going, you'll regret it.

Jade flushed hot and cold, unable to move. Further along the quiet street, an older man was walking his dog, while a young woman in office attire rushed in the direction of the station. Neither seemed suspicious, but Jade had to stop herself from breaking into a run.

She hurried to Iris's apartment block and reached for the doorbell.

Wait!

Iris had likely been raped by the victim, which made her a suspect, and she had a direct connection to two other suspects: Curtis and Danny. She could have colluded with either of them. Further, she'd switched from a public venue to her home at the last minute. This could be a trap.

Surely not. Iris was her friend. Although more and more it seemed friendship meant nothing to her cronies.

Jade wavered. Go in or leave? The World of Writing was messing with her head.

A surge of anger caught her by surprise. This was her job. She refused to be intimidated. Gripping her personal alarm in one hand, she pressed the doorbell with the other. As she waited, she pulled her jacket tighter against the wind.

Iris buzzed her in, and Jade, on high alert, caught the elevator to level three.

The door swung open to reveal Iris, classy as ever, in jeans, knee-high boots and a dusty-pink sweater. Jade hid her nerves behind a big smile, thumb poised on the button of her personal alarm.

Iris ushered Jade into the open-plan living area. 'Thanks for changing venues at the last minute, I just ... coffee? Oh no, you don't do coffee. How about tea? I have English breakfast, peppermint, chamomile.'

'Chamomile, please. You have the place looking great.' The bright, airy living room showed no signs of an ambush, only an eclectic mix of furniture covered in primary colours and floral prints. Jade would never have put them together, but it worked. Through an open door, she spotted a bright blue drum kit but no sign of Danny. Iris's bedroom door was shut.

Pages of digital art covered a large pinboard. Jade stepped closer. They told the story of a battle between a female warrior in a lime green, figure-hugging costume and an orange dragon. Although not exactly a self-portrait – the warrior had green hair and eyes to match her outfit – something in the angle of her head, mischievous lip curl, and sassy confidence echoed Iris's personality.

'These yours? They're amazing.'

Iris waved as if to brush it off, but a faint flush betrayed her pleasure at the compliment. 'Just some ideas I'm working on.' She brought their drinks, and they settled into a pair of armchairs. 'I have to get back to work, and I'm sure you do too, so I'll get straight to the point.'

Unable to focus on conversation, Jade jumped up. 'I need to use the restroom first.'

Even as Iris told her she was going the wrong way, pulse pounding, she barged into Iris's room. Oh, thank God, no one hid inside. A bold abstract painting in similar tones to the warrior woman dominated the room.

Jade retreated, heat rushing to her face. 'I'm so sorry, got mixed up.'

She tentatively pushed open the remaining door, and a rush of relief left her giddy. All clear in the bathroom. Inside, she took a few moments to compose herself, tucked the personal alarm into the pocket of her jacket, flushed the toilet, and washed her hands.

Finally able to relax, Jade slipped off her jacket and retook her seat next to Iris. 'Sorry about that.'

Iris jumped right in. 'If I wanted to have something published in the news anonymously, how would I do it?'

Jade switched gears, instantly ready for a scoop. 'You could use an anonymous tip line. Most of the big newspapers have one. They won't publish anything without proof, so you'll need to verify the information.' She tried to catch Iris's eyes, but Iris stared outside at the canopy of the street oaks, their branches bowing to the ferocious wind. 'Or you could tell me, and I can protect your identity.'

As if Iris felt the chill from outdoors, she folded her arms and hunched her shoulders. 'I'm not sure, I...'

Jade waited. Silence often spurred sources to open up as they rushed to fill the void in the discussion.

This trick didn't work for Iris, so Jade offered a prompt. 'Is it about Nick's murder?'

'No, well, not exactly. It's ... the thing is, I don't want to get caught up in a bunch of questions about the past.'

Jade went for the jugular. 'Is this about Nick? Did he hurt you?'

'Did he get you too?' Iris seemed almost hopeful, as if eager to find an ally, someone who understood her trauma.

'No, but Elena once made a weird comment. More of a warning, if you know what I mean.' As when talking to Curtis, Jade left out Peter as the middleman.

Iris nodded. Normally, she came across as composed and confident, but today, her vulnerability made Jade want to wrap her in a hug.

'Do you want to tell me what happened?' Jade asked gently.

Iris rubbed the arm of her chair, obviously uncertain, until she seemed to overcome her internal resistance. 'It happened just after we'd broken up. I didn't tell anyone right away. We'd been dating, so I figured everyone would assume implied consent.' She crossed her arms again.

'I'm so sorry you had to go through it alone.'

'I told Elena about a month after, and she offered great support, but then she...'

'Yeah.'

Jade longed to reach out and erase Iris's pain, or better yet, to rewind the clock and prevent the rape, but she could only offer words. 'If you said no, it was a crime. Even in marriage, you must consent. That's why they brought in marital rape laws.'

'People judge, you know how it is.'

'You'll get none of that from me.'

Iris gave a nod of gratitude. 'Nick was lovely while we were dating, but – I know this sounds horrible – I got bored with him. Of course, I didn't use that reason to end things. I just said our relationship no longer worked for me.' Now Iris had started talking, she seemed unable to stop.

'How'd he take it?'

Iris rubbed her hands on her jeans. 'Didn't say much, kept it in, but I could see he was upset.'

'So, what went wrong?'

Iris returned her gaze to the treetops. 'He came over to pick up his things – some clothes and stuff.'

'He came here?'

'No. The old place. I couldn't bear to stay there after what happened.'

'You told Danny?'

'What? Hell no!' Iris grimaced. 'Can you imagine how he'd react? With his temper? When our lease came up, I made excuses why I wanted to move.'

A sensitive soul like Danny might have guessed. He could be remarkably perceptive.

'The day Nick dropped in to get his things, he came into my room and made a move as if we'd never broken up. I pushed him away, but he laughed as if I were kidding. I told him to stop messing around, and ... I fought back, but Nick's stronger than he looks, and ... you can guess the rest.' Iris maintained her composure, but patches of red flushed her cheeks, and she played with the bottom edge of her sweater. 'After that, I avoided being alone with him again.' She sipped her coffee. 'I never thought something like this would happen to me.'

Jade didn't ask why Iris had never accused Nick publicly; she wouldn't want to re-live that private hell inside a courtroom either, and questioning it could be mistaken for judgement.

Iris rubbed her hands on her knees. 'I'm sick of hearing all this bullshit on the news about how lovely Nick was. His parents and brother all talk about his kind nature. What a crock. They have no clue he was capable of cruelty. It's tragic he died, but part of me is relieved, like now he can't hurt anyone else, you know?'

Jade nodded. 'A bit like karmic justice.'

'I want the world to know what he did.'

'I get it, I do, but the timing's risky. If it comes out that he hurt you, it'll implicate you in his murder. Or Curtis. Even Danny.'

'That's why I want to stay anonymous.'

'If an accusation of rape comes out in relation to a murder, journos will interview everyone who knew him to find out who it was. They'll find you. Then they'll turn it into a motive. Trust me, that's what I'd do.' Jade realised how callous it sounded and wanted to apologise for her profession, but she knew she couldn't change it, so the best she could do was warn Iris and stop her making a colossal mistake. 'Curtis has already been questioned for Nick's murder. This'll only give the police more ammunition. Rape's a compelling motive for murder, and you're his girlfriend.'

'Curtis didn't do it.'

'How do you know?'

'Is this off the record?'

Jade nodded, already knowing she'd regret it; Iris's pent-up energy suggested she was burning to reveal another monstrous secret.

'You swear?'

'I'm here as a friend, not a journalist.'

'This'll all come out, but I don't want to be the one who spills. It makes all of us look bad.'

Jade itched to hear more. 'How can you be so sure Curtis didn't do it?'

'Because I was there.'

'What?' All the colours around Jade – the bold chairs, the graphic artwork, the waving branches outside – faded as she focused on Iris.

'We were all there: Curtis, Danny, Steve and me. Moira too.'

Jade's world tilted off kilter. She'd spoken to all of them about Nick's murder, and not one of them had breathed a word. What kind of mad world had she stepped into?

Chapter 27

I Want to Break Free

Danny, the day of Nick's death

I SAT AT MY COMPUTER, the hours stretching long in front of me. Curtis had arranged a seven o'clock meeting about the future of the company, so I remained stuck at work longer than usual in my tiny office with room only for my desk and a couple of visitor's chairs. On my right, a window overlooked the street. On my left, a frosted-glass door led to the rest of the floor. I faced a wall of tacky art with inspirational mottos – exactly the sort of hackneyed positivity that dragged me down.

Curtis had been vague about the agenda for tonight's meeting, which put me on edge. When we'd first worked together, I'd been privy to everything, though he'd confided in me less since Elena had died. Today, something ominous bled through the lack of detail in the agenda, and my imagination filled the gaps with everything from layoffs to some sort of ASIC investigation. The air crackled with tension, violins playing tremolo, waiting for a chance to steal the spotlight.

All day, Curtis had been irritable, far from his usual cheery self, so when Iris popped her head inside my office with a work question, I took the opportunity to ask what had him so riled.

'How the hell should I know?' she snapped, unusually short-tempered – trying on my schtick for size.

I got up and beckoned her inside. 'Are you two okay?' I lived in hope that Iris would recognise Curtis as a user and break up with him, but I had to tread carefully because nothing guaranteed a relationship's survival better than family opposition.

'We had a bit of a tiff, that's all. We'll get over it.' She slumped into the chair in front of my desk, so I returned to my spot, hiding my delight, and observed her over the papers strewn on my desk.

I couldn't concentrate with mess around me, so periodically, I threw everything into drawers, leaving only my computer and the pages I was working on, but today, I didn't have the energy.

'Have you tried talking to him about it?'

She shot me a glare, obviously disinterested in my relationship advice – hardly surprising given I hadn't dated since Elena had died. Come to think of it, I hadn't dated since I'd fallen for Elena, although I'd had plenty of girlfriends before then.

'Why do you reckon Curtis asked Nick to prepare the report for tonight?' she asked.

I raised my eyebrows at the change of topic. 'You're jealous of Nick?'

Iris's hollow laugh sounded foreign from her mouth. 'Jealous? Hardly. I'm just not sure why Curtis asked him to write this report instead of you or me.'

'Me neither.'

'Nick is...' Iris seemed lost for the right word. 'What do you guys see in him? Why have you been friends for so long?'

'He's just one of the gang. Always comes to my gigs. Works hard. Good company. He's harmless enough.' Some friendships become a habit, and you never stop to ask why you connected in the first place.

Iris scoffed.

'What's going on?' I doubted Iris worried about petty professional rivalry. Maybe this had something to do with their brief time together, although that happened years ago now. 'If you don't like him, why'd you date him?'

Normally, I can read Iris – the benefit of being a twin – but I couldn't interpret the look flashing across her face, somewhere between pain and restraint. When men say they don't understand women, I bet they have an expression exactly like this in mind. 'Good question. I think I just needed a warm body. Or I was vying for Curtis's attention.'

I opened my mouth to reply, but she'd been more candid than expected, and words failed me.

'You know what? You're right. I should speak to Curtis.' She got up and rushed to his office, leaving me wondering what the hell just happened.

While Iris could be flighty in romance, I relied on her to keep me grounded. She helped me manage my temper – like the time the guy who got me suspended at school asked for a rematch, and she made me walk away. But since she'd been enmeshed with Curtis, we'd been unable to discuss my concerns about him and his company. I'd kept my worries hidden, even though hoarding my emotions had never worked in my favour.

Determined to view Nick through a fresh lens, I went to the boardroom where he'd been holed up since lunchtime, working on the presentation in question.

He changed his screen as soon as I stepped inside and asked, 'How're you going?'

Observing Nick clinically, I couldn't see how he'd attracted Iris with his mousy hair, rounded stomach and serious demeanour. She had a type: exceptional men, whether in looks, sport or business. She was a standout herself, and like attracted like. Nick blended in.

I pulled myself back to the conversation. 'All good. What's on the agenda for tonight?'

Nick assumed a secretive air. 'I could tell you, but then I'd have to kill you.'

I rolled my eyes. Talk about corny. 'Are we going to be stuck here half the night? I've got things to do.' I surveyed the room for hints, but the whiteboard had been scrubbed clean, and the board table sat empty except for Nick's laptop.

'Not my call, mate. Curtis is in charge.'

No wonder Curtis kept him around; Nick was a yes-man.

He surprised me with a question of his own. 'Why are you working for Curtis? You should be out there playing music. What makes you sit in an office juggling numbers?'

How could I explain? After I'd first realised Curtis had tricked me into placing illegal trades, I'd wanted to leave, but staying near Curtis kept me close to Elena. And I admit, although I'd been critical of Elena for continuing to date Curtis, he still held the magnetic charisma that had drawn me to him in high school. Once ensnared in Curtis's orbit, people found it almost impossible to escape– just ask Elena. She'd taken a handful of pills to elude him.

After she died, I became too lethargic to make changes, not to mention fearful of being out of work. In my state, nobody else would have employed me. It took about a year to regain any sort of emotional balance, and by then, I'd developed a stronger reason to stick around: revenge.

I could spin this to make me sound like a hero and say I was fighting for truth, justice and the rights of all those mums and dads Curtis had ripped off in the stock market, but that'd be a lie. Curtis deserved to pay for using Elena and me, for keeping us apart and for contributing to Elena's fragile state of mind. To hold him to account, I needed to catch him out with further crimes – which I knew he'd commit because, as my father used to say, a leopard doesn't change its spots. I'd hoped to build my case, itching to blow the whole thing sky high, but he must have been good at covering his tracks because I still didn't have any damning evidence.

Obviously, I couldn't tell Nick any of that, so I shrugged and offered a throwaway line. 'It pays the bills.' Only Curtis didn't pay me nearly enough. No salary could ever reimburse what he owed me. 'What about you? It must be hard seeing Iris with Curtis. Why are you still here?'

'*Pftt*. Iris and I didn't last long. It finished before it began. We're both fine with it.'

A bang against the window made us jump. A crow bounced off the glass and flapped away.

Nick laughed. 'Weird. Speaking of strange things, I don't suppose you've seen my phone. I can't find it anywhere.'

Surprising – Nick was one of the most organised people I knew, suitable for his role in operations. I, on the other hand, was constantly searching for something – phone, keys, wallet – so I knew what to do. 'Want me to call it?'

'Please.'

I rang his number, but it went to a message about being switched off or not in a mobile phone area.

Nick seemed at a loss. 'Must've run out of charge. I haven't seen it since last night. When I couldn't find it at home, I figured I'd left it at work, but it's not here.'

'It'll turn up.'

'You don't think someone's nicked it?'

'More likely you've dropped it somewhere. Last time I lost my phone, I found it in the fridge.' I do random shit like that when I'm preoccupied.

'I haven't been anywhere except home and work, but I don't have time to search right now. It's a pain in the butt. I need it.'

I could tell I'd get no more sense out of him. Usually, I saw him as a pushover, but every now and then, he toughened up. This was one of those times. The steely glint in his eyes showed he wouldn't divulge anything further about the meeting, so I left, none the wiser and no less concerned. His silence gave me a heavy sense of foreboding. I guessed I wouldn't come out of this evening's meeting with my secrets intact.

After Elena had passed away, taking her bounty of insider knowledge with her, we'd stopped trading. I kept expecting Bean-Blitz to perish. In the natural order of justice, we'd have fallen like roadkill on the highway of IT startups. But we didn't. We launched our accounting program – I still didn't understand what differentiated it from others on the market – and kept growing, raking in cash. I knew Curtis wasn't achieving excellence by following the rules, and this time, I refused to fall prey to his Machiavellian schemes. I documented everything. When ready, I'd throw him to the ASIC wolves. The problem? I couldn't find fault in the accounts.

Along the way, I'd created two issues. First, I'd been careless, and my investigations had left a trail. If my snooping had gone undetected, everything would have been okay, but the second issue arose when Curtis caught me tracking his moves and sent Nick after me as swiftly as chorus follows verse. He didn't find anything else, because by then, I'd grown wilier and had left no further trace.

How did I know all this? Well, I didn't become the office spy without finding all the best listening spots. From the lunchroom, conveniently tucked next to Curtis's office, I could hear most of what he said, even though years of hitting drums had shot my hearing. Curtis complained about the noise from the lunchroom, so why he hadn't twigged that sound travelled both ways staggered me, but either he remained unaware of this vulnerability or didn't care, so nobody fixed it. That's where I'd heard him tell Nick to get on my case.

So now, with Curtis and Iris at odds, I headed to the lunchroom to eavesdrop.

Chapter 28

Angry Young Man

I TOOK my laptop and set up in the lunchroom with an open jar of crackers beside me. I'd been so preoccupied by Nick's pending presentation that I'd forgotten to eat. Also, I needed to appear to be here for a reason besides eavesdropping on my sister and her boyfriend. I didn't like to think of myself as sneaky, but I had to admit to a leaning in that direction. As a kid, not a silly season went by when I didn't already know what Mum and Dad were giving me well before we opened gifts on Christmas morning. In fact, that's how I discovered Santa's true identity, a revelation that left me morose with disappointment. I should have stopped being nosy after that experience, but I was a slow learner.

Settling at the blond wood table, I admired the row of jars on the kitchen bench Iris had bought to house treats: Mint Slices, M&Ms, liquorice allsorts, soy crisps and the crackers in front of me. Iris could be quite the mother hen when she set her mind to it. Besides a toaster and kettle, she'd insisted on a coffee machine of mammoth proportions that kept our staff fully caffeinated and productive.

I turned my attention to the task at hand, exhilarated by my mission. At first, I couldn't hear my targets, so I strained my ears harder. Iris was speaking so softly the crunch of crackers in my mouth blocked her out. Reluctantly, I swallowed my mouthful and pushed the rest aside.

I soon forgot my rumbling stomach when Iris said, 'I don't understand why you're so protective of him.' Given our previous conversation, I assumed she meant Nick.

'Because I trust him.' Whether Curtis intended it or not, the implication he didn't trust the rest of us made me grit my teeth.

'Trust? Ha! How well do you really know him?'

'This again? For Christ's sake, Nick and I have been friends since high school. Since before I met you.' Wow! Curtis was flying close to the sun, almost as if trying to wind Iris up. My blood pressure rose on her behalf.

'Fine. Have you ever wondered why he hasn't kept a girlfriend for more than a couple of months?' The sharp edge in her voice sliced through the walls.

'You're not going to make this awkward, are you? I can't refuse to hire any man you've dated.'

I bristled. He made it sound as if she'd dated half of Melbourne. In Iris's place, I'd have decked him. I paced to the window and licked the salt from my lips, suddenly thirsty. A cloudless sky hung over the quiet morning.

Fortunately, Iris could control her temper better than I could. 'Would you refuse to hire any man who's raped me?'

Her words rang in my ears. Raped? Iris was *raped*? I had to exert every inch of self-control to stop from running to her and wrapping my arms around her to shield her from further harm. Did she mean Nick? Surely, that little weasel wouldn't dare. He wasn't the type.

But who was the type?

Curtis was obviously having trouble processing too. 'What? Nick *raped* you?'

A silence followed, and I assumed Iris nodded because Curtis asked, 'When? What happened?'

The enormity of Iris's revelation hit me, and I recognised the extent of my intrusion. It was bad enough to spy on company secrets, but this? Iris was baring her soul about a horrifying experience, and much as I desperately wanted to hear her reply, I respected her enough to leave.

On autopilot, I closed my laptop, having not read a single word, put away the jar, without eating another cracker, and returned to my office.

I felt sullied, an unwitting voyeur to my sister's worst nightmare. Already, I itched to scrub what I'd heard from my brain. It couldn't be true. My beautiful, darling sister Iris. Violated against her will by that hideous ogre I'd called a friend.

Nick. Not less than an hour earlier, I'd called him harmless. What a joke! He was as harmless as a tiger snake. I wanted to find him and slice him apart, ball by ball.

I glanced at the boardroom where that dirty scum was still preparing who knew what bombshells for our meeting and thought about killing him. I could run over the bastard. Or shoot him. Stab him. Jump on his fallen body and empty the air from his lungs. Only I didn't have a gun. A knife? We had a bread knife in the lunchroom. A butcher's knife would be better. I had the perfect one in my kitchen. In fact, I'd recently sharpened it. To save the trip home, I could bash him. Usually, I saw myself more as poet than boxer, but today, with anger searing my veins, I'd beat him for sure. Or I could strangle him. Surprise him from behind and wrap a tie around his neck. I didn't wear ties. A phone lead? I could garrotte him.

The mere prospect of ending Nick's worthless life gave me satisfaction, but inevitably, I'd be caught, and then I'd have to explain to Iris why I'd done it. I could never admit I'd overheard her revelation to Curtis.

I'd also face the small matter of going to jail for murder. No, if I were going to kill him, I needed to avoid detection. Poisoning? That wouldn't offer the satisfaction of inflicting pain with my bare hands.

I must have stayed at my desk plotting murder for hours because the next time I checked my watch, it read six o'clock. The office had emptied. Far from receding, the anger simmering inside me continued its crescendo. If Nick made the mistake of coming within ten metres of me, he wouldn't live to make his seven o'clock presentation. I had to escape before my head blew, so I told Curtis I'd run and get pizza for everyone. Grabbing my company credit card and the dregs of my self-composure, I took the lift downstairs.

Outside, the cold breeze acted as a small antidote to the fire raging inside me. I reached Heavenly Crust, our local pizza shop on Toorak Road, but didn't go inside. I kept walking, blindly, pushing past meandering pedestrians. Before I could face Nick again, or Iris, or Curtis, I had to restore some balance in my brain.

It was all too much.

No woman should have to endure unwelcome overtures. No man had the right to inflict them. I knew I was stating the obvious, but the obvious needed to be stated. I'd always seen rape as something that happened to women I didn't know. How naïve. I saw Iris as one of the strongest people I knew. The smartest. The bravest. How could this have happened to her? Not since the night of Elena's death had I felt so helpless. So impotent. My sister had suffered this physical and emotional pain alone. It ripped my heart apart.

Weaving in and out of foot traffic, I started shivering. I'd forgotten to put on a jacket. Good. I wanted to feel things, to experience tactile, real sensations, comfortable or not. I turned back and stopped at Heavenly Crust. Inside, sensory overload battered me: the heat, the smell of yeast and melted cheese, the orders called to the kitchen. Holding back claustrophobia, I lined up at the counter. When my turn came, I ordered a random selection of pizzas, one each for the six of us in the meeting.

I could have asked for delivery, but I wasn't ready to go back, wouldn't be able to stop abuse flying out my mouth at Nick. Too hot in the restaurant, I waited outside, listening to the idle chatter of passersby: who'd be home for dinner, a work mistake, a promotion, the desire to go to Fiji, and the blisters on someone's feet.

The random details of people's lives – small, painful or aspirational – helped me stay sane.

The pizza joint called my number, and I picked up the six boxes, relishing the scalding heat on my forearms. It was close on seven when I returned upstairs, fully loaded.

I went to the lunchroom to gather plates and napkins. Anything to get my mind off Nick raping my sister. My brain could only handle minutiae. Plates. Napkins. Cutlery, although I preferred to eat pizza with my hands, so I could feel it as well as taste it. The cheese. The grease. The bread base. Anything to avoid facing Nick. Fucking Nick.

I was counting plates when I heard the commotion – shouting and hollering from the boardroom.

'Help!'

'Somebody call an ambulance!'

'No, wait!'

I left the napkins, plates and cutlery, and went running.

When I reached the boardroom, Iris, Curtis, Steve and Moira were standing around something on the floor.

I stepped forward.

Nick lay there, deathly still. The chair he'd been sitting on earlier had been upended beside him, and a bruise had formed across his throat. A phone charging cable lay beside him.

He was in exactly the state I'd wished on him an hour earlier: dead.

Chapter 29

Under Pressure

NORMALLY, I loved the office at night. The floor-to-ceiling windows reflected the lights, so the view vanished as if the outside world ceased to exist, leaving us in a capsule suspended in space. It had a numbing effect on me. I wished I were one of those people who sailed through life on an even keel, but emotions pressed at me, always nagging. Often, I only survived the day by pounding my drum kit. Sometimes, even this didn't work, and then, everything hurt.

The night Elena died, I nearly buckled under the pressure. It happened only weeks after we'd slept together, and I couldn't help blaming myself at least in part for her frame of mind. I never should have bowed to temptation and led her to cheat on Curtis. Three years later, guilt still tore shreds in my soul – it wasn't lost on me that in one of my last conversations with Elena, she'd said, 'The guilt's killing me. I'm sick to my stomach.' I knew exactly what she meant.

I'm not saying I have some kind of monopoly on emotional pain, just that I experience things deeply, and the weird nighttime office anaesthesia effect usually worked. But not tonight.

Curtis, Iris, Steve, Moira and I stood in a semicircle around Nick. An inane detail popped into my head: I should have ordered only five pizzas. I clung to the life raft of the familiar because I sure as hell couldn't process the reality of Nick's current state: dead, just as I'd hoped. Nor could anyone else, judging by the silent gaping faces around me.

Moira broke free of her stupor first. 'Has anyone checked his pulse?'

'I did.' Iris's voice croaked as she stood over her rapist, face so pale I worried for her health. 'Nothing.' God, could she have done it? She had a damn strong motive.

'What the hell happened?' Moira asked.

Iris stated the obvious. 'He's been strangled.'

'Who did this?' Moira demanded. 'Come on, who did this?'

We responded with silence, shuffling feet and downcast eyes.

'Curtis?' she asked.

'Fuck! It wasn't me.'

'Steve? ... Danny? ... Iris?' She turned to us one after the other, only to be met by denials.

'Has anyone called the ambulance?' Again, Moira took the initiative.

Steve cleared his throat. 'We were questioning whether—'

'He's worried the company will be put under a microscope if the body's found here.' Curtis kept his tone level, but his hands shook like crockery in an earthquake. If I had to put money on it, I'd bet those hands had wrapped the cable around Nick's neck and stolen his last breaths. And who could blame him after what Iris had told him? He'd saved me the trouble.

A bleak thought crossed my mind: could I have done this? I'd lost hours during the day fantasizing about killing Nick. Had I willed him dead long enough and hard enough that it had happened? Perhaps I'd done it in a blackout rage and wiped it from my mind.

Moira's eyes darted between us, taking our measure, but I couldn't meet her gaze.

She reached a decision. 'Steve's right. Bad enough Nick works for us, but a murder in the office would bring a stronger focus. If the authorities dig into our finances, the company could go down, and some of our people with it. I vote we move the body. He's already dead. It won't make any difference to him if he's found somewhere else.'

I wasn't sure whether Moira taking charge or her suggestion shocked me more. I'd viewed her through the lens of a stereotypical housewife, and in doing so, I'd massively underestimated her. Move the body? She was nuts. And something else – how did she know about the insider trading? Her response seemed extreme. Surely if the government prosecuted Curtis and me for insider trading, the whole company wouldn't fail. And who cared about the company when one of us had laid Nick flat on the boardroom floor?

I didn't have time to process any of it because the shocks kept coming. My sister, the sweet kid with whom I'd shared Mars Bars and climbed trees, said, 'She's right. Let's dump him in the Yarra.' Her face glimmered with an emotion I couldn't immediately identify, but it approached glee. What had become of her? Did surviving violence fundamentally change a person?

Iris turned to Curtis, and her expression morphed into something I did recognise. I'd seen the same puppy dog adoration on Elena's face. How did Curtis inspire this excessive loyalty? Why didn't women view him as a greedy, self-serving criminal?

Or – my mind raced faster than my best drumroll – what if Iris knew Curtis had killed Nick to avenge her, and she was protecting him? It made perfect sense. If the police got their hands on the cable and checked it for fingerprints, Curtis would go down. I'm ashamed to say, I almost grinned. If I couldn't get Curtis for financial crimes, perhaps I could get him for this. At last. True, I applauded his motives, but murder? I had to stop this debacle before it went further.

I took my phone from my pocket. 'We need to call the police. They'll investigate the company no matter where Nick's found, but if they get us for moving the body, we'll go down for sure.'

'You haven't thought this through. We need to act like a

team.' Steve seemed remarkably insistent. Hell, did I have it wrong? Had he killed Nick? My suspicions switched so quickly they gave me whiplash.

But I wasn't giving in. 'Stuff that! One of you is a murderer.' Nick had been strangled, and we were debating whether to call the authorities. Even my sister seemed to have slipped into this alternative universe of optional morality.

Moira reached a calming hand to my arm and drew me aside. I'd never noticed her quiet influence before, but I followed her without question.

She leant close and lowered her voice. 'Think about what you just said. One of them is a murderer. Do you want to be next?'

Light flecks appeared in my peripheral vision, and I struggled for air. I couldn't pass out, not now. Was Moira helping me or threatening me?

'I need water.' I had to get away from these people before I lost my grip on reality.

As I made to leave, she gently prised the phone out of my hand. Too intent on escape to stop her, I stumbled back to the lunchroom.

The smell of pizza induced a wave of nausea, and I nearly vomited. I reached the sink, poured a glass of water and gulped it down. Resting my hands on the edge of the bench, I hung my head low and took long, slow breaths. Moira had a point. If I held out against the others, the murderer might get desperate enough to stop me.

Who the hell was it? Curtis or Iris could have killed him as revenge for the rape. Steve and Moira, both board members, seemed more concerned about what an investigation would reveal about the company. What if Nick had done what I'd tried and failed to do: figured out how BeanBlitz was making so much money? What if Steve or Moira had killed Nick to prevent him from exposing company secrets deeper than the trading? And where did Curtis stand on the company front? I'd deemed him responsible for all our wrongdoings, but what if one of the others had exploited our finances without his knowledge? He'd commissioned Nick to deliver a report, so even as CEO, there must have been things he didn't understand. My head reeled, a ticking time-bomb.

'Are you okay?'

I spun to see Iris at the door, strong yet fragile. I'd known her since our mother's womb, yet she seemed like a stranger. Until today, I'd had no idea she'd been assaulted by someone I'd considered a friend. Someone who'd lost his life in our company boardroom, for all I knew, by my sister or her boyfriend's hand.

What if Iris did it? Surely, she wouldn't kill me to stop me from calling the police. Would she? And – I staggered at the thought – would I cover up Nick's death to protect her?

I groaned. 'What are we going to do?'

She wrapped her arms around me, comforting me as she always did: when I'd fallen off my bike, when our dog Wilfred died, and when Aria Belle had scrapped my song from her album. But today, I wasn't sure who was comforting whom.

'I'm scared, Danny. Just do as they say.'

So, I did. Because it might have been her, and when it came down to it, that was all I needed to know.

When I returned to the boardroom, we swore an oath never to tell. But even as the words spilled out our mouths, I recognised it was only a matter of time before one of us caved and called the police. The only questions were: who'd break first, and what would it mean for the rest of us?

All hopes of using the cable as evidence evaporated when, continuing her meteoric rise to leadership, Moira wiped it clean and said she'd get rid of it. Far from the old dear I'd previously mistaken her for, she turned out to be a lioness.

I also longed to get my hands on Nick's presentation. Unless being a rapist had made him a target, what he'd planned to say in our meeting probably got him killed. But the conference table had nothing on it.

'Where's his laptop?' I asked.

Curtis shrugged, and the others mumbled they had no idea. Someone was lying; I'd seen it here earlier.

I strode to Nick's office, only to confirm what I expected: no laptop. Earlier in the day, Nick had said his phone was missing. Coincidence? More likely, someone had systematically cut Nick off from all forms of electronic communication. The police could search the building and the suspects' cars and houses to find the missing items, but we'd agreed no cops. Reckless! I'd gone along with this travesty to protect Iris, but the missing laptop steered my suspicion towards Moira or Steve. Just look at how she'd taken control under pressure. She still had my phone. If not a criminal mastermind, she should be.

I wiped my damp hands on my trousers. Iris was right: we couldn't risk crossing these people – we had to go along with it.

We bundled Nick's body in black plastic Curtis found in the storeroom. Moira made us wear latex gloves from the cleaner's cupboard. I'd heard bodies went into rigor mortis after death, but it obviously takes a while to kick in, because Nick's arms and legs flopped around, which freaked me out as I kept thinking he was coming back to life. It made the worst possible kind of job even more challenging – physically and emotionally.

By the time we'd gaffer-taped the shroud around him and carried him to the boot of Curtis's car, he'd gone cold. To stop going into meltdown, I focused on the task in front of me. *Don't think. Don't feel. Act.*

We voted against putting Nick in the Yarra as Iris had suggested because of too many obstacles: how to put him in the water undetected, how to keep his body under the surface and how to control when he'd reappear. Instead, we drove to the outer suburbs – any place far from South Yarra – arguing all the way about how to dispose of the corpse.

In the end, Curtis swung the car into the parking lot out the back of a supermarket in Lilydale, switched off the lights and cruised to the darkest corner near the industrial bins. He left the engine idling in a low growl and popped the boot.

Movement caught my side-vision, sending my pulse skyrocketing. I spun around to see a stray cat disappearing soundlessly into the night.

With Moira and Iris on lookout, Curtis, Steve and I heaved Nick out of the boot. We almost dropped him, staggering under his bulk. When people talk about a dead weight, they're not kidding. Complaining and grumbling, we recovered and battled on to the row of bins. It stank of rotting meat.

Don't think. Don't feel. Act.

Steve used his shoulder to prop open the middle bin. We struggled to lift Nick high enough, but on the count of three, we hoisted him up. I'll never forget the sight of him rolling over the edge, the horrible thump as he landed on a bed of trash. The lid shut with a thud of finality.

Without wasting a second, we scuttled back to our car and drove away. The whole thing lasted less than five minutes.

We assumed he'd be discovered before the rubbish truck came. In fact, we wanted him to be found so his family could have a chance to say goodbye. Hopefully, by then, we'd have bought enough time to remove all evidence of the crime from the office and to let the trail run cold.

Chapter 30

Stand By Your Man

Jade, now

JADE PERCHED on the edge of an armchair in Iris's apartment and tried to make sense of what Iris had told her. 'You were all there when Nick died? At the office. And you didn't tell the police?' Earlier, Jade had promised no judgement, but she struggled not to sound incredulous.

Iris squirmed. 'I know how it sounds, but if you'd been there, you'd understand. The fear. The need to protect each other. You think you know how you'll behave in a given situation, but something like this? Nothing prepares you for finding a dead body.'

Jade flinched at the memory of Elena on her bedroom floor.

Iris's hand flew to her mouth. 'Oh God, I'm sorry. You've been there. The point is, if you'd given me this situation as a hypothetical, I'd have expected to respond differently. Hear me out.'

'Go ahead.'

'Curtis called a meeting to reveal the results of a study Nick had done. Moira and Steve were busy during the day, so Curtis scheduled it after work. Everyone else had left, only Danny and the ones I've mentioned remained.'

'What was the study about?' Jade itched to take notes, but she'd promised to stay off the record. Outside, the wind blew on, unabated.

'That's a bit of a mystery. Curtis had asked him to check some details of our company finances, but Nick had been cagey about what he'd found. Even Curtis didn't know the results.'

'That sounds a bit odd.'

'I know. Danny and I weren't happy about it. I was fuming about Curtis trusting Nick, of all people, over us. We argued. That's why I finally told Curtis about the rape.' Even sitting, Iris held a warrior woman stance reminiscent of the graphic art images on the wall.

'How'd he react?'

'Bloody furious. I had to calm him down and make him promise not to tell anyone.' Iris rubbed her hands on her jeans. 'I was tempted to let him confront Nick, but in his state, it would've ended in disaster. Well, it *did* end in disaster but not because of Curtis.'

Jade tried to picture the scene. 'So, you stayed back for a meeting, then what happened?'

'Curtis and I were in his office. After I told him, he became all protective and didn't want me to be alone.'

'Where were the others?'

'Nick spent the day in the boardroom, preparing. I'm not sure exactly when Moira arrived – it must have been quite late – but Steve got there earlier and did a walk around. He often went from office to office to chat to people and see what they were up to, but most other employees had gone home by then, so he probably ended up in the lunchroom. Danny went out to get pizza.

'When it was almost time for the meeting, Curtis went to the boardroom while I finished writing an email. I heard him shout and went running. Nick lay on the floor. Strangled.' Iris's hands reached to her neck. 'Curtis wouldn't have had time to do it. It can't have been him.'

Jade tried to align this with Steve's version of events. Danny hadn't mentioned any of it. Nor Moira – although Jade now understood how Moira had known the murder happened in the boardroom. Even Curtis hadn't said a word. Jade had guessed

Danny and Curtis were hiding something, but she had no idea their secret was this colossal. The extent of her friends' lies hit with brute force.

'Oh, my God. That night at the Rock 'n' Barrell, when Nick never showed up, you guys already knew he was dead. You said he was missing!' She stood and paced by the window, heat rushing to her face. A fresh wave of disorientation washed over her. Her so-called friends had lied to her and excluded her.

She watched the swaying trees. 'Everything you guys have said to me since then has been bullshit.' Hot tears of fury ran down her cheeks. She brushed them away, humiliated by the sign of weakness, and faced Iris. 'What the fuck? How can you expect me to believe a word you say?'

Iris bowed her head. 'Because I'm telling you now.'

'Why didn't you tell me at the start?'

'We couldn't burden you with this. The fewer people who knew, the better.'

'If you'd gone to the police, you wouldn't have had this terrible secret. Why didn't you?' Jade knew they were going in circles, but this was the critical question, the one they kept returning to.

Iris had the glazed appearance of someone lost in the past. 'I was terrified. One of us was a killer, and I sure as hell didn't want to be next. To make it worse, if the police discovered the body in the office, and put BeanBlitz under scrutiny, the insider trading would've come out – I know Danny told you about it – and Danny and Curtis would've gone to jail. We panicked and decided to dump the body. Stupid, I know, but we weren't in our right minds.'

Stupid wasn't nearly strong enough. Reckless. Rash. Not to mention criminal. Some sort of crazy groupthink must have taken hold of them. Jade only hoped they hadn't conspired to murder Nick. They'd already broken their pact of silence – Steve had told her a version of events, now Iris. Not that their word counted for much.

Zain's advice about the need for impartiality broke through her racing thoughts. This – Jade's raw emotion – demonstrated why he'd cautioned her about taking on this story. She needed to calm down and think rationally, or she'd miss things. Iris was opening up, at least in part, and as a journalist, Jade needed to seize this opportunity.

She pushed her hurt aside and retook her seat next to Iris. 'So, who did it? Who killed him?'

'I don't know. We asked each other, but everyone denied it. Any one of them could've done it. Except Curtis.'

Jade's eyes strayed to Iris, warrior woman, on the pinboard. Who was she protecting? 'You must have a theory, who's most likely?'

'It can't have been Danny – he was out getting pizza. Besides, you know him; he wouldn't hurt a soul. Moira, too, she's a marshmallow. I'd put my money on Steve. I used to love the man, but now he scares the crap out of me.'

'Why would Steve have done it?'

'Nick must've found something to implicate him. The next day, Steve threatened to tell the police Curtis did it, despite our agreement. The only reason for him to cast blame elsewhere was his own guilt.'

Steve had blamed Curtis for the murder, but why had he only shared a partial truth and left out the pact? To protect the others or himself? 'Did Danny tell you our concerns about Elena's death?'

'You mean the possibility that the same person who killed Nick also killed Elena?'

'Yes. What do you think?'

'I can see where you're coming from, but I don't buy it. Steve would never have harmed Elena.'

Jade agreed, although an element of doubt remained. She turned her mind back to the night of Nick's murder. 'Aside from the six of you, was anyone else in the office when it happened?'

'No.'

'How good is your office security? Can anyone walk in?'

'It's card access only, unless someone tailgated in.' Iris checked her watch. 'You won't tell anyone, will you?'

'No, but you should. Your pact won't last. As you said, Steve's already threatened to break it.' And Jade knew he'd carried out his threat.

'I'll think about it. But right now, I need to go back to work.'

'What about the rape? Do you want me to write about it with you as an anonymous source?'

Iris picked at the cuticle on her thumb. 'Let's hold off for now. I don't want to implicate Curtis, or me. Sorry to waste your time.'

'Not at all. If you change your mind, or just want to talk, let me know. I'll do anything I can to help. And Iris, I'm saying this as a friend, please speak to the police about moving the body. I know you've committed a crime, but it's more important to find out who killed Nick.'

Iris didn't make any promises, but at least she didn't refuse. She went to hug Jade, but Jade hesitated, so she held back. 'We're good, right?'

'Of course.' Jade needed time for her wounded feelings to mend, but she didn't want to lose a friend, so she pulled Iris in for a quick embrace.

They left the building together to face the brewing storm.

Jade caught the train home, constantly checking for anyone following her as she reassessed all she knew in light of Iris's bombshell. Unless someone had snuck in, she could whittle her suspect list down to five: Curtis, Danny, Iris, Steve and Moira. She couldn't dismiss the possibility they'd colluded. At the very least, they'd conspired to move Nick's body. And likely, one of them had sent those emails from The World of Writing.

Their wild pact only benefitted the murderer, and soon, it would disintegrate into every person for themselves. Jade shuddered. This would not end well. She tried to understand why they'd gone along with it. What Iris had told her made partial sense, but Jade searched for what Iris hadn't revealed. She'd admitted she wanted to save Danny and Steve from charges of insider trading, but if she knew – or thought she knew – the identity of the murderer, she had a much more compelling reason to keep quiet. Jade couldn't imagine Iris going to such an extreme to shield Steve or Moira, but she'd been awfully insistent Curtis didn't do it, and she'd step up to protect him for sure, especially if he'd choked Nick in retaliation for the rape. Hell, they could have killed him together. Or Danny could have done it, and Iris would do anything for her twin.

Jade stared out the train window, the fences blurring as they rushed along, and the overwhelming sense of betrayal she'd so carefully squashed seeped back. She pulled Elena's charm bracelet out from under her sleeve. Since she'd rediscovered it, she'd only taken it off for showers. What she would give for even a single day with Elena! The dull ache of missing her best friend remained ever-present, but today, it acquired a sharper, more insistent pull because she had nobody left to turn to. Not a single friend she could trust. Her mother always told her to get out and socialise more, but why bother? She'd lost contact with her school friends, her university friends had drifted apart, and of the tight-knit group she kept up with, Nick – a rapist – was dead, while Curtis, Danny and Iris had conspired to hide his body. And she hadn't lost sight of the fact that whoever had killed Nick might also have sent Elena to an early grave.

Chapter 31

Time Warp

Jade hurried home from the station, hoping to reach shelter before the storm broke. Even as she reeled from the impact of Iris's confession, she recognised she was sitting on one hell of a story, if only she knew the ending. She could plot how to write it and verify the facts, so she'd be ready to publish if she could persuade Iris and the others to release her from her promises. A twinge of moral discomfort made her acknowledge that her friends hadn't trusted her with their secrets sooner for good reason – not personal, but survival. All the same, Curtis's snide remark, *Always after a good story, I suppose*, still rankled.

As she turned onto her side street lined with apartments, she accepted she no longer belonged to the inner circle. Whether intentional or not, they'd alienated her. Knowing her friends had thrown Nick's body into a dumpster made her physically ill. One of them – or Steve or Moira – had killed him. If she knew too much, could she be next?

She reached the concrete carpark of her cream brick apartment, and the hair rose on her arms. A man stood waiting by her tiny courtyard, facing away from her, a small black bag slung over his shoulder. People rarely came to her door, and she wasn't expecting visitors or a delivery. Instinct screamed for her to run.

She glanced around to find company, only to find the street deserted, the carpark empty. Backing away, she reached into her bag for her phone. She considered calling the police. But what could she say? A man was standing at her gate. So what? Perhaps she was being paranoid. He could be an innocent visitor. His untidy hair looked vaguely familiar.

Then again, someone had followed her under the bridge that day in the city. And she'd had those warning emails. She let go of her phone and picked up her alarm. She must remember to thank her dad for it. What a champion.

Jade prepared to run as the man turned.

Thank God! Relief flowed as she recognised Peter, Elena's dad. She only wavered a second before dismissing him as a threat – he hadn't made the suspect list for Nick's murder.

She stepped forward. 'Hi.'

'Hello, Jade, my apologies for turning up unannounced, but I didn't have your phone number.' He offered a shy grin.

'I'm happy to see you.'

'I tried to catch you after lunch yesterday, but I couldn't keep up. You mentioned this apartment, so I popped in hoping to find you at home.'

This explained Jade's tail around Southbank – behaviour somewhere between resourceful and creepy. Rather than following her around, he could have asked Moira for her number. He must be keen to see her. 'No need to apologise, come in.'

She took him to the kitchen, put on the kettle and cleared space on her small dining table. 'Sorry about the mess.' If only she'd made time to stack the dishwasher and wipe the bench before she'd hurried out of the house that morning.

Peter waved her concerns away. 'Don't worry about it.'

When the tea was ready, in Jade's favourite 'Don't Mess with Texas' mugs, they settled at the table.

'Is everything okay?' She sat forward, hoping for information about Elena.

He rubbed his forefinger over a knot in the pockmarked pine.

'I can't talk freely in front of Moira. That's why I'm here. There are things you should know.'

'About Elena?'

'Yes, but not in the way you might think.' Peter's hands trembled, making Jade want to reassure him. 'You seem determined to find some hidden motive behind her death, and I ... it's time you know the truth.'

The truth. Ha! He spoke as if the truth took solid form, when it proved elusive as the wind.

'We haven't always been straight with you, Moira and I.'

Jade pushed her mug away. Not more secrets. She'd never have suspected Peter of deceit, but apparently, everyone she knew lied with abandon.

Peter swallowed, making his Adam's apple bob up and down. 'It's my fault. It's all my fault.'

Jade covered his wrinkled hand with her own.

A crack of thunder made them jump. She retracted her arm as the rain started in earnest, pounding Jade's window like an intruder trying to break in.

Peter sipped his tea. 'I love a good storm. Makes it so cosy inside. And I came prepared.' He gestured to the umbrella poking out from the bag beside him.

'Why don't you start at the beginning?'

'The other day, you asked about my heart, which threw me because my heart's fine. Always has been.'

Jade wondered whether Peter was losing his memory. 'But you had a heart attack ... I was there. I saw you carted away in an ambulance. It was—'

'It wasn't that.'

A torrent of rain battered the camellias in Jade's tiny courtyard, tearing off red petals. 'Then what happened?'

Peter closed his eyes and took a deep breath. 'An overdose of sleeping pills.'

Jade had the sensation of time slowing, as though she could follow each raindrop from its release in the sky to its splash on the ground. 'Oh, Peter, I'm so sorry, I had no idea.'

His face hardened. 'Moira insisted we call it a heart attack, always so conscious of what people thought. Saw the whole thing as shameful. Elena was too young to understand, and Moira didn't want to poison her mind with talk of suicide, didn't think it was fair to make her grapple with what I'd done. I had no energy to argue, so I agreed.'

Jade waded through her shock to find something supportive to say. 'I'm glad you made it through.'

He grimaced. 'I've always battled depression. People don't understand. They think they can tell you to snap out of it, and you'll cheer up like that'—he clicked his fingers—'but it's not so simple, it's more than just feeling sad.'

Jade nodded. 'Do you have a counsellor?'

'Yes. Wouldn't be alive if not for him. And my medication.' He drained the rest of his tea, and Jade offered a top up.

She rose and crossed the few steps to the kitchen, grateful for the break in conversation. All these years, Moira had known Peter's troubles and kept them secret. Jade told herself Moira, traumatised by her husband's brush with death, had done what she believed best to protect her daughter. All the same, Jade's chest felt hollow. She understood an adult keeping traumatic details from a teenage girl to make life more bearable, but Jade had spoken to Moira about Elena's death just this week, and Peter's history was highly relevant. Jade struggled to grasp why Moira hadn't told her.

Jade reached to a high shelf in the pantry to find treats she'd tucked away for emergency use. Chocolate biscuits wouldn't cure depression, but they couldn't do any harm.

Back at the table, with two steaming cups of tea and a brave smile, she pointed to the Tim Tams. 'After my time in Houston, I still rank these as the best chocolate biscuits in the world.'

Peter raised his tea. 'I'll drink to that.'

'Thank you for telling me what happened.'

He avoided eye contact. 'There's more.'

Jade's hands tingled with apprehension.

'My overdose triggered the breakdown of our marriage. We'd been unhappy for years, but Moira lost patience with me after that.' He sipped his tea.

'I'm so sorry—'

Peter held up a shaky hand. 'Again, my fault. I'—he sighed—'I met a woman. Maybe I misdirected my anger with Moira, or I needed comfort, or maybe I'm just making excuses. Whatever, when Moira found out I'd been unfaithful, she bailed.'

'That must have been difficult.'

He nodded slowly. 'The point is, I didn't have to follow Moira's directives any longer, so just before Elena finished high school, I told her about my illness. If we had cancer or heart disease in the family, it would've been part of her medical history. Depression should be the same.'

'Absolutely.' Jade couldn't agree more.

She wished Elena had told her. Her gaze jumped from her spinner ring to the photo of Elena on the bookshelf to her charm bracelet. Elena resided everywhere. 'I know it's childish to react like this, but it hurts she didn't tell me. Surely, she'd have known I wouldn't judge.'

Peter's voice wavered. 'I made her promise not to tell Moira that I'd told her. It wasn't worth the grief. I figured Elena and I could hold this secret, and nobody else needed to know.' Tears trickled down his sun-spotted cheeks. 'Don't be too hard on her, she was only seventeen, and … depression doesn't do logic.'

Still, Elena – Jade's yardstick for all other friendships, the person she'd spent the last three years trying to understand – hadn't shared this profound, impactful family trait. Jade had always told Elena about her crushes and breakups. Elena had cried on Jade's shoulder after she'd failed her driver's license test. They'd celebrated together when they'd landed their first jobs. But all along, this mammoth omission had laid between them.

Peter's face crumpled. 'Do you think … do you think she

killed herself because I told her? That she'd have been better off not knowing?'

His words shocked Jade out of her selfishness. Peter suffered depression. He'd made at least one suicide attempt, and he'd suffered the loss of his daughter. She needed to stop nursing her bruised feelings and focus on him.

Ill-equipped for the depth of this conversation, she chose her next words carefully. 'Have you discussed this with your counsellor?'

He nodded.

'What did he say?' Jade kept her voice steady.

'He doesn't think talking about it would have caused her to do it. If anything, he says I should've opened up sooner. Either way, I failed her.'

'You didn't fail her. She loved you. Always. And if she suffered depression, she was damn good at hiding it. Even when she behaved strangely near the end, I never guessed for a minute she was thinking about ending it. I missed the signs.'

'We depressives cover our tracks. I'm never more humorous than when I'm in pain.'

'Are you going to be okay after talking about this again?' Another tragedy would be unbearable.

Peter gave a grim smile. 'It's tough, but I'll be alright.'

'Please call anytime if you need to talk. Can I give you my number?'

Peter picked up his phone, and they swapped details. 'I'm sorry to take you by surprise with all this. I imagine it's hard to take in.'

An understatement. Jade was trembling. 'It's a lot but thank you. We still must consider the possibility that Elena didn't do it, that someone forced her. Someone let themselves into our apartment that day. I found our spare key in her room, and Elena never used it.'

Peter didn't argue, but she read the disbelief in his eyes. 'I should go, thank you for seeing me.'

'Thank you for coming.'

They treaded along the cheap rental carpet to the door. He pulled the black umbrella out of his bag, and Jade watched as he headed into the rain under a small circle of protection.

As soon as she closed the door behind him, worn down by the strain of reining in her emotions, she sank into a heap on the floor and let her tears run for Elena, who'd kept all her pain and suffering to herself, never speaking of her father's attempted suicide or the injustice of being implicated in insider trading by her boyfriend. She cried for all Iris had endured at Nick's hands. And she wept over the lies Moira, Steve, Danny, Iris and Curtis had told her. Peter too. Falsehoods that had left her with the vertiginous sense of being an outsider, of not knowing her friends anymore.

As her sobs subsided, she reached a decision. Zain was right; she couldn't write an article about Nick's murder. Her relationships with the players made it too hard to remain objective. But it didn't mean she would give up. Far from it. Story or no story, she needed to find out what had happened to put her demons to rest.

Chapter 32

Glory Days

AFTER PETER LEFT, thoughts of Elena kept Jade from focusing on her article about a proposed development near Elsternwick Park. Her new understanding of Peter's history made the chance Elena had been suffering depression more likely – a fact Jade would have known all along if Moira hadn't covered it up. Jade tried to understand whether Moira had failed to make the connection between Peter's suicide attempt and Elena's, or if she'd been barricading herself from the awful possibility she'd failed Elena by not acknowledging her mental illness. The whole situation was fraught with angst.

Jade retrieved her keepsakes box from behind the living room couch. Hopefully, something in it might give a clue to Elena's state of mind – although if Jade's murder theory were right, there'd be nothing to find.

She took out the items she'd sorted previously and dug deeper, finding a slew of report cards, school concert programs, certificates of achievement for math and science competitions, netball medals, English essays, a couple of love letters from her high school boyfriends and a red notebook. A swimming certificate made her shiver at the memory of the survival program at the Brighton Baths when they'd jumped in fully clothed, leaving her goose bumped and blue-lipped. Melbourne waters were always too cold for her.

Jade opened the notebook. In primary school, Jade and Elena loved pretending to be detectives. They'd roamed the neighbourhood, jotting down license plate numbers and observing the comings and goings. Her young handwriting verged on indecipherable, but she scanned page after page. A report on Pets in Crisis expressed concern about (a) the treatment of the Labrador three doors down from Jade's house and (b) the aggressive poodle that lived between Jade's and Elena's places. Next came the number plates, each linked to its owner's house, any anomalies flagged. Jade chuckled at the earnestness of her younger self and set the notebook aside.

A fat elastic band held together the last batch of papers, a collection of letters. Jade unfolded the first page and studied the small, precise handwriting. She recognised the i's dotted with circles and the wide-looped y's but searched for the signature all the same – Elena.

After Moira had married Steve, they'd taken Elena on expensive holidays, and Elena had sent letters from every one of them. Would they offer any clues to a history of depression? Jade picked them up and ordered them by date.

First up: Disneyland, California. This had seemed impossibly glamorous to Jade, who'd never left Australia. That same break, her family had driven to Pambula, a seaside town up the coast. While she'd loved the beach, her 15-year-old self had been flooded with jealousy. Only now could Jade see those trips hadn't brought Elena happiness.

Next: Paris, then London.

A stray photo showed Elena with Moira out the front of an old wooden hut surrounded by towering gumtrees and a flower bed crowded with daffodils. Jade couldn't remember where it had been taken. Steve often scouted properties, so he might have rented it or added it to his portfolio but never bothered to revisit it. Although – Jade strained to think back – Steve had discussed buying a hobby farm. She recalled something unique about it, something that gave it the potential to be a money-spinner. Perhaps he'd planned to flip the place, or it had an orchard, or ... no, she couldn't remember.

The phone rang – Gina – so Jade picked up. 'Hi Mum, how are you going?'

'We've found a place.' Gina sounded exuberant, as if announcing a pregnancy.

'What do you mean?' Jade was still trying to recall how Steve had planned to make a quick buck.

'In Mansfield, darling, keep up.'

'Right.' Jade still couldn't believe her parents were seriously contemplating a country pad; Gina belonged in the city.

'Your father's head over heels. It's in a nice, quiet area and has a spectacular view over Lake Eildon. This could be the one.'

'Oh, right, so—'

'We'd like you to come and look at it. Are you free on the weekend?'

'Sure, I—'

'Fabulous. I'll tell Keith, he'll be over the moon. I better go. I've got to get to my next class. Chat soon.'

Feeling as if she'd spun too hard on a merry-go-round, Jade hung up and picked up Elena's letters. Elena went to Port Douglas in Far North Queensland for her last holiday before she finished school.

Dear Jade,

We walked on Four Mile Beach this morning. So weird. It's only four kilometres. How silly is that? Some people argue, 'What's in a name?' See, I do pay attention in English. Ha! What a load of crap! Romeo and Juliet – just a bunch of pathetic kids making pathetic decisions.

Mum was stressed about crocodiles, but we didn't see any. I wish we lived up here. The sunshine makes me feel free.

Jade considered the implications of this. Was Elena craving vitamin D? Because a lack of it could cause lethargy. Or was Jade reading too much into it?

Mum and Steve had a fight. They tried to hide it, but every time they thought I couldn't hear, they started arguing again.

Hmmm. Fighting parents could make any child unhappy, but that showed a normal response to a situation, not evidence of depression.

He wants to buy some land here and build a whole block of apartments. Can you believe it? A whole block! Mum said we can't afford it, but Steve said we'd only keep one of them – the penthouse, how cool is that? – and sell the rest. He promised to name the building after Mum, but she told him no, so I guess it won't happen.

He's hiding something. Last night, he left his laptop open, and when I peeked at it, he slammed the lid shut. It was some sort of financial report. Big numbers. I caught a few company names based on famous places: Eiffel Trifle and The Sydney Opera Mouse. He's definitely doing something dodgy. When I get back, let's check it out.

Wish you were here. Miss you lots.
Love,
Elena

Jade read the words, then read them again, trying to remember if they'd done any sleuthing after Elena returned. She checked her notebook, but the dates petered out after the year they'd reached high school. Usually, Jade and Elena did detective work together, but if an opportunity had arisen, Elena wouldn't have shied away from flying solo. Still, if she had, she'd have told Jade about it afterwards.

Elena's letter showed she hadn't trusted Steve, but she'd been protective of her mother after her first divorce and could have wrongly assumed Steve was involved in something shady. More recently, Iris and Curtis had voiced suspicions about Steve. Even Jade's mother thought he was shifty: *Their holidays. All those properties.* But as far as Jade could see, his greatest crime was being a clever businessman. His shrewd investments in the property market had made him a fortune.

Jade made a note to investigate Steve's finances further, then glanced at the time. Crap! If she didn't write her article in the next few hours, she'd be out of a job. She bundled everything back in the box and took her laptop to the dining table.

Chapter 33

Twisted Logic

By late afternoon, Jade had filed her article about the Elsternwick development. Her heart hadn't been in it, so it lacked her usual flair.

With that task out of the way, she refocused on Nick's murder. The crime appeared to be interwoven with a web of financial corruption that had ensnared Elena. Jade had narrowed her suspect list to the players at the office the night of Nick's death: Iris, Danny, Curtis, Moira and Steve. With this new information in mind, she wanted to interview each of them again. She'd heard Iris's perspective, and Steve wasn't available, but she could speak to the others.

She'd start with Moira, a woman known for her pearls and twinsets, her love of pomp and ceremony. Jade's new cynical outlook on trust made her question whether Moira's prim façade covered up her true self. For all Jade knew, Moira could be the mastermind behind BeanBlitz's financial success, or perhaps Curtis and Steve were using her as a pawn. Besides Nick's murder, Jade also wanted to speak to Moira about Elena. If they addressed Peter's truth together, they could reassess their speculation about Elena's death.

When Jade phoned, Moira answered almost immediately. 'Thank God you called. I didn't want to bother you, b-but—'

'But what?'

'I'm scared.' Her voice dropped to a whisper. 'I think Curtis is following me.'

Jade stood and scanned her courtyard, but nobody was there. The rain had stopped, and camellia petals dotted the ground. 'What happened?'

'I went to yoga this morning. When I got home, I saw a grey SUV parked across the street. I could've sworn Curtis sat in the front seat, but when I started towards him, the car roared away so fast it left skid marks.'

'Sounds like Curtis. Did you check the number plate?'

'Didn't think of it.'

Moira might be over-reacting, but if Curtis had killed Nick, he was dangerous. 'If it happens again, write down the number and call the police.'

'I don't want the police. I want to speak to Curtis myself.' Moira spoke softly, but her venom carried across the line.

'Why?'

'I want to know what that criminal did to my Elena.'

Jade paced from the open plan living space to her bedroom and back again, wishing she'd kept her theory about Elena to herself. A confrontation between Curtis and Moira would not end well. She rushed to patch over her mistake. 'I'm no longer sure anyone hurt Elena. Why don't I come over so we can discuss it? I hoped to have a chat anyway.'

'Thank you. I'd appreciate that.'

Within half an hour, Jade pulled up in front of Moira's house and perused the street for Curtis's grey SUV in case he'd returned. Seeing no sign of him, she grabbed her handbag and hastened to the front steps of the familiar clinker brick house Moira had kept in her divorce from Peter. She'd rented it out until the demise of her second marriage, then returned.

Moira must have been peering out the window because she

opened the door before Jade had lifted her hand to ring the bell. They played out the same old double-kiss, although it lacked its usual warmth. Moira, in a neat pantsuit, led Jade to the sitting room, where they settled on a floral couch. An urn on the hearth showed Moira didn't use the fireplace – too bad, Jade could have used the meditative effect of the flames, not to mention the heat.

'I'm so glad you called. I've been dying to talk about Nick, and yoga wasn't the place. They're all terrible gossips. I've been meeting the same women for twenty years, so trust me, I know.' Moira's words fell out of her mouth so quickly they ran into one another. 'I can't understand why the police haven't arrested Curtis. He's a menace to society.' She jumped up. 'Oh, how rude of me. I forgot to offer you a drink. Tea? Peppermint's your favourite, isn't it?'

'Thank you, and yes, peppermint would be lovely.'

Moira bustled to the kitchen, leaving Jade to admire the vase of freshly cut wattle on the coffee table. It seemed falsely cheerful in the middle of winter, but apparently some varieties blossomed before spring. Jade pondered whether a motherly person like Moira, so hospitable, could be a murderer – it didn't seem possible. Then she dismissed her naivety. Everyone at BeanBlitz that night shared some culpability, assuming Iris had told the truth.

Jade stepped to the window and saw her car parked out the front, but thankfully, Curtis – if it had been him – hadn't returned.

Moira came back with their refreshments just as Jade questioned whether she should drink anything prepared by a suspected murderer. She shook her head as if to reset her overactive imagination. The tea would be fine. She perched on the edge of the couch, staring at the arrangement of pinecones in the fireplace to mentally prepare for the difficult conversation to follow.

Tired of all the lies, she took the direct approach. 'The night of Nick's murder.'

Moira's shoulders tensed. 'What about it?'

'I know you were there.'

Moira's eyes contracted to pinpricks of fear. 'No, I wasn't.'

'I believe a group of you moved the body.'

'What?'

Jade had expected Moira's denial – she was a master of sweeping uncomfortable truths under the carpet – still, her patience wore down. 'Moira, please, I'm here as a friend, not a journalist. I just want to understand.'

'Who told you this nonsense?'

'I can't say. Look, I'm not accusing you of anything, and I'm not about to run to the police. This is all off the record. What happened?'

Moira studied Jade coolly, as if assessing her through new eyes, no longer through a soft motherly lens but with the sharp focus of an equal, weighing up whether to approach her as friend or foe. 'I didn't see anything. I arrived late, and by the time I got there, everyone was already in the boardroom.'

'Who's everyone?'

'Curtis, Steve, Iris, Danny ... and Nick.' At least that much appeared consistent with Iris's story.

'What did Nick look like? Could you tell what had happened?'

'I'm no forensic expert, but obviously, he'd been strangled. He had a bruise across his neck.' Moira drew a finger across her own throat, then winced. 'I haven't seen many dead bodies, but I'll never forget that bruise as long as I live.'

Jade swallowed. 'Why'd you agree to move the body? No offence, but from a distance, it sounds like madness.'

'Madness is a good description. We panicked.' Moira blinked rapidly as if trying to rid herself of the memory. 'It felt surreal, like a dreadful nightmare.' She closed her eyes as if to block it all out, then continued. 'A killer was among us, and I didn't want to be their next victim. Nobody trusted anyone else.'

'Did you ask who did it?'

Moira gave a condescending stare. 'Of course, but nobody confessed. I don't know if you've ever been scared for your life, but intense fear changes you. I didn't want to push the point and have someone come after me.'

Jade had experienced mortal fear, and tapping into her memory of that horror, she pictured Nick's colleagues eying each other with suspicion – all except one, who'd have had a completely different emotional response. 'Who do you think did it?'

'It would've taken some strength to kill a man that way, so not Iris. And Danny hasn't got the balls.'

Jade noted Moira's uncharacteristic crassness. Was her mask slipping? Also, Danny might be lean, but he must have serious upper-body strength from all that drumming. 'So, who then? That only leaves Steve or Curtis.'

'It had to be Curtis. That lowlife used my Elena to get information for insider trading. He's a criminal. He suggested getting rid of the body, and we were too afraid to argue. That's why Steve went into hiding – terrified he'd be next because he could bury Curtis, and Curtis knew it. And that man still roams free. Shameful! Mark my words: more blood will be shed before this is over.' Moira spread her hands like an oracle.

Jade experienced a powerful urge to run far from this grieving mother with her bubbling brew of anger, denial and fear. The links between the clues tugged at Jade as though leading her to some logical conclusion, but she couldn't yet put it together. Before she could leave, she had one last issue to explore with Moira.

'Let's put Nick's murder aside for one minute. We need to talk about Elena.' Jade stared at the coffee table, where pollen from the wattle dusted a circle at the base of the vase. 'Peter paid me a visit.'

Moira's shoulders stiffened. 'What did he want? Did he remember something about Curtis?'

'He wanted to inform me about Elena's medical history.'

'Did he now?' Moira sat ramrod straight. 'And what lies did he tell you?'

'He explained about the night he tried to take his own life. Not a heart attack.' Jade kept her voice level and free of accusation.

Moira's eyes darted around the room from the floor to the framed photo of Elena on the mantelpiece to the window – everywhere except at Jade. 'I couldn't have told anyone what really happened. Imagine the impact on Elena. How would she have felt if she knew her father didn't want to be with her? Didn't want to live?'

Jade immediately regretted causing Moira such obvious pain. She drew on her journalism training, the need to ask tough questions, but the task demanded so much more of her when she knew and cared for her interviewees. She struggled to compartmentalise her emotions the way her job demanded. Not for the first time, Jade contemplated a career change. 'I know how bad it felt after Elena took her life, so yes, I understand why you wanted to keep it from her. We were only kids.'

'I was dealing with a very sick man. I had to protect my daughter. I didn't want her to get any'—Moira picked up her tea with trembling hands—'any ideas.' She nodded at Jade's cup. 'Drink up, it's getting cold.'

Jade took a sip, but it had cooled to lukewarm, so she put it down again. 'I get it, I do, but why keep it hidden for so long? You could've told me when I first mentioned rethinking what had happened to Elena. Don't you realise Steve's mental illness is relevant?' Despite her best efforts, a note of indignation bled into her voice.

'Mental illness. You make it sound as if he has cancer. He made choices, Jade. Choices that hurt everyone around him.'

'Mental illness isn't a choice. Depression, anxiety, bipolar disorder – these conditions require care and treatment, exactly like cancer. If we'd known about Peter's issues back then, we might've been able to help Elena. She could've had counselling.'

'So, it's my fault?'

'I didn't mean that.' Jade was handling this all wrong. Did she blame Moira? That wasn't fair. She needed to slow down and stop being reactive. 'When Peter tried to suicide, society didn't understand mental illness as well. It held an element of shame—'

Moira's eyes flashed. 'It wasn't about shame, it was self-preservation. How I could get out of bed in the morning. I had to take care of Peter. Get Elena off to school every day. If everybody knew, their kindness would've undone me. I didn't want people asking if he was okay, if I was okay. With that kind of scrutiny, I'd have been constantly reduced to tears.'

Jade softened. 'I'm sorry for bringing this up. It must have been incredibly hard. I know you couldn't have told me back then. It's just, I've been running around asking questions about Elena's death when it was probably suicide all along.'

Moira leant forward, eyeing Jade with open contempt. 'I couldn't betray Peter. His health is confidential. *You* said you didn't believe Elena suicided. *You* brought up Curtis's involvement. *You're* the one questioning every detail like the tablets and the keys.'

'Right, but I didn't have all the facts.' Jade's head throbbed. Moira had suffered enough. First, her husband attempted suicide, then her daughter succeeded. There was no shortcut to understanding the complexity of depression. No wonder Moira had spent so long in denial. No wonder she hoped for absolution by way of a murder verdict. Jade wanted the same.

After taking a final sip, Moira placed her cup back on its saucer with a clink. 'I suppose you won't see this through then – to find out once and for all what happened?'

'What more can we do?'

Moira paced to the mantelpiece and traced a finger around the frame of Elena's photo. 'I want one final discussion with Curtis. To force the truth.'

'Maybe we should accept Elena suicided.'

'It's time you left.' Moira returned to the couch and stood over Jade.

'Moira, please—'

She leant in close. 'And next time you run around casting blame, take a long, hard look at yourself.'

'I wasn't blaming you, I—'

Moira stabbed a finger at Jade. 'Elena told me you threatened to move out. How do you think that affected her? You owe it to her to find out what happened.'

Without giving Jade a chance to respond, Moira showed her to the door.

Blood pounding in her ears, Jade stumbled to her car. She sat in the driver's seat, her worst nightmare replaying in her mind.

Chapter 34

Fight Song

Jade, the day of Elena's death

JADE ATE BREAKFAST, feeling sluggish, eyes gritty from lack of sleep after Elena and Curtis had stayed up late drinking with friends. They'd done this several nights a week for months. Each time, Jade brought it up with Elena in the morning, but it made no difference. At work, Jade could barely stay awake and had trouble stringing words together – a death sentence for a journalist. She didn't know how Elena managed her demanding job, but somehow, she flourished and remained enamoured with Curtis.

Something had to change. If not, Jade would have to move out. She wanted to make things right, but her attempts at negotiation had failed, and she didn't know what else to try.

She sat in the kitchen waiting for Elena, toying with the spinning ring on her forefinger, her twenty-fourth birthday present from Elena. The wide sterling silver base held three thin spinners: one gold, one silver and one rose gold. Rings represented something infinite, and that's how Jade saw her friendship with Elena, but living together had put their bond at risk. Moving out might offer the best chance of saving their relationship.

Elena's door creaked open, and Jade braced. In her experience, little good ever came from arguments, but she needed to stay strong.

Elena came into the kitchen, hair dishevelled, and took the orange juice from the fridge. 'I suppose you're going to tell me off again.'

'I'm not your mother,' Jade shot back, immediately chastising herself. 'But you can't keep doing this.'

'Doing what?'

'Keeping me awake all night when I have to work the next day.'

Elena rolled her eyes.

'Why are you being so selfish?' Jade's voice rose – not quite to a yell, but close. Her patience was fast unravelling. 'I'm too tired to argue. It's time I find somewhere else to live.'

Elena froze. 'What?'

'We've had the same conversation a million times, but nothing changes.'

'You can't leave me.' Elena's lip quivered.

Jade steeled herself. She couldn't be a pushover, or they'd never move forward. 'Don't play the emo card. That's not fair.'

'Fine. Move out. See if I care.'

They glared at each other. Jade's spoon hovered over her bowl of cereal, and Elena clutched her glass like she wanted to crush it.

Jade yearned to reach out, to tell Elena she'd stay, and they'd still be best friends – the words hovered, ready to come out, but she bit them back. She couldn't keep living with no sleep. She had to stay firm.

Elena waited, as if expecting Jade to backtrack.

Jade wavered. The injured look on Elena's face nearly made her crumble. Hopefully, the shock of Jade's suggestion would be the catalyst to make Elena more considerate, and they'd work it out before Jade packed her bags.

Elena stormed out, muttering, 'Fuck you!' She said it low under her breath, but loud enough to sting.

Chapter 35

Everybody Hurts

ALL DAY AT WORK, Jade stewed over her argument with Elena, the taste of regret bitter on her tongue. They needed to find a way through this. By the time Jade arrived home that night, a rehearsed apology played on her lips.

She called, 'Hello,' but only silence greeted her.

Strange. Elena usually came home before seven. Her keys were hanging on their hook by the door. She must be sulking in her room.

Jade wandered down the hall and knocked on Elena's door. 'You there?'

Still no response.

Jade tentatively cracked the door and peered around, chewing the inside of her cheek, wishing she'd kept her mouth shut. She never should have fought with Elena. If she'd been more patient and—

Jade's mouth dropped open. Elena lay on the floor, face down, red hair splayed across the carpet as though she'd fallen on her way to the door. She stayed perfectly still.

Jade knelt beside Elena and shook her. 'What're you doing? Wake up.' Was this some kind of sick joke? A prank? Elena loved melodrama, much like Jade's mum. It was okay. Any moment, she'd sit up and carry on as normal.

A cold stone formed in the pit of Jade's stomach. 'Elena? Stop messing with me.'

Jade's eyes swivelled around the room, absorbing information.

A glass of water on the bedside table.

Empty.

Two sheets of blister pill packs beside it.

Empty.

Oh, hell, no!

She forced herself to keep looking.

A key lay beside the pill packets, the spare key with its koala keyring.

Her stomach churned as she rolled Elena onto her back. Elena felt warm, but looked pale, too pale. Grey more than white. Jade watched for her breath. Please move ... please move.

Elena's chest didn't rise. Didn't fall. She remained perfectly, awfully still.

'No, Elena, no!'

Jade had never seen a dead body, but instinctively she knew her friend was gone or near to it. She searched through her brain fog for logic, staring at her friend in disbelief.

She had to act. Fast. She'd done mouth-to-mouth training at school, even practiced on a dummy. She wanted to start right away, but the instructor had said to call emergency services first.

'I'll be right back.' She sprinted to the kitchen bench, grabbed her phone from her handbag and dialled triple zero as she raced back to Elena.

The operator answered, 'Fire, police, or ambulance?'

'Ambulance.'

In the seconds while she waited to be connected, Jade put the phone on speaker and placed it on the ground. She crouched beside Elena and positioned her for resuscitation.

At last, the operator asked, 'What's the nature of your emergency?'

'My friend. She's not breathing.'

'What happened?'

'I just got here. I thought she was asleep, but I can't wake her. She took pills.' Jade read the name on the packet. 'Ambien.'

'What's your address?'

Jade gave their street name and number. 'I need to go. CPR.' If not too late, she could—

'Ma'am, please stay on the line. Open the door so the paramedics can get in.'

Jade ran to open the front door, then returned to Elena's side.

Motionless, grey, silent Elena.

Airways.

Jade opened Elena's mouth. No obstructions, just a single amalgam filling. Airways clear.

Breathing.

Jade already knew Elena wasn't breathing.

Circulation.

She checked the pulse in Elena's neck. Nothing.

Three quick breaths.

Compressions. Fifteen times. She could feel Elena's ribs and worried about hurting her. She blinked tears from her eyes.

Then two more breaths. What was the rate? She did what felt right. Time slowed.

Compressions. When did Elena get so thin?

Breaths.

Something dug into her hand. The Eiffel Tower on the charm bracelet Elena had given her. Jade ignored it.

Compressions.

Breaths.

An invisible hand squeezed Jade's chest. Her skin prickled as though someone were poking thousands of needles in and out of her limbs. In and out. In and out.

Compressions.

Breaths.

Compressions.

Breaths.

How much longer could she keep doing this? Jade's arms hurt from pressing on Elena's chest. Elena didn't respond.

The wail of an ambulance sounded in the distance, or was that the screaming in her head?

It came closer. Louder. Thank God.

Compressions.

Breaths.

The siren stopped. Car doors opened, closed. Voices.

'I'm in here. Quick. In here!'

Footsteps in the passageway.

A calm voice. 'You can stop now. We'll take over.'

Elena still hadn't responded. Jade couldn't stop. If she stopped, Elena might die.

The voice again. 'Please, ma'am, move out the way.'

'But—'

'You've done everything you can.' The paramedic, gentle but strong, guided Jade away.

Jade gazed, unseeing, as the strangers in uniform attended to Elena. They poked and prodded. Attached machines.

Elena didn't respond.

At some point, they pronounced her dead.

Police arrived. They questioned Jade.

Eventually, they left Jade alone with a new reality she found impossible to process: she was alive, and Elena was dead.

Chapter 36

The Lion's Den

Jade, now

JADE SAT in her car outside Moira's house, blinking tears. Was it her fault? Did she get the ratio of breaths to compressions wrong? Should she have started CPR before calling the ambulance?

If she'd arrived five minutes sooner...

If she hadn't told Elena she was moving out...

If she'd been a better friend...

Most likely Elena suicided, but Moira was right: Jade had to see this through. At the very least, she needed to know who killed Nick.

Jade buckled up, trying to figure out her next move. Since she'd found out who was present the night of Nick's death, Jade had discussed it with Moira and Iris. Steve remained in witness protection, which left Danny and Curtis. Now she knew more, she could probe deeper with them.

Rather than risk being alone with either of them, she decided to play it safe and approach them together. She called Danny on handsfree, planning to enlist his help. If she openly took his side, perhaps he'd reveal more than he intended.

He answered as she started driving and after brief greetings, Jade asked, 'How're you going?'

'I'm anxious. Curtis has been questioned again. I'm worried he's going to pin the whole insider trading thing on me.'

'Why would he do that?' Jade reached the end of Moira's street and slowed to a stop, eying the gridlocked road ahead. She glanced at the clock – just after half past three – school home time.

'To get himself off the hook. He's supposed to be my mate, but under pressure, he's always put himself first. Also … I know Iris spoke to you about the night of Nick's death, so I guess you have questions for me.'

'Why didn't you tell me what happened?' Her indignation rose, and her voice followed suit. 'For fuck's sake, Danny, we spent a whole night together at the Ruby Room, and all you gave me was info about Curtis's insider trading. That's not the act of a friend.'

'I am your friend. That's partly why I didn't tell you. What we'd done was bad enough. I didn't want to make you an accessory after the fact. And we had a pact. If I broke their confidence, you'd never trust me with your secrets.'

He had a point. The steam dissipated from Jade's argument, leaving her with a residual sense of exclusion. 'My trust in you – in all of you – has worn thin.' Jade found a break in the traffic – she didn't stand a chance against the brutal mums at school pickup – and turned right.

'I'm sorry. I hope you can forgive me.'

'Whatever. Just don't lie to me again.' Jade braked hard as a hunched grey-haired woman stepped off the footpath in front of her. The old woman dawdled across the road, oblivious Jade had nearly run her over.

'Done.'

Jade took a punt. 'Would you come with me to speak to Curtis? From what Iris says, he couldn't have killed Nick, but Moira reckons she spotted him parked out the front of her place this afternoon, and when she approached him, he drove away.'

'Creepy.' Danny paused. 'Can you come into the office? We're both here now.'

Perfect. Not only could she interview the murder suspects, but she'd see the crime scene. It might not offer any insights, but morbid curiosity drew her in. 'On my way.'

She turned onto Beach Road in the stretch known as the Golden Mile, lined with mansions new and old. Familiar landmarks flew by – the Brighton baths and the yacht club – but she was sailing through uncharted waters with Danny.

'Call me when you get here, and I'll come down to let you in. Just one question – is it worth the risk? If Curtis killed Nick and thinks we can prove it, won't that put us in his sights?'

Jade realised she had reached a crossroads. She could walk away and leave solving the murder to the police, or she could use her position of familiarity with the suspects to crack it. She glanced at Elena's bracelet and pictured her friend, teenage detective, notebook in hand, and knew she'd be one hundred per cent behind Jade. 'I understand if you don't want to come with me, but I need to know.'

Danny only hesitated a beat before saying, 'Okay. See you soon.'

Chapter 37

Who's the Thief?

HALF AN HOUR LATER, Danny met Jade on the BeanBlitz office ground floor. He used his swipe card in the lift and pressed level five. 'You haven't changed your mind?'

Heart racing, Jade clutched her handbag tighter, trying to act normal with Danny so he'd trust her. 'Let's do this. Is Curtis acting suspicious in any way?'

Danny flicked his hair out of his eyes. 'He's keeping to himself except for Iris. Like he doesn't trust anyone else. He's standoffish with me.'

The elevator opened to a foyer with the BeanBlitz logo plastered large on the glass door. Danny swiped again and led Jade into reception. A massive arrangement of peonies, lilies and hydrangeas adorned the desk, and their powerful perfume made her lightheaded.

The receptionist, a young woman with skin smooth as a porcelain doll, looked up from her computer. 'Hi, Danny. You want to sign in your guest?'

'Yes, please.'

The receptionist handed Jade a clipboard. 'Please fill this out.'

Jade completed the form in exchange for a pass, which she

clipped to the neck of her shirt. She agreed with Iris's assessment: it'd be hard for someone to sneak into their office.

Danny led Jade to an open-plan area, where around twenty office workers created a hive of activity. Sleek furnishings and a million-dollar view across the city lent the space an air of luxury.

Danny inclined his head at the corner office. 'There he is.'

As they wandered towards Curtis, Jade noted the offices on two sides of the floor. Iris sat in one of them, hard to miss in a bold top with triangles in various shades of blues and greens. Engrossed in a phone call, she gave a distracted wave.

Danny pointed out the boardroom – the murder scene – and Jade slowed. The frosted glass walls obstructed her view, although she could see the outline of pot plants and a large table.

'Did the police process the boardroom as a crime scene?' Jade imagined them using luminol and UV light to identify blood stains or other bodily fluids.

'Yes, end of last week. They took all the cables and anything that could be used for strangulation, but they won't find anything.'

Jade itched to examine the room, but after the police search, she doubted any clues remained. 'Nick must have left electronic evidence. Files and emails.'

Danny stopped, his face a mask of concentration. 'As far as I know, the police never found his laptop or phone.'

'Wouldn't his work have been backed up on the company server or something?'

'The police checked all that, but I don't know what they found.'

Jade suppressed a shiver; whoever had killed Nick had been meticulous in cleaning up after themselves. 'What was Nick's job?'

'Operations. More like an office manager, really. He knew everything that went on in this place.'

As Jade and Danny entered the spacious corner office, Curtis exchanged a brief nod with Danny, who positioned himself, arms crossed, in front of a wall-mounted whiteboard covered with scrawled lists and reminders.

Curtis came out from behind his desk. His cursory welcome didn't invite a hug. 'What can I do for the two of you?' His tone was light, but his eyes were dark. Evidently, he hadn't forgiven Jade for driving Steve away from Sorrento.

Jade matched his tone. 'Just a quick chat.'

'What, so you can feature me in some article?' Curtis sniffed. 'No, thanks.'

That stung, but Jade kept her reaction in check. 'I'm not after a story. I just want to know what happened.'

Curtis gave Danny a quizzical glance, and Danny returned a small nod. With obvious reluctance, Curtis gestured to the round glass worktable and chairs in front of his desk. The black faux leather chairs creaked as they sat. 'Let's make this quick. I'm busy.'

Jade placed a hand on the tabletop and launched in. 'I've spoken to Iris about the night of the murder.'

'I know.' Curtis's foot jigged, visible through the glass tabletop. 'If I had my time again, I'd report Nick's death right away.'

Jade took the opening. 'Why didn't you?'

'When we found him dead, I freaked out.' Curtis lowered his head. 'I figured if the police found the body here, they'd investigate BeanBlitz and expose the insider trading. With the threat of jail time, I panicked. Now the police have uncovered the trading, the risk we took seems even more pointless.'

Danny huffed, prompting Curtis to say, 'We all agreed to do it, so don't play innocent.' His expression shifted to contrition. 'Mate, I'm sorry I involved you in that trading. When the police questioned me, I told them you only ever followed my instructions, so you should be off the hook.'

Jade hid her surprise. Of all Curtis's possible reactions, she hadn't expected him to take responsibility for his crimes.

Danny seemed similarly taken aback. 'I ... well, thank you, I guess. Really, Elena deserves the apology, but it's a bit late for that.'

All three bowed their heads.

Jade sighed. 'If Elena were here, she'd figure out who killed Nick before any of us.'

The others muttered their agreement. Jade stared at Curtis's desk, where a globe hovered in mid-air above a base using a trick of magnetic forces, and wished she could find similar magic for the case.

She turned to Curtis. 'Best guess? Do you still think Steve did it?'

He tilted his head. 'I do. I suspected when Steve pointed the finger at me, and he confirmed it when he went off-grid. I can't believe you drove off with him that day. Where'd you take him?'

Jade teetered on the brink of telling him. She'd been hurt about the others excluding her from their pact because it implied they couldn't rely on her, yet here she was withholding information from them. But truth be told, she didn't trust them, and she didn't want to put Steve at risk, so she lied. 'I dropped him off at home.'

Curtis eyed her with suspicion. 'Well, he's not there. I've been back every day since. I've even driven to Sorrento again.'

'Why do you reckon he did it?' she asked.

'For the past two years, someone's been stealing from the business, so I had Nick do some checking – not specifically on Steve, but on all the key players: Moira, Iris, even you, Danny.' He flashed Danny an apologetic glance.

Danny scowled. 'What happened to trust, man? It's bad enough you spied on me, but Iris? Why are you dating her if you think she's a thief?'

Curtis held up his hands. 'Just covering all bases. Nick was about to give me his report when it all went to shit.'

But Danny didn't let up. 'Why'd you ask him to write that report?' The flare of anger in his eyes confirmed to Jade he knew about the rape.

Curtis's jaw clenched before he answered. 'He was so meticulous I knew he'd notice anything wrong in the accounts. Obviously, now, I feel shit about it. I reckon that's what got him killed. He told me he'd found something but never had the chance to elaborate. If he'd found something about Steve, and Steve knew he'd been rumbled, there's his motive.'

Thanks to Jade, Steve was in witness protection, so she couldn't question him. Had she been played? She reconsidered the past week, imagining Steve as the bad guy. Silhouetted against the window in his Sorrento house with his Cary Grant looks and honeyed voice, he'd been nervous, no question. 'Why was Steve so scared of you? Why'd he run to Sorrento?'

Curtis shrugged. 'He must have panicked like the rest of us about covering his ass for moving the body. Stress brings out the worst in people. If he killed Nick, he'd have had even more to hide.'

Jade still couldn't make it stack up. 'If that's why he ran, why'd you chase him?'

'Before he went, I had second thoughts and suggested we go to the police. When I brought it up, he threatened to point the finger at me. I wanted to find out what game he was playing.'

Jade recalled the scene outside Steve's Sorrento house. 'You had a gun tucked in the back of your jeans. That sounds like more than a casual chat.' And if squeaky clean, why did Curtis own a firearm? And how did he get it?

'You saw that?' Curtis scoffed. 'You spent too long in Texas. We live in Australia, not America. That wasn't real, it was a toy I took along to scare Steve. If he'd killed Nick, I needed at least the illusion of protection.'

No doubt about it, Curtis was smooth, not to mention super-smart. Even Jade's mother would applaud his clear-eyed honesty act. Unless he wasn't performing. Jade was inclined to take his word about the gun, but she questioned the rest.

She examined the possibility of Steve being the murderer from all angles, but struggled to remain objective. Steve was like family; she found it almost as hard to reconcile the idea of him being a killer as her own father being a suspect. Sure, the way Steve splashed money around made her cringe, and she preferred Peter, but he'd always treated her well. It made even less sense when she applied the same logic she'd used with Curtis about Elena's death.

'Do you think'—Jade turned to Danny, then back to Curtis—'if Steve killed Nick, is it possible he also hurt Elena?'

'Back to that?' Curtis crossed his arms. 'Unlikely. He was truly cut up about her death.'

Danny eyeballed Curtis. 'Or he was upset because he'd killed her.' His angst over Elena's death hovered near the surface. 'Did you have anything to do with her death?'

'Seriously? Why does everyone want to pin everything on me? No, I didn't kill Elena. She suicided.'

Danny maintained eye contact. 'Why did you go to Moira's earlier today?' His persistence impressed Jade.

Curtis baulked, perhaps caught off-guard by the change of topic or surprised Danny was standing up to him. He turned to the whiteboard as if the answer lay somewhere among the multi-coloured notes. 'I wanted to speak to Steve, and I figured if he came out of hiding, he'd go to Moira. He regretted their breakup, and they still had a bond, at least that's what he's told me. And the way she fawns all over him, it's clear she's still in love.'

Jade had observed the same. 'Did Moira know you'd involved Elena in insider trading?' Her conversations with Moira showed this to be true, but she wanted Curtis's take.

He drew back. 'God, I hope not. She'd kill me if she thought I'd hurt Elena. Unless Steve told her, I can't imagine she'd have worked it out. She was more a figurehead than a head for figures, if you know what I mean.'

Jade understood his implication, but knew Moira was more switched on than anyone seemed to realise. What's more, Moira knew Curtis had abused Elena's trust, and she'd wanted to talk to Curtis in person. 'Don't underestimate Moira. Be careful.'

'I can handle her.' Curtis stood. 'We're done here.'

'Wait.' Jade had the sensation of sand slipping between her fingers. 'I might be able to help get you off the hook. What evidence do you need? If you can prove Nick's report revealed something about Steve, that might be enough.'

Curtis gave her a disparaging look as if to say, *Don't insult me. I've already thought of that.* 'The murderer stole Nick's laptop and phone, so we don't know what Nick wanted to say.'

'Weren't the files backed up?'

'We've checked but found nothing.'

'And he didn't tell you anything?'

'Nick was a perfectionist. He never sent so much as a text until completely happy with his work. For this project, he hinted he had dirt on someone but wouldn't tell me who. I figured he was enjoying the power play, so I didn't press him. I wish I had. My guess is Steve, but for all I know, one of the others had a rotten secret.' His eyes darted to Danny, who glowered back at him.

Jade recalled her brief visit to Steve's Brighton home. Could Nick's laptop or phone have been stashed there? If only she'd known to look. If she went back, she could do a proper search.

Go back? Should she?

Curtis's phone dinged. He read the message and frowned. 'I need to check on something.'

Her time was up, so without further resistance, Jade slung her handbag over her shoulder, said goodbye to Curtis and walked with Danny to the lift foyer.

Danny, clearly agitated, checked they were alone and repositioned himself so he could see into reception. 'Curtis had Nick check me out. Me! He was the one arranging dodgy deals.'

Jade understood his outrage and didn't want to stoke it further. 'Yeah, rude.'

He stepped closer to Jade. 'What do you think? Is Curtis a murderer?'

'I didn't pick any signs of lying, but he always sounds

convincing. He's a shit-hot liar. And if Nick threatened to go public about the trading, he had motive.' He also knew about the rape, but Jade didn't mention it. If Danny knew about Iris as she suspected, she wanted to see whether he'd reveal that information himself.

Danny rolled his eyes. 'Don't tell me Curtis has conned you, too. He's always had a way with women.'

Jade snorted a bit too loudly. She could hardly claim immunity to Curtis's charm. 'What about Steve? Could he have hurt Nick or Elena?'

Danny shrugged. 'You've known him longer.'

'He seemed really frightened when I saw him at Sorrento.'

'He had reason to be. Curtis was coming to silence him or force him to testify.'

Jade tried to untangle the logic. If Steve was guilty, why did he agree to witness protection? Surely, that's the last place he'd want to be. Then she realised the brilliance of it. He could tell the police his version of the story, and his alleged fear would implicate Curtis. Clever. He can't have planned it, though, because Jade had suggested witness protection, not Steve. The idea had fallen into his lap, and he'd run with it. 'Trouble is, I can see it either way: Steve or Curtis.' She didn't mention her suspicions about Iris. Or Danny.

'What about Moira?'

'She'd never have hurt Elena, and she wouldn't have pressed me so hard to find out what happened to her if she'd done so, but I reckon she's still hung up on Steve, so I wouldn't put it past her to lie to cover for him. Would she kill to protect him?' Jade tried to weigh it up. 'I don't think so, but they could be in it together.'

'Seems a bit far-fetched.' Danny spoke so quietly Jade struggled to hear him. 'Steve didn't use Elena. Curtis did. He had reason to hurt her. She hated all the lies. She'd confronted him about the insider trading and told him to stop.' Tears welled in his eyes.

'So, Curtis then. What happened the night of Nick's death?'

A couple of people entered the foyer, and Danny waited while they pressed the button and stepped into the lift.

When the doors closed, he said, 'Let's not talk about it here.'

Jade felt cheated, like she'd reached the end of a book, and the last chapters had been ripped out. 'Come back to my place.'

'I can't leave now. Tonight?'

Jade would have preferred sooner but hugged him and watched him return to work.

She pressed the button and waited, but before the lift arrived, the fire alarm sounded. *Whoop, whoop, whoop*!

An announcement blared, 'Attention please. The fire alarm has been activated. This is not a drill. Please proceed to the nearest fire escape and exit the building. Do not use the elevator. Stay calm and convene in the fire assembly point. I repeat: this is not a drill.'

Heaving a sigh, Jade opened the door to the fire escape.

Chapter 38

Cell Block Tango

JADE JOINED the office workers filing down the fire escape. They exuded an air of elation, as though savouring the interruption to their routine. Snippets of conversation echoed around the concrete stairwell: jokes about who'd burnt something in the lunchroom or gone for a smoke in the toilets; worries the delay would cause missed deadlines; grumbles about *another* drill, such a waste of time; and arrangements to go for coffee.

'Sign off before you leave.' The fire warden, carrying a clipboard and wearing a hardhat, waved them along. 'And this isn't a drill.'

Jade could sneak away – she'd already returned her pass – but what she'd first viewed as an irritating delay, she now saw as an opportunity. Curtis, Danny and Iris would also be evacuated, so she'd have another chance to discreetly interview them while they waited. She doubted Iris had killed Nick, but a detective Jade had worked with in Houston had told her never to overlook the outliers, and this advice had stayed with her.

Outside, they assembled in an area paved in bluestone next to a row of pencil pines in raised garden beds. Office buildings towered around them. The chaos while the fire warden tried to account for everyone prevented Jade from finding her friends. A fire truck pulled up, and firefighters leapt out and rushed to the entrance. As they strode in, Iris came out, a striking figure in her top with all the triangles. Even in the middle of a crisis, she looked chic.

Once Iris had checked in with the warden, Jade sidled up to her. 'Do you know what's happening?'

'Haven't heard. Just what we need – more drama.' Iris seemed unimpressed.

They found a spot near the edge, not trapped in the middle of the crowd.

'Where are the others?' Jade asked.

'Knowing Danny, he'll take his sweet time. And Curtis told me to go ahead, he had to grab something from his office. They'll get here soon enough.'

Jade had a vision of Curtis and Danny engulfed in flames and battled the urge to run and find them. 'Let's hope it's not a serious fire.'

Iris gave her a quizzical look. 'Why did you meet with them?'

Jade faltered, unwilling to explain her suspicions about Curtis or Danny. 'I saw Moira earlier, and she had some idea Curtis was stalking her.' She waved a hand to make light of it. 'I wanted to smooth things over. When I mentioned it to Danny, he suggested I come in and have a chat.' She smiled awkwardly, aware how peculiar it sounded.

Iris seemed confused, and her expression reminded Jade of one of Danny's – an uncanny reminder of their twinship. 'Is it true? Was Curtis stalking Moira?'

A few people pushed past Jade to get to the street, so she stepped further aside. 'Sort of, well, not really. He said he went to her place in the off-chance Steve came to visit.'

'We haven't seen Steve for days.'

'Exactly.' Jade didn't want to lie about Steve's whereabouts again, and she had a question for Iris better asked before the others arrived, so she changed tack. 'Did you ever tell anyone else what Nick did to you?'

'Why? Did someone say something?'

'No. I've just been thinking about his murder and—'

'You're making this bigger than it needs to be. Only you and Curtis know, and as I said, Curtis couldn't have killed Nick because I was with him.'

Jade had no time to respond because Danny arrived, hair rumpled like he'd just got out of bed.

'What took you so long?' Iris asked.

'I got cornered by Mel from payroll. You know how she likes to talk. I couldn't get across to you.'

'Mel, huh?' Iris put a hand on her hip.

Danny groaned. 'Don't even go there. I'm not interested, but she won't get the message.'

'Have you seen Curtis?' Jade asked.

'He told me to go ahead. Said he needed to find an important file or something. He seemed frazzled.' Danny checked over his shoulder. Jade followed his eyeline but saw no sign of Curtis amid the throng.

Iris took her phone from her pocket. 'I'll make sure he knows it's not a drill.' She dialled, held the phone to her ear, then deflated. 'Voicemail.'

She hung up and tried again, to no avail. 'What's he doing?'

Danny grabbed her arm as she moved towards the entrance. 'They won't let you back in.' Sure enough, the building manager, stationed at the door, turned away a couple of people who asked if they could grab their laptops.

Iris crossed her arms, concern etched on her face. 'Why's he taking so long?'

Jade's instinct for danger went into overdrive and, despite the cold, sweat formed on her upper lip. 'Maybe he's down here already but got caught talking, like Danny.'

They fanned out to check the crowd, but no success.

Iris went to speak to the fire warden.

'Anything?' Jade asked when she returned.

'They haven't checked him off but said the fire's under

control.' Iris shifted from one foot to the other. 'Apparently, someone had been smoking in the bathroom.'

Danny whistled. 'They won't win any prizes for productivity.'

Iris tried calling again and left a message. 'Curtis, where the hell are you? We're in the courtyard.'

They waited outside a further fifteen minutes before the firefighters came downstairs and the building manager announced the emergency had been resolved.

'Do you mind if I come back in with you?' Jade asked Danny. 'I want to make sure Curtis is okay.'

Danny nodded, and they hurried to catch up to Iris, who powered ahead. At the sight of a queue for the lift, they chose the stairs.

At level five, Jade didn't bother signing in. Breathless, they raced to the corner office. It appeared empty.

Iris ran behind the huge desk, the others a few steps behind. Chilled by her ashen face, Jade followed her gaze down. Curtis lay at Iris's feet, eyes open, unblinking. Blood had drenched his shirt and spattered all around him.

The metallic stench made Jade's limbs tingle. 'Oh my God, he's been shot.' She battled a wave of dizziness.

Danny and Iris gaped.

'Curtis!' Iris dropped to her knees and wrapped her arms around him. 'No, no, no. Curtis, wake up!'

'Check his pulse.' Jade took her phone from her handbag and dialled triple zero.

Iris put her fingers on Curtis's neck. 'I can't feel anything. Danny, help me.' She bent low and placed her cheek above Curtis's mouth. 'He's not breathing.'

Triple zero connected, and Jade asked for police and ambulance.

'Help!' Iris shouted. 'CPR, we need help.' She tried to position Curtis, but when she placed her hands over his chest to do compressions, they rested right on top of the gunshot wound. 'This isn't ... he can't be...'

Jade inhaled sharply at memories of trying to revive Elena.

Danny knelt next to Iris and wrapped his arm around her. 'It's too late. This is a crime scene. We shouldn't move anything. We're doing it properly this time.'

Iris bent over Curtis and clung to him, staining her top with his blood. 'I can't leave him.'

Danny remained by her side. 'Stay there, just don't touch anything else.'

Jade watched the scene as if from behind a dirty window, disconnected. Outside Curtis's office, a low murmur of voices grew as workers returned from downstairs. Inside it, a nightmare reigned.

She looked for the gun. No sign of it. A laptop sat on the desk. 'Where's his phone? The last time I saw him, he was texting.'

Danny checked around Curtis, and Iris patted his pockets, but found nothing.

Something glittered on the floor beside Curtis, and Jade pointed. 'What's that?'

Danny reached to pick it up but stopped. 'We shouldn't touch it.' He leant closer. 'It's a necklace. A silver dolphin on a chain, it's, oh my God…'

Jade stepped forward and gasped. 'You're kidding, it's—'

'What?' Iris asked.

Danny's voice cracked. 'It's Elena's necklace.'

Chapter 39

Aftershock

THE POLICE LOCKED down the BeanBlitz office and permitted nobody to leave until they'd been interviewed. Workers waited in the lunchroom or one of the offices while officers searched the common areas. Jade, in Danny's office with him and Iris, viewed this as pointless. Surely the murderer would have slipped away during the fire alarm – doubtless an exercise they'd triggered to clear the building. Then again, the police could identify anyone missing, which would tell them plenty – although if the killer had considered this they'd have remained behind.

Jade blinked, disoriented by her circular thinking and crushed by the all-too-familiar hand of grief. No matter his faults, Curtis had been charismatic and visionary. How could he be sprawled lifeless on the carpet, the blood drained out of him?

The detectives commandeered the boardroom and said they'd summon Iris, then Jade, then Danny as the first people on the scene.

Jade hated being on the other side of the interview table, particularly when the police delved into her connection with Elena after she identified the necklace found at the murder scene. Fear stirred deep in her core. She'd run around spouting her theory about the possibility of Curtis murdering Elena to anyone who would listen: Danny, Steve, Moira, Jade's parents and Curtis. Curtis couldn't tell tales any longer, but that only raised her concern. If the police learnt of her idea, they might view it as a motive for revenge. What a set-up.

Jade had been visiting the BeanBlitz office at the time of Curtis's death, invited by Danny. Had it been a trap? Danny had been late coming downstairs after the alarm, giving him time and opportunity to kill Curtis. Now she thought about it, Iris had been slow leaving the building too.

After Jade's interview, the police called Danny. As Jade passed him, they shared a look of solidarity, comrades in grief. The despair in his eyes brought tears to Jade's. Averting her gaze from Curtis's office, now cordoned off, she headed to the restroom, chin wobbling, barely holding herself together. A police officer manned the lift lobby. Jade stumbled past him, pushed through the door marked 'women' and let herself into a cubicle.

She put the toilet lid down and sat on it, sobbing quietly. Curtis had played a huge role in her life, from being her first crush to using Elena for profit. For several minutes, the tragedy of his death flattened her, leaving space for nothing else.

After the tears stopped, she stared blindly at the back of the door, drained from her meltdown. When her hands stopped shaking, she left the cubicle and washed her face, diving into her handbag for tissues to clean her smudged eyeliner. She patched up her makeup as best she could, wanting to speak to Iris and Danny before she went home.

Drawing on her dwindling emotional reserves, she found Iris in her office. 'Do you mind if I wait with you? I want to speak to Danny after they've finished with him.'

'Okay.' Iris gestured vaguely to one of the seats on the other side of her desk. A silver-framed photo of Curtis and Iris arm-in-arm on a beach at sunset sat in pride of place.

Jade's heart ached for her. 'Are you alright?'

Tears glistened on Iris's cheeks. Of course, she wasn't okay. Jade kicked herself for asking. Iris's bloodied triangle shirt had been replaced by a clean, white T-shirt, and she'd washed her hands, but her vacant expression seemed to indicate a lack of awareness of her surroundings. Jade lowered her eyes to respect her silent anguish.

Three of Jade's friends were dead. It didn't seem possible she could shed more tears, but they leaked out. Who was next? She wiped her cheeks, suddenly aware of the dank smell of her adrenaline-fueled sweat. She couldn't waste time wallowing; she needed to figure this out before they were all gone. While she'd floundered around trying to solve Nick's murder, the culprit, whether Nick's killer or someone else, had planned the next execution. If she'd worked smarter, been more objective and known whom to trust, she could have prevented this tragedy. She'd been completely wrong-footed, and now, beautiful Curtis was gone. Elena would have been gutted. Iris was gutted. And so was Jade. Curtis hadn't lived a perfect life ... he'd made terrible mistakes and hurt people he cared about, particularly Elena and Danny, and yet they'd all adored him.

If the same person had killed Curtis and Nick, Jade could narrow her suspect list to four, but she couldn't dismiss the option that Curtis had killed Nick, and someone else had killed him for revenge or some other motive.

More tears made Jade's eyes swim, but she refused to cry anymore. If she started again, she'd never stop, and she needed to focus. Taking a steadying breath, she tested other theories. Rather than setting up Jade, what if the killer had planted Elena's necklace to set up another person who'd want revenge for Elena: Moira or Danny. Or, rather than a setup, it could be an actual revenge killing.

'Do you think anyone believes Curtis killed Elena?' Jade asked before she could contain the question.

Iris didn't move her head, but her eyes slid across to Jade. 'Apart from you?'

Jade winced, aware she deserved the parry. 'For what it's worth, I've backed off that theory.'

Iris raised her eyebrows. 'A bit late now someone's gone and killed him for it.'

'We don't know that's the motive. It could be something else altogether. But if so, then who? Danny? Moira?'

Iris flushed. 'Don't try to pin this on Danny.'

'Never! So, Moira?'

'That mad bitch? She's the one who insisted we move Nick's body. Everything's gone wrong since then. We never should've listened to her.' Iris wiped her eyes, then busied her hands collecting documents and stacking them on her desk.

'Could she have killed Curtis?' To dislodge the image of Curtis on the floor, blood soaking into the carpet, Jade focussed on the police officers searching the floor. BeanBlitz workers filled the lunchroom and other offices, creating a low hum of chatter.

Iris paused, then said, 'I wouldn't put it past her.'

Logistically, Moira would have faced some challenges. Jade had left Moira's home that afternoon and gone straight to Bean-Blitz, so unless Moira had followed her and stayed out of sight, she wouldn't have had an opportunity to shoot Curtis.

Jade pulled her phone from her handbag and dialled Moira. No answer. Her stomach lurched, then she reasoned their meeting hadn't ended on good terms, so Moira could simply be avoiding her. She hung up without leaving a message.

'What if someone put the necklace there to frame me?'

Iris's scathing look could have skinned a cat. 'You really think this is all about you?'

Jade flushed. 'Okay, what if this has nothing to do with Elena, and the killer placed the necklace as a distraction. What about Nick's report? Or the insider trading?'

Iris reached for a tissue and wiped her nose. 'Curtis hasn't set a foot wrong since those trades, but he believed someone was skimming funds. That's what Nick was investigating. But as you know, Curtis never got Nick's report.'

Jade desperately grasped for a breakthrough. 'Did Curtis write up his concerns?'

'I don't think so.'

They both looked up as Danny returned from his interview, skin blotchy, eyes puffy.

Iris gestured for him to sit. 'How'd you get on?'

He remained standing. 'They want me to give them a few documents, like staff, client and supplier lists.'

The mention of lists made Jade think about who might have slipped away after the fire alarm. 'Do you have access to security logs showing the times people come and go from the building?'

'Yes, that's one of the reports the police asked for.' He inclined his head. 'Why?'

A jolt of adrenaline made Jade sit taller. 'Can we see them before you hand them over?'

'What for?' Danny asked.

'If anyone on the list isn't here now, they could've snuck away after the murder.' The word murder caught in Jade's throat. Someone had shot Curtis. She still couldn't grasp it.

'Do you suspect someone?' Danny persisted.

'Well, I—'

But Danny was already hurtling towards his office. Jade and Iris sped after him and watched over his shoulder as he sat at his computer, clicking buttons and opening windows.

Before long, he pulled up a log.

Jade skimmed the list. About halfway down, the data showed Moira Gillespie had entered the building at 4:32 p.m., exactly fifteen minutes after Jade had arrived.

Chapter 40

Money, Money, Money

DANNY TOOK the security log to the detectives while Jade waited in his office with Iris. The room's layout matched Iris's, although Danny had no personal items on display as if he'd only planned a temporary stay. Piles of papers, opened envelopes and several dirty mugs sprawled on the desk. A picture hung on the wall of a yacht drifting into a golden sunset with the words: Dare to dream.

The rush from finding Moira's name must have reenergised Iris, and she'd shed her lethargy like a winter coat. As soon as Danny stepped back in the office, she asked, 'What did they say?'

He started pacing. 'They sent an officer to find Moira. I just … she's so proper. Do you really think she's capable of killing a man?'

'Yes,' the women replied.

Danny held up his hands in surrender. 'Okay, okay.'

His attention strayed outside the door. Most employees had left after their interviews, so few people remained in the lunchroom, but a couple of police officers entered Iris's office.

Iris cursed under her breath. 'What the fuck?'

Jade startled at the venom in her tone. 'A search, I guess.'

'Don't look at me like that!' Iris glared at Jade and Danny.

'Curtis and I just have some, er, let's call them "love notes", and I don't want anyone to see them.'

She strode towards her office, but a police officer intercepted her. 'I'm sorry, ma'am. We're sealing all empty offices until they've been searched.'

Iris clenched her fists but outwardly reined in her temper and rejoined Danny and Jade.

'You okay?' Danny asked.

'As if it's not bad enough that my boyfriend's been murdered. Now, they're trawling through our private correspondence. It's'—she choked a sob—'it's an unacceptable invasion of privacy.'

Danny enveloped her in a hug, and Iris took several shaky breaths.

After a few moments, she pulled away and sat next to Jade. 'They damn well better get Moira for this.'

Jade followed her lead – better to redirect Iris's energy to the case than to feed her anger. 'Something doesn't sit right. Unless Moira wanted to get caught, why use her pass? She must've known the police would check the security logs. And Elena's necklace? She's too clever to leave an obvious link like that.'

Danny returned to his desk chair. 'She'd have known the necklace would implicate Jade or me – anyone who blamed Curtis for Elena's death, right?'

'Right,' Jade said, 'but she'd be at the top of that list, so—'

'Or'—Iris sent a vicious look Jade's way—'Moira wanted to make a statement and put Elena at the centre of it. She took her gun, raced in here, shot Curtis and left. That could be more important to her than doing time.'

Jade recalled her conversation with Moira at Talking Heads Café when she'd planted the seed of suspicion about Elena's death and felt dizzy at the repercussions. Had she led Moira into this?

Danny shook his head. 'That sounds like an impulsive act, but this attack was carefully orchestrated. The fire alarm didn't activate by accident.'

'So, what then?' Jade's thoughts and emotions battled for dominance. 'Someone's trying to frame Moira? If that's true, it's someone close to us. Someone with access to Elena's necklace.'

They sat quietly until Iris asked, 'Do you think it was the same person who killed Nick?'

If so, Jade's five suspects were down to four. And if Moira or Steve didn't do it, she was sitting in the room with the killer. Fifty-fifty odds. Her underarms prickled with sweat, and she reminded herself to retest every assumption.

Danny pushed his fringe off his face. 'That narrows it down to Moira or Steve.' Obviously, he'd followed a similar train of logic but discounted himself and his twin.

'But Steve's in—' Jade stopped. She hadn't told them about witness protection.

'Where the hell is he?' Danny turned to Jade. 'Have you seen him since Sorrento?'

Jade, guilt-stricken, wondered whether keeping Steve's whereabouts secret had been a huge mistake.

'When was that? A week ago?' Danny asked.

Iris's eyes widened. 'What if he's dead too?'

Danny grimaced. 'More likely, he's in hiding so he doesn't have to answer questions about Nick's murder.'

Unable to hold out any longer, Jade blurted, 'He's in witness protection.'

'What?' Danny and Iris responded in sync.

'I'm sorry I didn't tell you. If everyone knew, his safety would've been jeopardised. But after Curtis ... you need to know.' Jade noticed Danny's injured air, aware how hypocritical she sounded after she'd blasted him for not telling her about the pact.

'How did you find out?' he asked.

'I went to see Steve at Sorrento. When Curtis arrived, we thought he was going to hurt Steve, so we ran to the police.'

Iris blinked, her bewilderment making her seem younger than her years.

Danny spread his hands. 'If Steve's out of action, Moira must've killed Curtis.'

'Not necessarily.' Jade had given this a lot of thought. 'I assumed once in witness protection, he'd stay there, but it's voluntary, so he can leave if he wants to.' If only she could talk to Steve. 'Let's go back to motive. What made everyone so concerned about attracting attention to BeanBlitz? Iris, you said Curtis was worried about the accounts. Were you aware of anything illegal, Danny?'

'I looked but couldn't find anything. The business was growing faster than made sense. We attracted clients with hardly any marketing. They seemed to fall into our lap.'

Jade couldn't work it out. 'But for Curtis to believe someone was stealing from the company, wouldn't results have to be worse than expected?'

Iris stared at her office, where the search continued, then back at Jade. 'He wasn't worried about our income but said we were paying huge amounts for random services like graphic design or printing.'

'Why didn't he just check each of our suppliers?' Danny asked.

Iris shrugged. 'Maybe that's what he asked Nick to do.'

Jade was no businesswoman, but overpaying suppliers seemed a simple thing to track down. 'There must've been more to it.'

'There is.' Danny cleared his throat, casting an anxious glance at Iris. 'I did the same thing from the other direction. I figured we had too much income, so I made a list of our customers. The detectives have asked to see it.'

'And?' Jade asked as Iris glared at him.

Danny ran his hand through his hair, leaving it sticking out at odd angles. 'Most of our customers are regular trading companies, but some are shell companies, which means they don't actually operate as businesses.'

Jade didn't understand. 'Why's that significant?'

'Well, for a start'—Danny raised his eyebrows—'why does a

shell company need software to manage payroll if they have no staff? Or to track income if they provide no products or services?'

Jade followed his logic. 'Right. They're paying for something they won't use.'

Iris rounded on Danny. 'Why didn't you tell me you were checking into this?'

'You're his girlfriend. I couldn't compromise you.'

Iris flinched. 'You thought Curtis was cheating the system? I told you – he's been clean since that mess with Elena.'

'I wasn't blaming him.' Danny looked sheepish. 'I was trying to figure out why our company was growing so quickly.'

Jade sat forward. 'Stop arguing. We need to figure out who killed Nick and Curtis because otherwise, one of you could be next.'

Stunned into compliance, Iris said, 'No company would pay for an accounting program they don't need. There must be a catch. Are they getting something illicit – drugs? Arms? Human trafficking?'

Danny collected a pile of papers and tapped them on the desk to align them. 'That's what I've been trying to figure out. But we have no storage, no shipping, nothing that leads to a physical product.'

'Wait! I get it.' The puzzle pieces slotted together in Jade's head. 'On one hand, BeanBlitz is getting money from customers for something they're not using. On the other, it's paying unreasonable sums to suppliers for little of value.'

'But why? That makes no sense.' Iris turned to the door as a tall, gangly police officer approached. He looked too young to be in the job.

'Iris Wyatt?' he asked.

'Yes.'

'Please come with me. We have more questions.' The officer shuffled.

Danny stood. 'What's the problem? Iris has just lost her partner. She's already submitted to one police interview. Isn't that enough for today? Give her some time.'

'Why are you harassing me?' Iris asked, face streaked with mascara.

The officer clasped his hands behind his back. 'It won't take long.'

Danny stood firm, showing strength Jade admired. 'What's the problem? Tell us, then she can explain, and we can all move on.'

'Well, I—' The officer looked from Danny to Iris and back, clearly wanting to explain but unwilling to break procedure.

'What is it?' Iris had turned faintly green.

The officer crossed his arms. 'Just come with me.'

Jade turned to Iris. 'Answer their questions. But tell them what we discussed about the company. Ask them to get a financial expert to find connections between suppliers and customers. BeanBlitz is a money laundering haven. The question is, who's behind it?'

The puzzlement cleared from Iris's face, and she pulled back her shoulders. 'Okay. Let's go.' She followed the officer out the door.

Danny watched her leave, clearly baffled. 'What the hell just happened?'

Jade hadn't worked in business, but she'd studied money laundering for a story she'd written previously. 'Let's say Bill sells drugs for a living. He has a problem: any transactions he makes over ten thousand dollars attracts the attention of the Australian Tax Office, so he needs to clean his money.'

Danny nodded.

'Bill creates a shell company, Company A, which buys BeanBlitz software.' Jade picked up a mug and placed it in front of her to illustrate. 'He doesn't really care whether the software works or not, as long as it's a legitimate business expense.'

'That's great for BeanBlitz, but how does it help Bill?'

'He creates another shell company, Company B'—Jade took

another mug and put it next to the first—'which delivers graphic designs to BeanBlitz for as much as they paid for their software, less BeanBlitz's money laundering fee. This appears as legitimate business income for Bill, and *bam*. By going through BeanBlitz, he now has clean money.'

Danny stared out his window. 'So simple. How did I not see that?'

'It'd be easy to figure out if the customer and supplier companies were the same, but they're separate entities. I don't know how we can prove the income from Company A is offset against the payment to Company B.'

Danny stretched his arms. 'We need to search for links between them, like the same directors.'

'If that's what Nick had discovered, whoever's behind this would've been worried their scam had been found out.'

Iris appeared at the door, pale and drawn. 'They're acting like I'm their chief suspect.'

'What? That's crazy.' Danny clasped the arms of his desk chair so hard his knuckles turned white. 'What did they ask about?'

'They found Moira's access pass in my office.' Iris stifled a sob. 'They said Moira wouldn't have left it there, so they reckon I pinched her pass and swiped it to deflect blame. But that's not true. I've no idea how it got into my office. Someone's framing me.'

A million thoughts competed for Jade's attention. Iris had tried to access her office before the police searched it, ostensibly to find 'love notes', although she could have been after the pass. She'd been noticeably distracted while the search took place. But if Iris had cleverly planned this murder, using Moira's pass to implicate her, she wouldn't have tripped over something as basic as leaving the pass in her office. Did the police know something about Iris that Jade didn't, or had they pounced on the easiest suspect – the victim's intimate partner?

As the police had said, it seemed unlikely Moira would swipe into the office, murder Curtis, and stop to place her pass in Iris's office, unless, as Iris suggested, she'd planted it there to implicate Iris. A brilliant move.

A third option: if Danny killed Curtis, he'd woven an intricate web, first framing Moira with the necklace and pass, then sending the police down another blind alley by setting up his sister. But Jade couldn't believe Danny would harm Iris.

Which left Steve. If he'd ducked out of police protection, he could have used Moira's pass to frame her, then implicated Iris by leaving the pass in her office.

Jade tried to reassure Iris. 'They can't have enough evidence, or they'd arrest you. How'd they react to our money laundering theory?'

'They seemed sceptical but agreed to look into it.' Iris sank into a chair.

Danny sat back at his desk. 'So, what now?'

Jade stretched her arms. A headache was brewing, and she needed to get her blood circulating. 'I guess we wait for the police to do their thing. Their forensic accountants will figure this out faster than we can.'

'Stuff that,' Iris said.

'Right,' Danny agreed. 'If someone's framing Iris, we need to get on top of this.'

A tremor of excitement ran down Jade's legs. Could they figure this out? 'When you compile the other lists for the police, can you make copies for us?'

'Sure, and I'll study them all night if I have to.' He turned to his computer.

Jade and Iris sat quietly as Danny worked.

At last, he pushed back his chair. 'I've emailed it to them, but a hard copy's easier. Wait here, I'll grab it from the printer.'

He swept out of the office and crossed to the printer room. An officer stopped him, but once Danny embroidered the truth to say he was printing files for the detectives, they allowed him to pass.

A few minutes later, he emerged with a pile of papers.

Over the next hour, Jade, Danny and Iris studied the company names – so many that Jade's eyes glazed over: banks, government organizations, architecture firms, photography businesses and more. She had trouble focusing as her mind replayed the scene of Curtis with a gunshot to the heart, left to bleed out on his office floor. She took another unsteady breath and tried to read the page in front of her. The words blurred from tiredness and tears.

Recognizing her exhaustion, she conceded temporary defeat. The rest of the office staff had gone, leaving only the police. 'I need a break. Sleep on it and try again tomorrow?'

'Meet back here?' Danny asked.

'We can't. The police said we won't be allowed back in. It's a crime scene.' Iris teared up. 'Curtis isn't here to do it, so we should send a company-wide email to tell everyone to work from home until further notice.'

'I'll do it,' Danny offered.

Jade stood to leave. 'Let's get together in the morning. Come to my place if that works.'

The others agreed.

Hoping she hadn't just invited the murderer into her home, she made her way to the lift.

Chapter 41

Jigsaw

BACK HOME, Jade forced down a piece of toast and went to bed. Sleep came in fitful bursts between waking nightmares of the discovery of Curtis's bloodied body, her failed attempts at CPR on Elena and images of Nick with a phone charging cable tight around his neck. Tears soaked her pillow.

By four in the morning, she gave up and got out of bed. She sat on her worn couch with a pen and paper to make notes – a page for each of her four suspects, considering them for either or both of Nick's and Curtis's deaths. To round it out, she included the possibility Elena had been murdered. After a bit more thought, she added a page for Curtis in case he'd killed Nick and/or Elena.

First up, Iris. She had a compelling motive to kill Nick, her rapist, but Jade couldn't think why she'd have killed Curtis. Yes, intimate partners often murdered each other, but Jade hadn't noticed the pair being at odds. BeanBlitz's financial minefield seemed to be at the centre of it. It seemed unlikely Iris had been caught up in the money laundering, but if Curtis had found out she'd betrayed him in this way, it could have led to trouble. As for Elena, Jade couldn't see why Iris would have killed her except they'd been love rivals, a stretch.

To stay alert, Jade needed to move, so she used the strip of floorspace between the kitchen bench and the table to practice rumba walks, holding the notepad and pen, stopping to write when she had a clear thought.

Suspect two: Danny. Jade's stomach turned at the idea of him being a killer. She had a soft spot for him and saw him as a gentle soul. Still, he had a temper, and if he'd found out what Nick had done to Iris, enough said. He had a strong reason to kill Curtis, who'd set him and Elena up for insider trading, especially if he blamed Curtis for Elena's suicide. A wilder theory crossed her mind: perhaps Danny had killed Elena because he loved her, and she wouldn't leave Curtis, then he'd killed Curtis because Curtis had found out, but she immediately dismissed the idea – the early hour had made her as melodramatic as her mother.

Putting down her pen and notepad, she took some deep breaths and stretched her hands high above her head, to the side, then forward, hoping the blood flow would reach her brain. To relieve her stiff neck, she rolled her head back, to her chest, left, then right. Deep breaths.

Next, Moira, who hadn't returned Jade's calls. Besides the revenge motive, she could be involved in the money laundering and have killed Nick and Curtis to cover it up. Jade scoured her mind for reasons Moira might have hurt her daughter. Perhaps Elena had uncovered Moira's or Steve's involvement in money laundering and threatened to expose them. Or Elena had planned to go public about her own involvement in insider trading, and Moira couldn't bear the humiliation. But no matter how hard she tried, Jade couldn't find a ring of truth in any of it. It seemed unlikely Moira would disguise Elena's murder as suicide after she'd lied about Peter's overdose for so many years.

She found these intellectual gymnastics hard going, but more so, she hated the emotional wrench of viewing her friends as murderers. She couldn't believe – or didn't want to believe – any of them were capable of such heinous acts, but with three of her friends dead, the likelihood of an outsider seemed remote.

Suspect four, she turned to Steve. She couldn't see him committing a crime of passion, but money laundering seemed up his alley, and perhaps he'd kill Nick, Curtis or even Elena if they'd uncovered his scheme.

Finally, Curtis might have killed Nick to protect company secrets or for revenge over Iris's rape. He might have killed Elena if she'd threatened to turn him in over the insider trading.

Lists complete, Jade made a cup of tea and sat at the table, flipping between pages, pondering the three deaths together or separately, the potential suspects alone or with others. She sipped her drink, hoping to dislodge some logic or a memory that would make sense of it all.

A row of photos on the bookshelf caught her attention: her family the day of her graduation; her dance instructor from Houston; and Jade and Elena the night of a university ball, arms around each other. Elena, red tresses curled around her shoulders, had paired a low-cut electric blue dress with a stunning silver necklace. A rogue wave of grief hit Jade. She ached to have a heart-to-heart discussion with her friend. What would Elena do now?

Jade scanned the simple kitchen and crowded living area: the bookshelves, a small table and chairs, a wooden coffee table, and Jade's favourite, her threadbare but enveloping couch. The corner of Jade's trove of keepsakes poked out from behind it. She dragged out the box and placed it on the coffee table. Under the pile of Elena's letters, she saw her red detective notebook. If only the mysteries in her life were as simple as who owned the unfamiliar car parked down the street.

Maybe Elena's death wasn't a mystery. Suicide could not be ruled out. She had a family history of depression, and from what Peter had told Jade, that could be debilitating, a heavy blanket weighing a person down.

Even if Elena had taken her own life, that still left two murders. Both deaths had occurred in the BeanBlitz office, a company that survived on a foundation of financial trickery. Curtis had taken accountability for the insider trading, but who had masterminded the money laundering? To unravel the mess, Jade recalled everything she knew about money laundering: the methods, the clever accounting and the associated criminal element – drug cartels, arms dealers or other illegal traders. Whoever was using BeanBlitz for unscrupulous purposes probably hadn't stopped – or started – their financial crimes there. In a previous case, a family had used a chain of gyms, then they'd ventured into dance studios. The BeanBlitz launderer had covered their tracks within the company, but she could try to find one of their other avenues. Cash or service businesses.

Something Jade's mother had said came back to her: *Their holidays. All those properties.* Then it hit her: Steve was a real estate mogul, he had been for years, and property offered some of the best avenues to launder money.

Buzzing with excitement, Jade turned back to the box and took out Elena's letters, sifting through them until she found the one from Port Douglas.

...He wants to buy some land here and build a whole block of apartments. Can you believe it? A whole block! Mum said we can't afford it, but Steve said we'd only keep one of them – the penthouse, how cool is that? – and sell the rest. He promised to name the building after Mum...

He's hiding something. Last night, he left his laptop open, and when I peeked at it, he slammed the lid down. It was some sort of financial report. Big numbers. I caught a few company names based on famous places – Eiffel Trifle and The Sydney Opera Mouse. Do you think he's doing something dodgy? When I get back, let's check it out...

For the first time in days, Jade gave a genuine smile. A block of apartments would be a brilliant way to clean money, either through rental income paid in cash amounts below ten thousand dollars to avoid government scrutiny, or by buying and selling apartments to associated parties at artificially lowered or inflated prices, depending on the scheme. She needed to find out whether Steve had gone ahead with this plan. For sure, he'd developed other properties, like the one down the road from Elena's childhood home.

She checked Eiffel Trifle and The Sydney Opera Mouse against the BeanBlitz customer and supplier lists, but no joy.

If only she could talk to Steve and make him slip up and give himself away. She'd asked thousands of questions in her career to get people reveal themselves, yet he remained out of reach in witness protection – a situation that now seemed far too convenient. She considered searching his study now she knew to look for Nick's laptop or one of the murder weapons. Danny had told her they'd got rid of the cable, but Steve might have kept the gun. That tempered her enthusiasm.

An image of Curtis tucking a gun into the back of his jeans returned. He'd claimed the gun was fake, but if he'd lied, he could have been shot with his own firearm. Unless Steve owned the murder weapon.

Pushing that fear aside, she considered other evidence. Steve's bank statements would show real estate income and any transactions with BeanBlitz's suppliers or customers. She could also check for Moira's involvement.

To calm herself, she poured a glass of water and quenched her thirst. This sleuthing wasn't just a bit of sneaking around like she used to do with Elena. Nick's and Curtis's killer – possibly Elena's too – remained at large. Timing was critical. If Steve had stayed in witness protection, his house would be empty, and Jade could search freely, but if he'd left, he could already be at home.

The sensible option was to pass everything she knew to the police, yet Jade resisted. Iris had already told them the money laundering theory, and they hadn't shown much interest. Further, if they left it too long to search Steve's house, he'd have time to destroy the evidence. But most compelling of all, the thrill of the hunt magnetised her. Jade felt on the cusp of a discovery, and even though she'd resigned herself to not telling this story because of her personal connections, if she cracked the case, she'd jump back in the game and nail whoever did it to the wall.

So no, she wouldn't tell the police – she'd go to Steve's herself. To stay safe, she considered taking someone with her, although she didn't want to put anyone else at risk. And who could she trust? She swallowed the lump in her throat.

She needed to tell someone what she was doing. But who? Her parents would stop her from going. She couldn't expect Zain to help unless she had a story. Moira could be in it with Steve. Her choices narrowed to Danny or Iris, and she knew Danny better. It could backfire, but she had to choose someone.

She perched on the edge of the couch and called him, apologizing profusely for ringing so early in the morning. He assured her he hadn't slept either.

By the time she'd explained her idea, she was slightly breathless. 'If I go to Steve's, I might find enough to implicate him, Moira or both.'

Danny sounded husky. 'Tell the police. They can do a legal search, and it won't put you in danger.'

'True, but I know Steve so much better. I can spot things that won't mean anything to an outsider. Photographs. Mementos. Maybe something about the Port Douglas building Elena mentioned in the letter.'

'Did she give an address for the apartment?'

Jade picked up the well-creased sheet of paper. 'No. Steve said he'd name it for Moira, but she didn't agree.'

'What about the company names Elena saw on his laptop?'

Jade tapped the page. 'I already checked, and I couldn't find any overlap in the BeanBlitz files.'

'Bummer.'

'Right.'

'Don't go to Steve's. What if the police find you there? Or Steve comes home? Now Curtis is dead, the police might say he no longer needs protection.'

Jade contemplated this. 'Surely they'll think he's in even more trouble now two of his colleagues have been killed. If he's coming home soon, all the more reason for me to go now.'

'What if he arrives while you're there?'

'I'll tell him I'm watering the plants or checking the mail.' She recited it like lines for a play.

'Let me come with you.'

Jade bit her lip, sorely tempted to say yes. The more she thought about going back to Steve's, the tighter her chest became, but going together wasn't the smartest strategy. 'If Steve's there, and you're with me, we'll both be caught, but if you're on standby, and I don't call when we agree, you can get help.'

'Fine. I'll wait nearby, just a phone call away. But please, be careful.'

'I will, I promise. I'll call as soon as I'm out.'

Chapter 42

Headlong

AT FIVE IN THE MORNING, Jade parked in a side street around the corner from Steve's and ran through her plan once more. Touching Elena's bracelet for courage, she approached on foot, keeping watch for police or anyone suspicious. The cold air turned her breath to fog, a creepy sight under the streetlights. She zipped up her jacket – phone in one pocket, keys and personal alarm in the other – and paced the street twice before approaching the front door.

She tensed when she spotted the peace lily. The leaves stood upright, and the damp patch under the pot suggested a recent watering. The letterbox had been cleared. Perhaps a neighbour like Dorothy had stopped by, or more likely, Moira had assumed this responsibility. Had this other person or persons come and gone, or were they still inside? Jade couldn't think clearly, mind scrambled with fear.

She pulled her shoulders back and rang the doorbell. If Steve answered, she had her excuse ready: to check the mail and water the plants. A plausible excuse, if a little odd at this time of day.

The *ding-dong* echoed inside the house. Jade strained to hear any movement – footsteps, a rustle or a creaking door.

Nothing.

She rang again and waited.

Still, no response.

As she bent to retrieve the key from under the pot plant, a movement snagged Jade's peripheral vision. Blood hammered in her ears. Had the front curtain stirred?

She stared at the window. Everything stayed still. Man, she was jumpy. She reminded herself Danny was waiting on standby.

One last time, she scanned the street.

In continuous motion, she put the key in the lock and stepped inside. Sweat dampened her armpits as she switched on a light and turned to the alarm pad. Her finger hovered above the panel, poised to key in the code, but the alarm hadn't been set. Either someone was here, or the person who'd attended to the plant and letters had forgotten to reset it. The urge to run away seized her, but she pictured Elena and stayed firm.

'Hello?' she whispered.

'Hellooooo?' Louder now.

'Is anybody here?'

Silence.

To steady herself, she did a quick walk-through. One by one, she opened the doors and checked the rooms. In the bedrooms, nothing had changed from last time. In the spectacular back room, all the blinds except the one in front of the back door had been closed, obscuring the pool and striking garden art. A glance around showed no sign of anyone lurking. Her erratic pulse steadied but remained on high alert.

She made a beeline for the study, perched on the chair and focused on the desktop. Dust had collected on the stacks of papers at the back, so she didn't bother examining them. The closer piles had copies of the *Australian Financial Review*, management textbooks and several company annual reports.

Inside the drawers, pens were arranged by colour, sharpened pencils ready for action. She studied a couple of bank statements and a handful of receipts from the past three or four months –

some clothing, a weekly grocery shop and a trip to the hardware store.

The first bank statement, evidently Steve's personal account, had numerous withdrawals, none noteworthy. A single deposit covered an amount consistent with a salary. A healthy salary. Steve's finance company must be profitable. Her eyes snagged on a director's fee for BeanBlitz, also a healthy sum.

The next statement was for a business account. A variety of companies had made sizeable deposits: mechanics, cafés and entertainment venues. Several had incorporated the names of famous structures like the pyramids. Jade's heart pumped harder as she spotted The Eiffel Trifle and The Sydney Opera Mouse, the same companies Elena had noticed all those years ago. But that only proved Steve had a long-standing relationship with those companies; Jade had already checked the BeanBlitz supplier and customer lists.

Jade replaced the papers, closed the drawers and turned to the bookshelves. A cursory glance revealed nothing except Steve's interest in finance and economics, and the row of photo albums. The filing cabinet, the most likely hiding place for the laptop, was locked. Dammit! She searched the desk drawers for the key, but struck out. Maybe she should look among the keys in the kitchen.

But as she moved across the room, the back door clunked, and hurried footsteps approached. Heavy treads suggested a man. Jade's nerve endings burst into flames. Steve?

The footfalls came closer. She had to move. Now!

With no time to leave out the front, she crept behind the study door. Her near-silent tiptoes amplified in her ears.

The person reached the hallway. Jade remained still, willing him to pass. She prayed he'd continue to the front door and leave, then she could escape without being seen. Who the hell was it, and why had he come through the back door? He must have been out there the whole time.

The study door swung wider, and Jade flattened against the

wall. She nearly passed out as a tall dark-haired man rushed in. Steve.

He threw a package on the desk. Wrapped in a black plastic bag and secured with gaffer tape, it landed with a clunk. He dusted off flecks of something like paint in bold colours: white, pink and orange. Angled away from the door, he didn't notice Jade, although she stood less than two metres from him, hands in pockets, thumb on her personal alarm.

He tore off the tape. The sound ripped through the silence.

She longed to sneak out, but even a flicker in his side vision would betray her. The urge to swallow hit, but she resisted in case it made a sound.

He unwrapped the bag and pulled out a passport, a wad of cash and a plastic bag holding a stack of credit cards.

Hell! He was leaving the country.

Seconds ticked by. She held still.

He turned to pick up a backpack by the filing cabinet.

Jade tried to blend into the wall.

He had almost reached the door, Jade wondering at her luck, when he pulled a handgun from the back of his chinos and pointed it at her chest.

She squeezed her eyes shut, waiting for a bullet. Her personal alarm wouldn't help her now.

'Jade?'

She blinked her eyes open and somehow found her voice. 'Hi.'

'What the fuck are you doing here?' He glowered, gun steady.

Jade gulped. 'I came to bring in the mail and water the pot plants.'

'So why are you in the study?'

'I heard footsteps and hid. You went into police protection. I thought someone had broken in.' Her nerves remained fully charged, her pulse off the charts, booming in her ears.

'The police are waiting outside. I came in to grab a few things.'

Jade clocked the lie. She'd checked the street, and nobody had been there. He'd come in before her – the alarm had been turned off – and had been in the backyard when she arrived, most likely retrieving the package.

'Can you?' Jade gestured for him to lower the gun.

He tucked it back in his chinos and pulled his windcheater over it. 'Sorry. Instinct. I have enemies. You're damn lucky I didn't shoot you.' He laughed, a brittle hoot that turned his features sour, then narrowed his eyes, body taut, ready for action. 'Are you alone?'

'Yes, but I'm meeting Danny for breakfast.' Jade's instincts screamed for her to leave as quickly as possible. But how? One wrong move, and she'd have a bullet in her head. She needed to pretend to be on his side. 'Did the police tell you about Curtis?'

'What do you mean?'

She studied his reaction closely. 'He was shot. Yesterday.'

'What? They didn't tell me. What happened?' Steve's acting rated about as highly as Gina's – he did a decent impression of being surprised but didn't convince Jade.

'Someone set off the office fire alarm and murdered him while everyone was evacuated. You made a good move getting away, we're all in danger.'

'Do they know who did it?' Steve watched her with the same intensity she'd used on him.

'Not yet. The police questioned all of us.'

'You were there? Why?'

Jade hated being on the wrong side of the questions and struggled to keep her voice steady. She needed to get away. Now. 'I wanted to talk to Curtis.' She tried to sound conspiratorial. 'Do you still think he killed Nick? That would mean there are two murderers.'

Steve's blank expression gave nothing away. Apparently, he could act better than Jade's mum after all. Then he scowled. 'I saw him holding the cable, I tell you. That bastard killed Nick.'

Jade's eyes strayed to the desk where the money and passport lay bare. A mistake.

Steve followed her eye movement and stiffened. 'Christ!' Even his silver tongue couldn't dismiss the clear signs of going on the run. 'I wish you hadn't got mixed up in this. I tried to warn you.'

'The emails. You sent those emails?'

'Of course. If you'd paid attention, we wouldn't be here. But Curtis has implicated me in financial crimes, and I need to go away until things calm down. I can't let you go until I've had time to leave the country.'

The gun, the passport and Steve's behaviour confirmed his guilt, but Jade couldn't be sure whether for financial crimes or murder.

Jade eyed the door, but was too scared to move or use her alarm. If he'd killed before, he could do it again, and right now, the fierce glare on his face made him look ready to blast Jade into a grave right next to her friends.

Chapter 43

Bad to the Bone

BACKED into the corner behind the study door, Jade could only think about the gun tucked into Steve's chinos. She'd never noticed the grey roots in his hair until now.

Steve laid on his honey-voiced charm. 'Let's work together, and we can walk out of here without any trouble.'

'Agreed. I won't tell anyone I saw you.' Jade assumed her most sincere expression. She'd be on the phone to the police the minute she reached safety.

He smiled, but no warmth reached his eyes. 'I can't let you go right away.'

'Okay. You leave now, and I'll wait for ten minutes.' She was a child again, negotiating curfew.

'Nice try, but no. Give me your phone.' He held out his hand.

Jade reached into the pocket of her jacket and reluctantly handed over her umbilical cord to the outside world. He threw it under the desk. As she watched it drop, cold seeped further into her marrow.

'Come with me. Do as I say, and I'll let you go when we're out of the city.'

Out of the city? How far were they going?

Ding-dong. The doorbell. Hope flared. Jade wasn't yet due to check in with Danny, but he might have grown anxious and come early. Or Dorothy, the eagle-eyed neighbour, might have spotted something awry.

Steve merely checked his watch and smiled, as if expecting someone. He held his finger to his mouth. '*Shhh.*'

Someone rapped on the door. 'Steve, are you there? It's me!' Moira's warbly voice carried through the front door.

'About bloody time,' Steve muttered.

A surge of fury burned in Jade's chest. So, Moira *was* in on it with Steve.

'Hurry!' Moira called.

Steve took out the gun and held it in both hands. 'Answer the door. Let her in and close it behind her. If you run for it, I'll shoot.' He pushed Jade forward but remained half-hidden behind the study doorway.

Jade reached the door on shaky legs, prepared to play to Moira's sympathy. She pulled it open to see her friend's mother, pearls and all.

Moira gaped. 'What are you doing here?'

'Help me!' Jade mouthed. 'He's got a gun.'

But Moira wasn't paying attention. She swept past Jade, brushing the hallstand and sending an advertisement for pest control fluttering to the floor. 'Where's Steve?'

He emerged from the study, gun behind his back.

Jade closed the front door, a giant sob rising in her chest.

'What the hell's going on?' Moira asked.

Steve glared at Jade. 'She just turned up, was sneaking around.'

Moira addressed Jade. 'You've always been such a sticky beak, but this has nothing to do with you.' Then to Steve, 'Let's go! My car's out the front. The police will soon realise you've left their protection.'

Steve grinned. 'That won't be a problem.'

Moira smoothed her skirt. 'Stop smirking. This isn't a laughing matter. The police questioned me yesterday about

Curtis's death. Someone took my pass and tried to frame me. I can't afford to make them more suspicious.'

'Who said I was in witness protection?' Steve asked.

Jade clawed through her memories. 'I dropped you there myself.'

'Yeah, well, I didn't stay.' His smugness made Jade want to slap him. More freaking lies. Who knew where he'd been hiding all this time, free to roam and implicate others. And Curtis's murder? She'd attributed Steve a false alibi. He had to be the killer.

All colour drained from Moira's face. Whether his accomplice or not, clearly, he hadn't told her everything. 'Then where have you been? And why didn't you call sooner?'

'I don't have time for this shit!' Steve balled his free hand. 'Where's the car?'

'Out the front. Fuelled up and ready to go.' Moira held up the keys.

Jade flushed, incensed Moira was helping him. Elena would have been mortified.

'Stay here and lock up,' Steve told Moira before turning to Jade. 'You're coming with me.' He made a grab for the keys, but Moira pulled away, and his fingers swiped through the air. 'This isn't a game. Give them to me.'

Moira put her hands on her hips. 'You said we'd leave together.'

'I can't risk it now she's involved.' He jerked his head at Jade. 'I'll send for you once I'm clear.'

But Moira stood firm. 'There's no time to argue. Come with me. Now.'

The pulsing vein in Steve's temple looked ready to burst through the skin. 'No.'

'Why is she going with you?' Moira nodded at Jade.

'Because he's got a gun,' Jade said.

Moira eyed Steve up and down. 'Show me your hands.'

Steve opened his left hand. 'This is ridiculous. I need to go.'

'Show me the other one.' Moira pointed at his right side.

'I'm not a child. Fuck you!' He drew out the black handgun and pointed it at Moira.

The women backed away in a cloud of Moira's cloying floral perfume. Jade eyed the gun muzzle.

'Steve! What are you doing?' Moira asked, whey-faced.

'Calm down. I won't use it unless one of you does something stupid. Throw me the keys.'

'What have you done?' Moira had a look of dawning comprehension. 'Oh my God! Did you kill Nick? Curtis?'

Steve glared at her, defiant. 'Don't insult me.'

'You told me you'd been set up.' Moira pursed her lips. 'Oh, Steve. Why else would you lie about witness protection?'

'You're getting way ahead of yourself. The police wouldn't help me, so I did what I could to protect myself.' He held out his palm. 'The keys. I love you, Moira. Believe me or don't, but it's the truth.' His adoring smile came off as sleazy.

Moira regained some of her colour. 'If you love me, let me come with you.'

Steve shuffled, clearly losing patience. 'No.' He snatched the keys and shoved them into his pocket.

Moira held her head high. 'Fine, I'll stay, but who's to say I won't call the police?'

Jade inwardly applauded her, but Steve looked menacing.

'You won't. You're just as involved as I am. You'll go to jail.'

Voices came from the front door, and the trio froze.

'What the heck?' Steve motioned for the women to go into the study and followed them in.

The doorbell rang, and a voice came from outside. 'Jade?' Danny.

Oh, thank God. Jade had trusted the right person.

He pounded on the door.

'Jade, you there?' A woman's voice this time. Iris.

If Jade got out of this alive, she'd owe the twins big time.

Steve glared at her. 'Did you call your whole freaking fan club?'

'No, I—'

'Open that drawer.' He shoved Jade towards the desk.

She did as she was told.

'Take the gaffer tape.' He made Moira sit in the desk chair and signalled for Jade to tie her to it.

She did so, apologizing profusely and keeping the tape loose so Moira could make an easy escape.

Steve noticed and made her tighten it. With a gun pointed in their direction, they couldn't fight back.

'I'm so sorry,' Jade muttered, while at Steve's direction, she cut a piece of tape and covered Moira's mouth.

The older woman trembled.

'No chatting,' Steve whispered.

Danny and Iris kept hollering and knocking.

'I'll stay too.' Jade figured she'd be safer taped up in the house than on the run as Steve's hostage.

'No. You're with me. Grab that.' Steve pointed at the backpack resting against the filing cabinet. 'Put the cash and my passport inside. And those credit cards.' He nodded at the desk.

Jade searched for an opportunity to double-cross him, wishing she had a tracking device, but Steve had tossed her phone under the desk, and he was watching her too closely for her to retrieve it.

He snatched the backpack from Jade and slung it across his shoulder, then pulled Jade in front of him. 'We're going out the back. One sound, and you'll get a bullet.'

'But Moira's car's out the front.'

'We can't go that way, thanks to your friends. Where's your car?'

'Fischer Street.' A side street a minute's walk away.

'Let's go.' He nudged Jade towards the family room.

She walked ahead, listening for her friends. The knocking and calling had stopped. What were they doing? Could they get into the backyard, or would the side gates prevent access? She wished they'd call the police and stay away.

Steve poked the gun into her back as she passed the sea of kitchen bench tops and European appliances.

'Wait.' Steve opened a drawer and took out a bunch of keys. He shoved them into the backpack and nodded for her to keep going.

Jade stepped into the dark, wishing she'd waited for daylight before she came on this misguided mission. The water feature in the suburban oasis tinkled, making her want to pee. She searched the yard for an escape route but found none. Was that Iris's voice on the breeze?

Steve urged her on.

A gum tree in the corner of the garden shaded a collection of plush ferns and shrubs. One of its branches had fallen into the pool and floated like a misshapen corpse. The brightly coloured horse and foal statues caught the moonlight. The horse had a gaping wound in its ribs. Plaster and paint chips littered the ground. So that's where the pink and orange flecks on Steve's escape package had come from. Jade begrudgingly acknowledged the brilliance of his hiding place.

He prodded her again.

Jade startled at a clatter from the side of the house and the deep rumble of Danny's voice. He must be trying the side gates. She willed him away; she didn't want him and Iris anywhere near Steve and his gun.

Steve didn't seem bothered by the noise, so she assumed he'd locked the gates. He maintained his cool under pressure. No mistakes. Yet. For any chance of escape, she needed him to crack.

They followed an overgrown path behind the dense foliage to a gate in the back fence. A distant sound caught Jade's attention. She stiffened. A police siren? Or wishful thinking?

Steve kicked into a higher gear. 'Quick! Through the gate.' Not panicked, but a notch closer.

Jade fumbled with the bolt, clumsy with nerves. She jiggled it but couldn't free it, hands unsteady as she sensed Steve's impatience.

'Press your shoulder against it.' He stood so close she felt his breath hot on her neck. His deodorant barely masked his sweat.

Should she tackle him? Try to knock the gun out of his hand? But then what? He had a serious height and strength advantage and could easily overpower her. Her personal alarm would anger him, so she couldn't risk using it.

The wailing siren grew louder. The police were approaching. How long before they reached her? She needed to slow Steve down. But with her shoulder against the wooden slats, the bolt slid across, and she pulled the gate open.

Chapter 44

Shut Up and Drive

JADE STEPPED through Steve's back gate into a narrow, cobbled laneway. Trees overhung from adjoining properties, and three-foot-high weeds threatened a takeover.

Steve tugged the gate shut behind him. 'Turn right.'

Jade navigated the slippery cobblestones, careful not to turn an ankle. The sirens stopped, leaving an eerie silence in their wake. She tried to imagine what the police were doing. They'd find Moira soon. What would she tell them?

When they reached Fischer St, Steve took off his jacket and draped it over the gun, which he angled at Jade. He asked where her car was, and she pointed right. As he strolled alongside her like they were companions out for a chat, pressure built in Jade's head. Every step took her further from safety. She clutched the personal alarm in her pocket and weighed up whether to use it. The threat of a bullet made the decision for her.

Streetlights cast shadows from a sole early morning walker on the other side of the road. Jade tried to reach out to the lonely figure with her eyes, hoping he'd read her fear, but he hurried on, doubtless caught up in his own affairs.

When they reached the car, Steve told Jade to drive. He jumped in the passenger seat and threw his bag in the back.

Jade dared not resist. Her hope evaporated, and despair kicked in as she turned on the engine. She held no faith Steve would release her as promised. She might become his third victim. Fourth, if he'd killed Elena.

She glanced up and down the street, desperate for help, but it looked like an abandoned stage set. Lights in a few of the homes offered tantalizing signs of life, but nobody appeared.

Steve aimed the gun at her hip. 'Head to North Road.'

As the car picked up speed, a rush of tears filled Jade's eyes. Escape now seemed out of reach. 'Where are we going?'

'Just drive.'

She checked the fuel gauge, hoping for near empty, so they'd need to stop at a service station, but the meter read half full. For now, she could only follow instructions.

A car turned in front of Jade from a side street, and she braked hard, body thrumming with adrenaline.

Steve sucked a sharp breath. 'Careful.'

'That idiot pulled in front of me.' She should have collided with him, then she'd have had to stop.

'Shut up and focus on the road.'

She drove past Monash University and reached the highway, where Steve told her to turn.

'Please, let's pull over. Take my car and go on without me. I won't go to the police.' At least, not straight away. She didn't even have her phone. If she trekked to a service station, someone might let her make a call. The police could use her registration number to track Steve.

'I need you out of the game a bit longer.'

Jade had the sensation of dropping fifty floors in an elevator. 'Let me go. I don't care whether you get caught. I just want to go home.'

Steve nodded ahead. 'Keep driving.'

For almost an hour, Jade stayed at the wheel, on high alert. The sun rose, battling the overcast sky to cast bleak light as the land transitioned from suburbia to farmland. Steve directed her past Lilydale and through Yarra Glen.

The shock of Steve's betrayal gave way to bewilderment. The only people who hadn't lied to her – that she knew of – were her parents, but she now realised even they must have secrets, personal details she neither wanted to know nor needed to know. Would she ever see them again? If only she'd appreciated them more, instead of rolling her eyes at Gina's meddling. No matter how annoying her mother could be, Jade never questioned her love. Everyone else in her life seemed to lack authenticity. And Steve, who'd watched her grow up next to Elena, invited her to Sorrento for school holidays and taken photos before school dances, was kidnapping her. Clearly, her ability to judge people needed improvement.

Jade brushed self-pity aside as she frantically groped for an escape plan. She wished she had the skill to smash into a car or a tree and control the amount of damage, but she'd probably end up dead or, worse, hurt someone else. Steve would notice if she tried to attract another driver's attention. She could jump out of the car when they slowed for a turn … but he had a gun. He probably wouldn't use it in sight of other people, but she wasn't willing to take the risk.

Unable to craft a decent plan, Jade tried to work out how Steve had killed Curtis. He must have used Moira's pass to get into the BeanBlitz building, then placed it in Iris's office to frame her. He'd evidently hidden in the bathroom and triggered the alarm by smoking, but how could he have been certain Curtis would be the last person remaining in the office? If Curtis had evacuated with everyone else, the whole charade would have been for nothing.

Trapped next to Steve, she decided to ask a few questions. He might not answer, but he wouldn't shoot her while she was driving.

She kept her eyes forward. 'How'd you do it?'

'Do what?'

'Kill Curtis.'

'I didn't.'

Jade stayed quiet as they passed a winery, then farmland with cows grazing, her chaotic brain at odds with the peaceful landscape. 'We both know I'm not getting out of this alive, so it makes no difference if you tell me. You outsmarted us all. The setup with the fire alarm, using Moira's pass, even before that, the whole police protection thing, so we'd dismiss you as a suspect – brilliant!'

She risked a side-look at Steve to gauge his reaction and caught a glimmer of pride crossing his face.

But he didn't follow her lead. 'I'm not going to kill you.'

'Then tell me where we're going.'

'You'll see.'

'What I don't understand is how you kept Curtis in the office after everyone else had left.' Jade wondered whether to press him for an answer; a confession might lock in her death sentence. Still, curiosity pushed her on. If only she had her phone so she could record him.

He took so long to answer she thought he wasn't going to reply, so she added, 'I already know you did it, all you'd be doing is confirming the details.'

Finally, he chuckled. 'It wasn't as hard as it sounds.'

Jade took the cheerless win. Either his need to brag outweighed his fear of exposure, or he'd already decided her fate. Cold fury gripped her, and she made a silent promise: if she got out of this alive, she'd damn well write the best story of her life and expose the true Steve Gillespie to the world.

He tapped the gun and kept it trained on Jade. 'I texted to warn him I'd be setting off the alarm and said if he waited behind, I'd give him proof of who strangled Nick.'

Jade recalled her last meeting with Curtis. He'd received a message and said he needed to check on something. That must have been

Steve. Hopefully, the police could recover Curtis's text messages. His phone had been missing from the murder scene, but with a warrant, maybe they could access the data through his phone company.

'Who did you tell him killed Nick?'

'Iris.'

Jade's eyebrows shot up. Between this text message and Moira's pass, Steve had thoroughly framed Iris. No wonder the police had paid her so much attention, but Jade couldn't imagine Curtis accepting his girlfriend was a murderer. 'Why'd Curtis believe you?'

'I had evidence – Nick's phone. I sent the text from it and told him I'd found it at Iris's house.'

Jade slowed as the traffic in front of her backed up behind a tractor.

Steve harrumphed. 'Get off the road, you dickhead.'

But Jade needed to slow down so she could digest what Steve had said. He'd implicated himself not only in Curtis's murder but in Nick's. 'Why did you have Nick's phone?'

'I took it because he was investigating BeanBlitz's finances, and I wanted to see how much he knew. And before you ask, I knew his passcode because I'd watched him type it. His emails to Curtis didn't give much away, but I could see he'd figured out some financial details I didn't want made public.'

Jade assumed he meant his money laundering scheme, only he didn't know she'd worked it out too. 'I'm surprised Curtis agreed to see you. You'd put the police onto him, and I know he suspected you of Nick's murder.'

'Do you think I'm stupid? I didn't tell him it was me. Besides anything else, that would've left hard evidence. I signed the message from Moira.'

Jade shuddered at Steve's lack of remorse, his willingness to incriminate anyone. Again, she considered the situation from Curtis's perspective. 'How would Moira have had access to Iris's home?'

Steve scoffed. 'You're not very creative, are you? I told him I – Moira – went there to discuss Nick's death.'

The tractor turned off the highway, and Jade accelerated, as did her mind. 'But why would Iris leave Nick's phone lying around? And how would Moira have known it was his?'

'Curtis didn't ask as many questions as you. Besides, I told him we'd discuss everything when I arrived, and that I needed Iris out of the way. He had no reason to feel threatened by Moira. Then I stopped texting.'

Jade gave him begrudging respect. He'd thought of everything. However far-fetched it sounded, his plan had worked.

Up ahead, Jade spotted a white car with telltale blue signage approaching from the other direction. A police car. She tensed.

'Don't even think about it,' Steve warned.

But Jade was thinking about it. She couldn't think about anything else. The trouble was she couldn't take advantage of this perfect opportunity. Anything she did – honk the horn, flick her headlights or set off her personal alarm – would end with her being shot or injured in a car crash.

She watched helplessly as they crossed paths and carried on, Jade in the car with a murderer, the police heading away to attend to business.

Steve's shoulders relaxed. 'Good girl.'

Jade wanted to slap the patronizing smile right off his face. Instead, she asked, 'Why'd you leave Elena's necklace beside Curtis?'

'I need to thank you for that idea, sniffing around asking about Elena. What a brilliant way to complicate the investigation. More framing and misdirection. Loose ends for the police to sort out. And when I applied my mind to it, I could see your point. Curtis *was* to blame. He'd shamelessly exploited what Elena told him for his own gain.'

At least they agreed on this point. 'How'd you get the necklace?'

'Oh that'—he had the gall to chuckle—'that wasn't Elena's, but I know where she bought it. I got a replica.'

Jade slowed again, this time for the reduced speed limit as they approached Yea, a quaint country town. Steve directed her to bypass the main street. She longed to pull over, but they rejoined the main road before she could act, and she returned to a hundred kilometres an hour.

'At the time, were you aware Curtis had used Elena's information for the illegal trades?' she asked.

'Yes. Elena asked me about it.'

'What did she say?'

'She explained what had happened and wanted to know if she was liable. I told her the truth, and she freaked out. Curtis's fault. He deserved to pay for that.' Steve spoke with what seemed like real concern for Elena. Jade found it hard to reconcile this apparent emotion from someone who had just confessed to murder.

'You framed Moira with the necklace and her pass. How could you risk her taking the blame?'

'She didn't do it, so the police would never get enough evidence to put her away. I didn't set out to hurt her, just needed to take the heat off me.'

Acid rose in Jade's mouth at his calculated callousness. He had no idea what true love was. This new reality hurt. Her second father, a murderer. How must Moira feel? Although she deserved no sainthood – she'd tried to help Steve escape. By now, the police must have released her from her gaffer tape bindings. Jade hoped she'd grasped what Steve had done and would help the police track him down with her knowledge of his properties, habits and thought patterns because now Steve had unloaded his guilt onto Jade, her chances of coming out of this alive rested at an all-time low.

Jade eyed the peace symbol on Elena's charm bracelet, then drew her eyes back to the road. 'So, you did all this, Nick and

Curtis'—she didn't dare bring up Elena—'to avoid prosecution for financial crimes?'

'I sure as hell wasn't going down for that. Nick would've told everyone what I'd done. And Curtis had commissioned the report. He'd have persevered and exposed me. That jackass, who I helped, built up and treated like a son. I wanted to kill them together, but Nick called that meeting faster than expected, so I had to act quickly. Then I had to wait for things to cool down before I went back for Curtis.'

Jade had no words, but didn't need them because Steve went on. 'I planned to take Curtis out that day in Sorrento. I knew he'd track me down. But then you came and "rescued" me.' His hollow laugh made Jade want to knock him over the head. 'You cost me five days, but you did hand me the witness protection idea on a platter.' No question, Steve could improvise as well as a jazz musician.

Jade braked to take a corner, then sped up again. 'But you were already on the run after Nick. Why'd you care if Curtis exposed you? If you'd taken off, you'd be in the Caymans by now.'

'I needed to buy time. It's harder than it sounds to move money. If they'd uncovered what I'd done and frozen my accounts, I'd be penniless.' He showed no regret, merely stated cold, hard facts.

Jade could see plain as the road in front of her that he'd dispose of her with the same lack of emotion. She had to escape, because otherwise, she wouldn't live to help put him where he belonged: in a tiny, windowless cell.

Chapter 45

Hammer to Fall

JADE DROVE through Yarck and gazed longingly at a café boasting the best pies in Australia. A random memory popped into her head of being with Elena as youngsters at a similar café, gorging themselves on vanilla slices, or 'snot blocks' as they'd called them, in fits of laughter.

A short distance later, Steve directed Jade off the highway. They continued along smaller roads, overshadowed by enormous, densely packed gum trees, where landholdings grew larger, so property gates were spaced further apart. By the time they turned onto a dirt track, Jade, palms clammy, had lost her bearings, though she guessed they had arrived somewhere in the Strathbogie Ranges.

They rattled over the bumpy road for another ten minutes. Jade's pulse escalated as they departed from civilisation.

Steve directed her onto a driveway that climbed a small hill and pointed to the tiny cottage ahead. 'Park there.'

Trembling, Jade did as he said, praying she'd live to drive home again. She recognised the ramshackle structure from a photo in her keepsakes box – the one with Elena and Moira surrounded by eucalypts and daffodils. Perhaps Steve had bought the place as a hideaway; she guessed he'd stayed her under 'witness protection'.

The drive had lulled Steve into a calmer mood, but now he jumped out of the car, gun trained on Jade, and ordered her to hand over the keys. 'Follow the path.' He pointed to a track winding behind the building into the forest.

Jade's legs went weak. She saw no point in screaming; nobody would be within earshot. Even her personal alarm served little use. Desperate to stall, she asked, 'Does the hut have a bathroom?' She'd ransack the bathroom cabinet for anything useful as a weapon: tweezers or a pair of nail scissors. Besides, she really needed to go.

Steve vacillated, apparently torn over whether to grant the delay. 'Alright, but make it snappy.' He picked up the backpack from the backseat, took out the keys, tossed them to Jade, then strode forward, telling her to go inside.

The front door casing didn't fit the opening properly, and folded cardboard filled the gaps along the side. Gaffer tape patched the cracks in the stained-glass side panels featuring roses and leaves.

Inside, with Steve close behind, Jade took in the rustic multi-purpose room: a kitchenette, a small laminate table with four chairs and a worn couch, the seat cushions sagging almost to the frame. A jacket on the back of a chair, tea and coffee on the kitchen counter, and ashes in the fireplace confirmed this to be Steve's hideaway. The structure appeared home-built – a renovator's delight, or more realistically, a knockdown. Whoever had put it together must have run out of money or willpower by the time they got to the finishing touches because the ceiling had exposed rafters and the incomplete plastering revealed the wall framing and silver foil insulation behind it. The house displayed its full underbelly.

Steve dumped his backpack on the couch and shoved Jade towards the bathroom. 'Leave the door open.'

Damn! She wouldn't be able to check the cabinets with Steve

watching. The idea of relieving herself while he hovered gave Jade the creeps, but she had no choice.

The room had a hopelessly out-of-date pink toilet and basin, cracked floor tiles and mould in the shower. As she drew down her jeans, something crinkled in her pocket. She pulled her sweater low for privacy. Steve momentarily averted his eyes, and Jade took the opportunity to fish out the paper from her pocket. A receipt. She didn't have time to check the details, but it would leave a clue that she'd been here.

Once done, she checked whether Steve had lost interest, but he stood with face impassive, legs apart, gun at the ready, tracking her every move.

She turned to the basin, her back to Steve, and dropped the receipt behind a box of tissues. In water so cold it must have been bordering on ice, she washed her hands. Then she re-entered the living room.

Steve waved his weapon. 'Let's go.'

'Are you going to kill me?' She assumed he wouldn't be honest, but she didn't want to spend her last minutes in silence.

'Such a tacky question. You're a writer, can't you come up with something more original? I'm just going to keep you out of action for a while. Think of it as an escape room.' He checked his watch. 'Enough stalling.'

He hustled her out the door.

Jade breathed in the eucalyptus scent and hugged herself against the cold. She listened for signs of people – a car engine, voices or the hum of a generator – but bush sounds closed in around her, amplifying her remoteness. Magpies warbled, wind rustled the gumtrees, and a crackle in the undergrowth betrayed a small creature. Usually, Jade found nature's reverberations calming, but today she only heard sinister undertones. She wanted to shout, to turn on Steve and rip the gun out of his hands, but fear kept her quiet and obedient. Mouth dry, she trudged along the path behind the hut, trampling on leaves and twigs, pushing past fronds of bracken and stepping over puddles.

Surely by now, the police would know Steve had taken Jade, but would Moira cooperate? If so, would she remember this place and guess Steve had retreated here? The further he took her from the hut, the less hope Jade held that anyone would find her.

The track traversed the side of a hill, with the peak up to her left. To her right, the terrain sloped down to a creek that bubbled and frothed a warning. They traipsed to the top of the hill, then down the other side.

Jade slowed, anything to buy time and give others a chance to catch up. But hoping for rescue wouldn't save her; she needed to be proactive. Until now, she'd been compliant, but they were nearing the end of their journey. To survive, she needed to overthrow Steve with a surprise attack. His superior size, weight and strength meant she'd have to deliver a knockout blow first shot. One chance. She scanned for anything she could use as a weapon – a rock or a fallen branch. If she launched it at him with enough force, she could disable him. But if he saw her picking it up, he'd shoot her. Or—

'Go right.'

Jade took the turn, then stopped. The path ended at a makeshift, solid wood door that led into the side of a hill. The reason Steve had been attracted to this property came back to Jade with a gut-punch – one of the early owners had struck gold and dug a mine. The project had long since been abandoned, but what better way to dispose of a body than toss it down a mineshaft? Jade had read about such cases and didn't want to feature in a similar article.

If he threw her into a hole like that, even if she survived the fall, she'd never get out alive. Who knew its condition? It could cave in. And the Australian bush, much as she loved it, offered an arsenal of venomous spiders and snakes. Thank God it was winter, so snakes would be dormant. Jade had no idea whether they'd bite if disturbed, and she really didn't want to find out. Either way, once in the mine, she'd likely never see daylight again. It could be hours, days, even months before anyone found her. By then, Steve would be long gone, and Jade would be dead – if not from a spider bite, then from thirst. People could last weeks without food, but mere days without water.

The door looked as homemade as the hut. Two wooden fenceposts held it vertical against the hillside, and it could slide behind the posts to reveal the opening, although not to the left, as it sat flush against a protruding rock. A long metal rod through the right fencepost into the door acted as a lock. Jade held no hope she'd break her way out; she'd never bust through a door like that nor have the strength to bypass the metal rod.

She turned back to Steve. 'Please, don't ask me to go in there.'

At least he had the grace to look apologetic. 'You'll be fine. Once I'm safe, I'll tell Moira, and she can come and get you.'

Everything seemed to slow down now Jade could see the site she feared would become her final resting place. She couldn't depend on Steve to reveal her location to Moira – or anybody else. 'How long will that take? What about food and water?'

'This isn't the Sheraton.'

No kidding. 'What about snakes and spiders? God knows what's down there. You might as well shoot me now.'

'Don't tempt me.' He gestured to the door. 'Come on. Pull out that rod.'

Jade grasped the end of the metal rod and tugged. It came out easily.

'Now slide the door across.' Elena's stepdad was pure evil.

Jaw quivering, Jade examined the door. It must have been ages since anyone had opened it because grass and weeds had grown over the area to the right. Standing on the left, she made a half-hearted effort to shove it across. It didn't budge.

'Put some muscle into it,' Steve said.

'Asshole,' she muttered as she tried again.

It took all her strength to move the door a couple of inches. Then it jammed. Light fell through the small crack between the door and the rock, illuminating a path inside that ramped down at a steady angle until it disappeared into darkness. Goosebumps crept up Jade's arms and legs.

'It's stuck.' She stepped to the right side of the door to check what had stopped it and found a tussock of grass.

Steve growled, frustration building. 'Grab a rock or a piece of wood and clear the ground so it can slide. And don't get any ideas about using them to hit me. Any fast moves, and I'll shoot.' He took several steps back, presumably to avoid striking range.

Jade scoured the ground for digging implements, choosing what would make a suitable weapon rather than an effective spade. This could be the chance she needed; she couldn't blow it. A strong short stick could become a baton. Or she could throw a rock. Her aim would have to be perfect, which posed a problem; she'd never been much of a goal shooter in netball, playing centre or one of the attacks was more her speed.

She kicked a stone to dislodge it, rolled it over to get rid of the ants and earwigs, then picked it up. Flat, about the size of her hand, it had a sharp edge – better for digging than hurling. She held onto it but kept looking. A branch lay to the side of the path. After removing any insects, she broke away the twigs and thin end. It snapped too easily, so she tossed it away and found a thick, strong one that was almost perfect, although heavier than she'd like.

'That'll do,' Steve said. 'Come on. We haven't got all day.'

Jade returned to the door, pulse thudding in her ears. She placed the wood beside her. As she used the stone to dig around the grass roots, she grasped the irony that this tiny hole would give passage to her grave in the mine. All she had to do was burrow deep enough to allow the door to open – a task she resisted completing.

Facing away from Steve, she pulled out some grass but lodged a piece of rock in its place to block the door. She worked along the rest of the sliding path, alternating between the branch and the stone for digging.

Behind her, pacing footsteps spoke to Steve's building irritation, so his cross words – 'That's enough. Try again.' – came as no surprise.

Knees stiff from crouching, she used the branch to hoist herself up and shook out her legs. A mental image of Steve escaping to a non-extradition haven spurred a last-ditch effort at negotiation. 'Can we talk about this? Leave me here. I have no phone, no way to contact anybody until I walk to the closest town. Take my car and drive to an airport. By the time I'm out of here, you could be in the Caribbean.'

'Do as you're told, or you'll end up a lot worse off.'

Jade didn't doubt Steve would kill her. Curtis had been – in Steve's words – like a son to him, yet he'd shot the younger man. Jade now knew Steve's darkest secrets, so he'd have no hesitation using the gun on her. She meant nothing more to him than an uncomfortable reminder of Elena. Had he killed her too?

Although tempted to launch her attack, he remained too alert, so with the branch under her arm and the stone in her hand, she took her position on the left of the door and pushed. The door inched along, leaving Jade terrified her small rock wouldn't hold, but just as she was about to howl with despair, it jammed tight, leaving an opening too narrow for a person to slip through. She strained and pushed to no avail.

'What now?' Unable to contain his impatience any longer, Steve came forward and bent down to see why the door wasn't moving. He scrabbled at the ground.

Jade prepared to bash him with her stone, but he straightened and grasped the door. It slid across, revealing a path sloping down into the bowels of the hill. No telling how far it went. Small mercies it didn't drop straight down.

Steve checked the entrance and made the mistake of turning his back. Jade brought the stone down with every ounce of energy she could muster.

He must have caught her movement in his peripheral vision because he ducked. The blow missed his head and struck his shoulder, throwing him off balance. He toppled forward, landing with his upper body over the entrance.

Jade grabbed the branch from under her arm as he crawled back from the slope. Fear charged her muscles, and she swung at him as he staggered to his feet. She struck his arm, and he stumbled sideways. The gun slipped out of his hand.

Jade brought the branch down again, harder, on his head. He howled. She darted forward, and they both reached for the gun.

She seized it first.

Triumphant, she turned and ran.

A battle raged in her head: get away or ask for answers?

No time to think.

When she'd put ten metres between them, she turned and waved the gun. 'Stop, or I'll shoot.'

He paused, holding his head, eyes wide.

Panting, she steadied the gun with both hands. She'd never used a firearm in her life, but how hard could it be?

Steve held up his arms. 'Wait, we can work this out.'

Her blood burned hot. 'Answer one question, and we'll see.' She drew a deep breath. 'What happened to Elena?'

Steve raised his voice, each sentence escalating louder than the last. 'What's the matter with you? First, you accused Curtis of hurting her, now me. I didn't touch Elena. I loved her. I'd give anything to bring her back.' He drew to his full height, wincing – Jade must have done some damage. 'I'll admit, I've done some shitty things in my life, but never, ever, would I have hurt Elena.'

His reaction, so complete, so raw, made Jade believe him. He'd admitted to his other murders, so he had no reason to lie.

'What about the key? Do you know who put our spare key in her room? Someone came into our house that day, I know it.'

He gave an ugly sneer. 'Why don't you ask Moira about that?'

'Moira?'

He seemed to enjoy her confusion, and Jade didn't want to give him further satisfaction. She'd deal with Moira later. For now, she had to get away from Steve.

She eyed him warily. 'Lie down. Face to the ground.' If only she had some rope or that gaffer tape she'd used on Moira. She saw no point trying to lock him in the mine, as by the time she shifted the door shut, he'd escape. 'Hands behind your back.'

Steve laughed and stepped towards her. 'Don't be silly. Give me the gun.'

'Stop!' She fingered the trigger, hands quivering.

'Have you ever shot a person?' he scoffed. 'Have you even touched a gun before?'

His confidence unnerved her. Truely, she knew nothing about guns. She must be doing something wrong. 'One more step, and I'll shoot.'

She searched her mind for anything she'd ever heard about firing a weapon. A safety switch? Did she need to cock it? She'd read something about kickback.

In the time it took for her to glance down, Steve charged.

She closed her eyes and squeezed.

A feeble *click*. Shit!

As he reached her, she swung the gun at his head. It caught him hard on the temple, flew out of her hand and landed a few metres away.

Steve tumbled sideways, reaching an arm to bring her down with him.

She twisted to avoid falling. Too late.

They hit the ground together.

Crack! What the hell? A bone? Hers or Steve's?

Steve lay still. Knocked out? Dead?

She saw her deformed left leg before she felt it. Her foot stuck out at an unnatural angle. She didn't need a doctor to diagnose it was broken or dislocated. Why couldn't she feel any pain?

An ambulance, she needed an ambulance. So did Steve.

She reached for her phone but found her pocket empty. Dammit! She'd left her phone in Steve's study.

The pain hit. Searing stabs of heat.

She needed to get back to her car. To drive to get help. Steve had her keys. She tried to move, to grab them from his pocket, but waves of nausea hit her, the pain so intense she almost passed out. Who was she kidding? She couldn't get back to the car with her leg like this.

Help. They needed help before she lost consciousness. She pulled the personal alarm from her pocket and pressed the button. Her wonderful dad.

The piercing squeal hurt her ears. She kept her thumb on the buzzer.

Another worry hit with blazing urgency: she had to secure the gun in case Steve regained consciousness. If she fired all the bullets, Steve couldn't use them on her, and building on the noise from the alarm, maybe, just maybe, someone would hear the shots and send help. She returned the alarm to her pocket.

The gun lay a few metres away. Surely, she could move that far. She shuffled on her backside, trying not to jar her injured leg. Bolts of white light shot across her vision. She urged herself to keep going.

Shuffle. Rest. Shuffle. Rest.

After a few excruciating minutes, she clutched the gun. Lying back, she studied it for some kind of safety. Ah! She spotted a small switch on the frame. She pivoted the lever to expose the red dot. Ready for the kickback, she aimed the gun away from her and squeezed. *Click*.

What the hell? They made it look so easy in the movies.

She pulled back the slide, and something snapped into place. With both hands, she aimed at the sky and pulled the trigger again.

The gun jumped as the shot echoed in the forest. Something shot out to her right, and a wisp of smoke vanished into the air. A cartridge lay on the ground beside her. So that was what had popped out.

How many bullets did this gun have? She fired again, holding the gun firmly. And again. Three shots. Three ejected cartridges. Blinking to clear her clouded vision, she tried again. *Bang*!

Bang, bang, bang!

That made seven. How many more bullets? How much longer could she keep the whiteness in her vision at bay? Steve still hadn't moved, but she couldn't risk leaving any bullets in case he woke before she did.

Bang, bang, bang, bang!
Bang, bang, bang, bang!

Smoke filled her nostrils. On her sixteenth attempt, the gun clicked empty. Was that it? She squeezed again. *Click.* Thank God!

Should she check whether Steve was carrying extra ammunition?

Before she could decide, she blacked out.

Chapter 46

Death Defying

When Jade came to, the excruciating pain in her leg made her groan. Something encircled her arm. Steve? He was holding her down. She grasped wildly, trying to push him away.

A voice said, 'Relax, ma'am, I'm just taking your blood pressure.'

Jade blinked, and her hazy vision refocused. Men in blue uniforms hovered over her. Paramedics. Above the men, sun glinted through a canopy of trees. She was still in the bush. When she tried to move, her leg sent lightning bolts through her body. Pain crippled her and made her queasy.

She tried to sit up but fell back in agony. 'Where's Steve?' The spot where he'd been lying was empty. All this, and he'd got away? 'No, no, no. He's a—'

'He's on a stretcher on the way to the ambulance parked at the hut,' a paramedic told her. 'We couldn't drive up here.'

'Thank God! Was he hurt?'

'He was waking when we got here. Had a pretty good knock on the side of his head. They'll keep him under observation for signs of concussion, but he should be okay.'

'Tell them he's dangerous. He'll be desperate to get away.' Jade sank back and rested her head on the ground.

'Ma'am, the police are here too. They'll want to take your statement, but we need to get you into hospital to take care of your leg first. How's the pain on a scale of one to ten?'

'Eleven.'

'Here, suck on this.' He passed her a green whistle. 'It's a painkiller. Penthrox.'

Jade breathed it in. At first, it had no effect, but seconds later, it took the edge off the pain.

The next few hours passed in a blur of transport to hospital and medical procedures. They put her dislocated ankle back in position, set her broken leg and put it in plaster. It hurt so badly they had to put her under to do it. She kept wondering when she'd be able to dance again.

When she woke, pleasantly drowsy, she recognised the blue around her as hospital curtains. The piercing tang of antiseptic overrode all other smells. Jade felt no pain, just pure happiness. What drugs did they have her on?

A nurse came to check on her, and soon, an orderly transported Jade from recovery to a normal ward. She kept her eyes shut to stay cocooned in her blissed-out state as long as possible.

Some indeterminate amount of time later, a familiar voice whispered through her haze, 'Jade, honey, are you okay?'

Jade opened her eyes to see Gina leaning over her, and Keith close behind. 'Hey Mum, I'm great, but what's wrong with you?' Her voice slurred.

Gina looked to Keith, then back at Jade. Still in a whisper, Gina asked, 'What do you mean?'

Jade gestured to Gina's outfit: blue jeans and a simple black sweater. 'What happened to the Abba vibe? I didn't know you had any black in your wardrobe.'

'Oh, darling, I didn't have time to think about clothes. When

Danny called, we came straight away. We've been worried sick.' Gina wrapped Jade in a careful hug, trying not to hurt her.

'Mum, I'm fine. You can stop whispering.'

Keith pointed to Jade's leg. 'You're lucky you don't need surgery.'

Gina shuffled out of the way so Keith could embrace Jade. A sob escaped him, but he pulled himself back together, stood and wiped his eyes.

Jade had never seen him cry. Unsettled, she rushed to reassure him. 'Really, Dad, I'm okay. Thanks for that alarm. It must've helped.'

He grinned broadly.

'I've been speaking to Moira.' Gina's voice returned to its regular, well-projected volume. 'She told me all about it. Wait until I see Steve. I'll give him a piece of my mind.'

Jade recalled hitting Steve and him passing out cold. 'Have you heard how he is?' She didn't want to face murder charges. Surely, she could claim self-defence. Although, hadn't the paramedics said something about him waking up?

Keith, back in control of his emotions, said, 'They won't give us any details – privacy laws – but said he'll make a full recovery.' Jade breathed easier until Keith added, 'If they let me anywhere near the man, I'll knock his lights out.'

'God, Dad, don't do that.' The last thing she needed was another murderous father figure. 'How's Moira? Did she tell you Steve made me tie her up with gaffer tape.'

Gina looked ready to take down Steve herself. 'She did and she's fine. Physically. Psychologically, it's another story. She really cared about the bastard.'

Energy spent, Jade closed her eyes again as her parents continued showering her in love, care and concern.

They must have left once she slipped back to sleep because the next time she woke, Danny was sitting beside her. 'Thank God you're okay. How's your leg?'

Jade eyed the cast on top of the white hospital sheets. 'I don't know what they've got me on, but I'm high as a kite.'

A buzzer sounded outside the room – one of the many hospital sounds Jade soon learnt to tune out. Easy to do while the drugs made her euphoric.

Danny nudged her arm. 'You've been on the news.'

'Really? What'd they say?'

'That you're badass.'

Jade chuckled. 'No way. That's your language, not theirs.'

He laughed. 'Seriously, I'm just so happy you're alright.'

She gave his arm a grateful squeeze. 'Mum said you helped find me. I owe you.'

'When Iris and I came to Steve's, and you didn't respond to our knocks, we called the police. They broke in and found Moira. She was a mess.'

Jade cringed at the memory of her ordeal with Steve. 'I was scared nobody would find me at the mine. How'd you work it out?'

'Moira gave the police a list of Steve's properties and local members went to each one. When they got to the hut in the Strathbogies, they found evidence of a visitor. One thing didn't belong – a receipt for groceries, including feminine hygiene products. They figured that wasn't for Steve.' Jade grinned. 'Then they heard a weird squeal and gunshots. They found you near an abandoned mine.'

'Thank you so much.' Jade shifted her leg to find a more comfortable position.

'That's what friends are for.'

Danny's casual assumption of their relationship made her clasp his hand in hers. 'You're awesome.'

True, he'd kept the terrible secret about moving Nick's body, and for her part, she hadn't told him about Steve being in witness protection, yet their bond had survived, and he'd stepped up when it really counted. Perhaps Jade had formed idealistic expectations after her intense friendship with Elena. She hadn't appreciated how precarious those bonds could be, how petty grievances could blossom into colossal issues, how great the need for give and take. Her relationship with Danny wasn't perfect, but it came close enough.

'Yeah, I am pretty cool.' He laughed, then started talking in a torrent. 'After you told me about the Port Douglas apartments this morning, I searched online for any properties there with Moira in the name. Nothing. I tried Elena, same thing. But then I found The Gillespie Seaside Resort. Fifteen apartments. Sales data shows they've been turned over several times. The original prices of around a million dollars, doubled in subsequent sales. I checked for the owners and found two familiar company names: Llama Clothing Trading and Silver Gate Bridge. Both were on BeanBlitz's supplier list. This doesn't prove Steve was money laundering through us, but it shows his connection to some of the companies involved. I've given this information to the police. They're thrilled because if they get Steve, they'll also have evidence against his clients.' His voice held a note of pride.

'Impressive.'

A nurse came in and checked Jade's drip. 'The police want to take your statement. Are you up to it?'

'Sure. When can I go home?' Jade asked.

'The doctor will do a final examination after you've finished with the police. If all's well, we'll discharge you then.'

Danny said goodbye, promising to see her soon, and two detectives came to her bedside.

After their questions, the officers assured her kidnapping would be one of many charges they'd level at Steve.

By the time she'd finished her statement, the analgesic effect was wearing off – her euphoria had disappeared, and her eyelids drooped.

The doctor came, prescribed painkillers and signed off for her to go home.

Her parents took her downstairs in a wheelchair, and she struggled into the backseat of their car. They drove her to their house, insisting they look after her at least overnight. Sore and tired, Jade didn't argue.

On the way home, she studied the streets as if seeing them for the first time. Spring was still a few weeks away, but a few brave trees had already produced blossom buds. She spotted Moira's familiar gold BMW outside her parents' house. Jade's fingers curled when she remembered Steve had incriminated Moira over the spare key in Elena's bedroom.

'I forgot to warn you.' Gina gave an apologetic grimace. 'Moira asked when you'd be home. She's desperate to see you. I told her you're worn out, so she's promised to be brief.'

Jade groaned. Her leg was aching, and the rest of her body pulsed in sympathy. She longed to climb into bed and close her eyes, but plastered on a smile as Gina invited Moira inside.

Gina bustled around making tea and putting biscuits on a plate, then left Jade and Moira sitting alone at the kitchen table, Jade's leg elevated on a chair.

Moira took a phone out of her handbag and passed it to Jade. 'I grabbed this before the police could bag it for evidence.'

'Thank you.' Jade noticed multiple missed calls from Danny and Iris before she put it down.

Moira rubbed her bloodshot eyes. 'I'm so sorry. I should've seen through Steve, but I ... I still can't believe he's a killer.'

The knot of anger in Jade's stomach loosened a notch. She understood the difficulty of questioning a fundamental belief about someone close to you. If she hadn't begun by assuming Steve was telling the truth, she might have solved the case sooner. 'You love him, you always have.'

'In love with a murderer? What does that say about me?'

Jade opened her mouth to answer, but Moira's faraway expression showed she didn't expect a response.

Moira touched her pearls. 'Do you still think someone hurt Elena? Could Steve have done it?'

Jade's leg throbbed with pain. She needed more drugs. 'I asked Steve, and while he's conned me before, I believed him when he said he didn't hurt her. But ... he suggested you know why the spare key had been used that day.'

Silent tears trickled down Moira's face. Jade longed to reach out to her, to lessen her pain, but she needed an explanation.

Moira handed a few papers from her handbag across the table. 'At the beginning of all this, you asked for the autopsy results, but I ... I wasn't ready. Just be prepared, it's clinical and spares no details.'

Jade covered her surprise and steeled herself – she couldn't spend her life running away from her emotions. She tried to read objectively, although all the drugs in her system, not to mention the pain, made it hard to be clear-headed.

The conclusion was clear: Elena's death had been caused by the Ambien in her system. Two things grabbed Jade's attention. First, while Elena didn't take enough tablets to kill her, an allergic reaction had hastened her death.

Second, the medication had been prescribed to Moira to cure insomnia. All this time, Moira knew where Elena had found the tablets. Her obfuscation, her inability to accept what had happened, her pushing Jade came down to what? Guilt? Denial? Or maybe deep down she really wanted to reveal the truth.

Once, Moira's lies would have caused Jade blood-curdling anger, but rather than fury, profound sadness made her head heavy. Moira had done everything she could to avoid facing the truth. And Jade couldn't blame her because she'd done the same.

With the shock of a slap in the face, she finally understood her friend had died by her own hand. 'We need to accept that Elena took her own life, don't we?'

'There's more.' Tears streamed down Moira's face. 'The key. That was me. Elena had been having trouble sleeping, and I offered my pills. I dropped them off during the day, so I let myself in and left the key in her room. But I never imagined she'd take all those tablets. Not for one minute.'

Jade's empathy went into overdrive. 'You couldn't have known, I—'

Moira slumped. 'I made a stupid, terrible mistake.'

Jade's heart ached for her. 'Thank you for telling me. It must've been very difficult for you. At least now, I understand.' Moira's need to deflect blame must have been powerful for her to have gone along with Jade's theory about Elena's murder. It was far-fetched to imagine someone had chanced upon the tablets and forced Elena to take them in the few hours between when Moira had delivered them and when Elena came home from work.

'Nobody blames you,' Jade said.

Moira sniffed. 'I do.'

Jade wished she could remedy Moira's grief, but they each had to grapple with this in their own way. If nothing else, they now had answers: Steve had slaughtered Nick and Curtis for fear of going to jail for his financial crimes, which in turn had been committed out of greed. Elena suicided.

Did others' behaviour influence Elena's decision? Curtis's abuse of her trust, her love triangle with Danny and Curtis, Jade's anger, and Moira's denial of her mental health issues? Perhaps all this exacerbated Elena's problems, but the underlying issue – Elena's depression – remained. If she'd received the right help, the right medication, perhaps she'd still be here. Or maybe she wouldn't.

The women had little more to discuss, so Moira gave Jade a tentative hug and left.

Exhausted, Jade accepted Gina and Keith's help to climb into bed in her childhood bedroom with its familiar leaf-patterned curtains. The wall hangings had changed – framed headshots of Gina as a young actor had replaced Jade's posters of ballerinas and tango dancers, and a bulb mirror had been added above the dressing table. In this safe space, where new mingled comfortably with old, Jade drifted off to sleep.

Chapter 47

I'm Sorry

Jade, one month later

JADE AND DANNY walked in silence, Jade on crutches, Danny with his arms full of flowers. They reached Elena's grave and stopped. Danny handed Jade the daffodils, and she bent over to place them on the grave.

Danny sank to his knees to rest a single red rose among the others. 'I know she loved daffodils, but I wanted to show her that I...'

Jade's lips trembled, and she only managed a brief, 'I get it,' as he stood.

The pair held hands in solidarity. Trust was complicated. Everyone had secrets, sometimes with good reason, sometimes not. Nobody could get it right all the time.

Jade and Danny had spent far too much time at cemeteries lately. They'd been ambivalent about going to Nick's funeral after finding out about the rape, but Iris had needed closure, so the trio had gone together. Iris had opted not to tell anyone else what Nick had done, preferring for his family to mourn him without suffering the weight of his crimes. Jade's grief for Curtis had been complicated too. So much anguish.

A kookaburra in an overhanging gum tree gave a throaty

laugh and took off into the overcast sky, perhaps in search of its mate.

'What's your perfume?' Danny drew her hand to his nose to sniff her wrist. 'No, wait, let me guess. Dolce & Gabbana's Dolce Garden?'

Jade smiled. 'Yes. Elena's favourite.'

'I know.' He released her hand and took out his phone. 'Do you mind if I play a song?'

'Not at all. What is it?'

'Something new I wrote. This isn't a proper recording, but Sammy helped me pull it together. It's called "I'm Sorry".' He pressed play and placed his phone next to the flowers.

Jade bowed her head as she listened to Danny's pain in song.

I cannot bear to see,
The hurt look in your eyes,
Your eyes accuse me,
I did not wish to,
I did not try to,
To cause this crazy mess.

Jade wiped her eyes as a magpie carolled alongside the melancholic piano solo. A slow rhythm on the drums gave a sense of the inevitable.

Danny remained still, eyes down, as if tumbled in the wash of music, until the last chords faded away. His face reflected the song's poignancy, the call of regret.

Jade wrapped an arm around him for a quick hug, one of her crutches trapped between them. 'It's beautiful. Elena would've loved it. She'd be thrilled you're composing again.'

'I wish I could play it for her.'

Jade hoped he'd keep songwriting now he'd resumed, and that the process would be cathartic. 'She'll hear it. Wherever she is, she'll know you wrote it for her.'

'That's a nice thought.' He pocketed his phone, looking

around as if surprised to find himself surrounded by graves, fresh sea air and tea-trees in sandy soil. 'Have you heard from Moira?'

'We've caught up a couple of times. She'll likely be charged for moving Nick's body and for her part in the money laundering. She knew all about it.' Jade saw Moira more clearly now – the way she manipulated people from behind the mask of grieving mother. Jade had a hard time reconciling these hard truths.

Danny raised his eyebrows. 'I reckon she orchestrated the whole scheme. She's a heap smarter than she lets on. How she fell for Steve, I'll never know.'

Steve had been charged with Nick's and Curtis's murders, and although the case had yet to go to trial, everything pointed to a guilty verdict.

'I'm just glad he recovered from my attack. Much as I hate what he did, I wouldn't want to have killed a man, self-defence or not.' Jade had battled nightmares, waking in sweats, thinking she'd been sentenced to life imprisonment in Steve's goldmine for his murder. 'Speaking of, what's happened about the insider trading? Will you be charged?'

Danny ran his hand through his hair, and it flopped back down over his forehead. 'The police interviewed me a few times, but my lawyer says I have a good chance of getting off because I didn't know where Curtis's information came from. The charges for moving the body will be harder to fight. Moira, Iris and I will all face that. My lawyer will argue mitigating circumstances, but no question, we showed bad judgement. I wish I'd played it differently, but you can't go back in time.'

'If only.'

'Hey, I saw your article in the paper.'

'And?' After breaking the salacious crime story about Nick's and Curtis's murders, Jade had written a feature article about depression. She'd interviewed psychologists, psychiatrists and patients. By talking about her experience with Elena, she'd given it a personal touch, and in doing so, felt she was honouring her friend. Zain had given his full support and was encouraging her to write more feature pieces.

'I reckon your writing's a bit like my music. It helps you figure things out when life gets too chaotic.'

'Then I better keep writing because I still have heaps to learn.'

'Well, you're looking good, in fact'—he studied her more closely—'you have a bit of a glow. Has something happened?' Dawning comprehension animated his face. 'You've met someone, haven't you?'

Jade couldn't stop grinning. 'Maybe.'

'Come on, spill, what's his name?'

'Brett. He's ... I like him.'

'Is he the chicken korma you've been waiting for?'

'We'll see. I'm not saying anymore. I don't want to jinx it. Speaking of chaos, I heard there's a chance BeanBlitz will go under.'

Danny shrugged. 'It's too soon to say. Iris has taken the reins, and hopefully, she'll bring things back under control. But I've resigned.'

Jade's eyebrows shot up. 'Wow. Congratulations, I think ... is that a good thing?'

'Seeing our friends die put things into perspective. You know how it is. I need to get back to my first love – music.'

'Hearing your song'—Jade pointed to Danny's pocket where he'd put his phone—'you have a gift.'

'I'll probably end up old and broke, but I'll be happy doing it.'

'I get it. I haven't exactly made my fortune putting words on the page. Speaking of happy. My parents are delirious with joy. Their offer on that place in Mansfield has been accepted. They settle in a couple of months.'

Danny chuckled. 'I can just see your mum in workpants and a flannel shirt.'

'Yeah, she's already planning her costumes for Gina, the

farmer. She reckons she's starring in the next *Man from Snowy River*.'

'She'd do that so well.'

Jade laughed. 'I must admit, the place is pretty cool. You'll have to come and stay.'

'You're on.'

'Should we head to the pub?'

'Sounds like a plan.'

They walked back to the car, Jade proficient with her crutches. Something caught on her sleeve, and she reached to free Elena's bracelet. She fingered the charms. A dove had its wings spread as if soaring high and free. All this time, she'd never fully appreciated why Elena had given her the jewellery, such a beautiful gesture. Jade had wondered if it was a goodbye gift, but now she believed it.

A flock of seagulls flew overhead, their mournful squawks drawing Jade's attention. She looked up to see sunbeams battling their way through heavy clouds. It was time to accept the past. To move on.

Acknowledgments

Writing can be a lonely endeavour, but I'm blessed with many dear friends and family who support me along the way. I give them my sincere thanks.

The team at Next Chapter believe in my series and have brought another of my manuscripts to life.

My talented sister, of Susan Bradfield Photography, took the cover image and author photo. My niece, Mia Bradfield, is the running girl. I deeply appreciate their enthusiasm and skill.

My amazing writing groups offer tremendous support: Wings Goddesses, Bayside Women Writers, Expat Writers, Pen Pals, Brisbane Writing Crew and Debut Crew 2024.

I had the privilege of spending a week as a writer-in-residence at Varuna, the National Writers' House, with five other fabulous writers, where I had uninterrupted time to work on this manuscript.

The brilliant Nadine Davidoff's edits lifted *A Killer Among Friends* to a higher level. I feel so lucky to work with her and to have her insight for all my novels.

I have marvellous writing colleagues, whose feedback made this book more vivid. They went over and above as beta readers, but more importantly, their friendships keep me sane and add colour and richness to my life. Bella Ellwood-Clayton, my book wife, is always ready to discuss any element of the writing journey, particularly characterization. Lisa Heidke shares her wisdom and experience. Her laugh-out-loud sense of humour is a gift. Sue Anderson's careful thought and keen understanding of human nature ensures no detail is overlooked. Kate Murdoch has an artist's eye for crafting visuals in writing. Sarah Hawthorn always brings left-field ideas to the party. Diane Clarke offers considered feedback that adds impact and finesse. Sarah Bourne asks all the right questions. Katelin Farnsworth read an early draft and gave me the confidence to keep going.

Lynne Elder did a sensitivity read for issues relating to mental health, and I thank her and her husband, Andy, for sharing their experience and emotional wisdom.

My friends Sandra and John Lording helped me to understand various elements of policing, and I appreciate our entertaining conversations about how to get away with murder. Any mistakes are my own.

My childhood best friend, Sally Nicholes, now heads a family law firm that leads the field. Our adventures as kids created a whole slew of fond memories. We really did run around the neighbourhood jotting down number plates, intent on uncovering criminal behaviour. More recently, she introduced me to Andrew Palmer, who saved me from committing legal blasphemy with a court scene full of errors. I deleted that chapter before the final drafts.

Marc Hakala taught me how to shoot a gun. He and his wife, Kerri, have also taught me a thing or two about friendship.

Music plays a huge part in this book, and Danny Finley shared his love of rock music, his insight to the industry and allowed me to use his name.

Tim Bradfield helped me figure out some of the details relating to financial crimes, which he most emphatically did not condone.

The Barton clan have stood beside me for this journey. Special thanks to John, Judy and Chris.

Dad offers never-ending support, and Mum's influence is everlasting. Catherine, Susan and Trev are always there for me.

Matthew goes on many walks and talks with me, when we solve all my plot issues and so much more. What would I do without him? Morgan offers feedback and insights. Firmi shares a unique perspective on the world.

My partner in crime, Andrew, provides endless (mis)adventures, and he allowed me to recreate his ankle injury! He is also an outstanding editor, who picks up all things practical and any word that isn't quite right.

About the Author

Andrea Barton, award-winning author of the Jade Riley Mysteries, runs the book editing company Brightside Story Studio. She is Vice President of Mansfield Readers and Writers Festival. Her writing credits include *The Winding Narrative* blog, short stories, picture books, stage productions and anthologies about expatriate life.

An electrical engineer turned career consultant, Andrea spent twelve years enjoying the exhilaration and dislocation of life as an expat in Nigeria, USA and Qatar with her husband and two children. Now repatriated in Australia, she commutes between Melbourne and Mansfield in the Victorian High Country. Along the way, she developed a passion for ballroom and Latin dance, helped to build a school, got bogged in both the Qatari and Australian deserts and had an accidental hallucinogenic experience in Peru.

When she's not writing, thinking about writing or discussing writing, she loves photography, theatre and spending time with family and friends.

To learn more about Andrea Barton and discover more Next Chapter authors, visit our website at www.nextchapter.pub.

Publisher contact information
Next Chapter
2-5-6 SANNO
SANNO BRIDGE
143-0023 Ota-Ku
Tokyo, Japan
https://nextchapter.pub

Printed in Dunstable, United Kingdom